The Rich Man
of Pietermaritzburg

Aflame Books
2 The Green
Laverstock
Wiltshire
SP1 1QS
United Kingdom
email: info@aflamebooks.com

ISBN: 9780955233999
First published in 2008 by Aflame Books

First published in isiZulu as *Inkinsela Yase Mgungundlovu* by
Shuter & Shooter Publishers, 1961

First published in isiZulu as *Inkinsela yase Mungungundlovu,*
by Shuter & Shooter, Pietermaritzburg, 1961

Cover design by Zuluspice www.zuluspice.com

Printed in Poland
www.polskabook.pl

Sibusiso Nyembezi

Translated by Sandile Ngidi

Nyanyadu in northern Natal is an old place, a pretty famous place in fact. The name of the place is taken from that of the enchanting Nyanyadu Mountain, nearby. If you are travelling to this place, either from Durban in the south or Johannesburg in the north, the best route to take is one that goes straight to the town of Dundee. In this town you would board the bus to Nyanyadu that goes once a day – on Sundays there is no bus at all. The bus leaves Dundee at lunchtime, zigzags through the white suburbs until it exits the town. Then you will see it blowing up the winds beside the legendary Mpathe Mountain which is believed to harbour money left by ghosts at its summit. It will keep on travelling, stopping only to let some passengers alight. Some would have come to Dundee by the buses from Zululand, others would have come by buses from Msinga. Many would have come to town by bus to do their grocery shopping and various errands. Now, everyone is on the way home. The bus keeps on picking some up along the way. It carries on until it reaches the black township of Longlands. When it leaves Longlands it is already on its way to its depot at Ngisana store.

When people alight temporarily at the store it is because they have to buy a few items that they forgot to buy in Dundee. Some get off to check on their mail at the local post office. Some do not enter the store at all. They hit the ground running, immediately they alight, to Devon, Lady Bank, the nearby tents, some to the Wesleyan Mission and others down to Mzinyathi. For these people, travelling long distances on foot is nothing unpleasant or worth complaining about. Women simply put their luggage on their heads while men use their shoulders. Few are the lucky ones whose reception party consists of a horse and wagon. On some days, the bus goes beyond the store. It passes Lady Bank and Wills on its way to Stein's place, until it stops at the distant Flint's place. Things are much better than in days gone by – there is now a new bus from Hathanga to Nyanyadu.

Nevertheless, the story being told here happened a long time ago at Nyanyadu, long before the arrival of modern modes of travel, it happened in days when people were living miserable lives when it came to public transport. In those days, people's desperation would be most acute if someone was sick – it was virtually impossible to rush that person to a doctor. In those days, people going to Nyanyadu would alight at Dannhauser station, then take a bus owned by an Indian businessman to continue the trip. On getting off, their luggage either on their heads or shoulders, they would finish the last lap of their trip on foot.

Quite a few of the people preferred alighting at Glencoe and taking the Vryheid train that would drop them at Tayside. Tayside is a tiny, one-shop and basically barren station. It is from this station that people would usually proceed to Nyanyadu on foot, horse or donkey carts if they were lucky – some were even met by ox-wagons. Like the spoils of Christmas Day, a car was a rarity in those days.

In those days it was even difficult to collect mail. It was collected three times a week from Tayside. In the morning, outgoing mail would be taken away in the same mailbag that would bring incoming mail in the afternoon. If one had a postal order notice one needed to wait until the next mail day before collecting the cash. The mail days were Monday, Wednesday and Friday. Even telegrams were sent via the mailbag – there was no alternative method for sending them, no matter how urgent it was. Anyone whose letter could not wait for the mailbag would go on foot, by bicycle or on horse-back to Tayside. Life at Nyanyadu was really tough.

One Wednesday afternoon, Nyanyadu resident Mr Zeph Mkhwanazi received a letter in the mailbag from Tayside. It was summer, and most people were busy tilling the soil, often waking up at the crack of dawn, like birds, so that by sunrise they would already have covered a lot of ground. A prominent Nyanyadu resident, Mr Lushozi, was the one who received the mailbag in the area. Mail day was a big day. On this day, girls would dress up in their best clothes, do their hair and rub bath soap on their legs for an alluring shine. As for the boys, mail day was just another day, they would stay dusty and let their khaki shirts hang aimlessly. They usually arrived first at Lushozi's house, often before the mailbag had been brought.

On that day, as usual, by the time the mailbag came, young girls and boys were already milling around to collect the mail. Among them was a young college student, Themba Mkhwanazi, the oldest child of Mr Mkhwanazi and his wife maNtuli. He was almost 20, no longer so young really. Although he was not tall, his muscular build made up for it — he was clearly a well-fed young man. He even wore long trousers, as college boys often did in those days. His light complexion was attributable to his maternal genes. Themba had also come in search of his family's mail. Indeed, as soon as he found it he went straight home.

The Mkhwanazi home was modern, with a big lounge, four bedrooms, a kitchen and a dining room. A verandah on both sides of the house also helped enhance its beauty, although the windows were rather small for a house that size. Like most old houses of the time, the Mkhwanazi house had the obligatory pillars on the verandah. The red corrugated iron roof was rusty and leaking. Unlike most houses in Nyanyadu, which were essentially mud huts, this house had green-brick walls that would have only needed firing in a kiln to make them red. Numerous pictures hung on the walls and some had faded over time. These were mainly pictures of the

Mkhwanazi family and their relatives. One was of Mkhwanazi and maNtuli on their wedding day.

It wasn't surprising that the pictures were dusty, since no one bothered to clean them regularly. Nailed to the wall in the dining room, there were also pictures of factory workers in uniform. Nothing hung in the other rooms, except clothes in the bedrooms.

Outside one of the rooms was an old, dilapidated and useless water tank that had resisted all efforts to repair it. Consequently, they fetched water on their heads from the well on the hill above the house, using small drum containers. The house was painted, although the paint was wearing off in places. The Mkhwanazi house was undoubtedly among the finest in Nyanyadu.

The yard was big, and fenced. The fence was old, and crumbling here and there. At times – even if the fence was supposed to be standing – donkeys would simply encroach on the yard as they pleased. There were two gates, the small one at the front and the big one at the back used by carts and ox-wagons. Next to the house, outside the gate, was a cattle and sheep shed. There was also a wagon and tool shed for the head of the household. In the yard, there were countless chickens and a few black pigs. It was clear to all that the household was relatively well off, and headed by a strong man. The garden had two peach trees and a *hananadi* tree that chickens often used as shelter on hot sunny days. In one distant part of the garden there was a *halibhoma* plant.

Among the letters Themba had brought, one had a Pietermaritzburg stamp – it was for his father. When Mkhwanazi studied the envelope before opening the letter, he couldn't make out the handwriting at all. He tried hard to think of who the writer could be, but to no avail. He finally opened it to find out who had written to him from Pietermaritzburg, for he was not a regular traveller, and even Pietermaritzburg was not that familiar to him. The place he knew well was the Mzinyathi district. He would usually only go as far as Dannhauser and Dundee and even nearby

Newcastle was as Johannesburg to him, as he considered it very far away.

Mkhwanazi was without doubt a fully grown man and his beard in the fashion of Napoleon the Third, said as much. He was strongly built, though average in height. The coarseness of his hands was proof that this was a man who worked hard with his hands. He liked to wear a khaki shirt and trousers. The sleeves of the shirt were always rolled up because this was a hard-working man. He would put a leather belt around his waist. He would only wear a coat in bad weather, when he was going to church or to a meeting. When it came to footwear, he preferred boots for doing physically demanding work in the fields. He would usually wear his shoes without any socks, or put on old ones that exposed his toes. At times he would just hit the road barefoot, and hardly give a damn about it. Since he hardly ever shaved his beard, its scruffiness had become his trademark. He had a dark-skinned complexion.

Nyanyadu was his birthplace, where he had grown up and married a local girl from the Ntuli household, daughter of Mabhozomela. When he told his childhood stories, Mkhwanazi said that when he and other boys were looking after cattle in the fields, they often saw buffaloes grazing along the nearby Mzinyathi River. He said that in those days the grass was extremely high – to the point of making a 10-year-old boy walking in the dense grass forest virtually invisible. Today, the same place is barren. Now, huge *dongas* narrate the curse of soil erosion on these lands. These *dongas* resemble wrinkles on an elderly face, a beaten face. Soil is eroded from the walls like rotten meat when it shrinks from the bones. Then heavy rains come and wash it away. He went to school here at Nyanyadu, and since in those days schools went only as far as Standard Four, he stopped schooling at that point. Even though Standard Four was his highest class, he was regarded as a learned and civilised person. He could read isiZulu with impeccable ease, but battled with English. Mkhwanazi regarded himself as part of an educated elite and

11

felt threatened by those who had attained college education.

As he opened the letter, his eye hurried towards its end. When he read the name he frowned in disbelief, as he had never in his life heard of such a name and surname. The sender had signed himself as Mr C.C. Ndebenkulu. It amazed him to learn that there were people whose last name was Ndebenkulu, or 'the one endowed with long lips'. He couldn't quite work out the tribe or clan of the Ndebenkulu people. He decided to continue reading the letter.

2 Blue Arcade
High Street
Pietermaritzburg.

Mr Zeph Mkhwanazi
Nyanyadu School
P O Tayside

Mr Mkhwanazi,
Inasmuch as you do not know me Mr Mkhwanazi so it is the case with me, I do not know you either. Be that as it may, in the event you are an avid newspaper reader, you probably have read about me and the work I do to uplift my people. Here in the big cities there are just too many ways in which people get help, they are just too many to count. On the other hand, people in rural areas continue to live in abject poverty because no one in the big city has the interests of rural people at heart. It is precisely for this reason that I have seen it my duty to come to the rural areas and bring progress to people in these areas as they are after all the most needy and the most neglected.

In a conversation with an associate who knows your area pretty well I realised that I could not ignore his sincere appeal that the people of Nyanyadu would benefit tremendously from my benevolence. I had no option but to heed his call. He also gave me your name Mkhwanazi thanks to your intelligence and ability to see things much quicker than most people. I'm quoting his words almost verbatim, his direct words echo in my ears to this day. It is for this reason that I have written to you,

Mkhwanazi. My wish is to meet the men next Monday the 13th. Do pardon me for putting a fixed date already – hopefully you will understand that had my schedule been less taxing, I would have done things differently. The truth is that no other date would actually be convenient for me. My associate says the best route is to travel to Tayside where you will then receive me. Since there is no train to Vryheid on Sunday, I will catch a train at Pietermaritzburg on Friday evening and alight at Tayside on Saturday morning. I trust that you will manage to organise the meeting on my behalf and to also receive me at the station.

The undersigned,

C.C. Ndebenkulu, Esq.

When Mkhwanazi had finished reading the letter he frowned in bewilderment and shouted, "Gracious me!" He then re-read the letter that was the cause of his confusion.

As Mkhwanazi had just come back from the *mielie* fields, his wife maNtuli entering the room, put a pot of sour milk on the table in front of him. MaNtuli was also getting old and her hair was gradually going grey. She was the eldest child of Mabhozomela Ntuli, who was also a resident of Nyanyadu. She was light-skinned and also slightly taller than average, like her husband. She was of normal build and pleasantly proportioned. She was a hard-working whirlwind of a person and barely sat down to rest. As for her temper! She could be a chilli-tempered little monster. At times, even Mkhwanazi was at the receiving end of her rage. Among maNtuli's children, Themba had inherited her temperament. However, when the weather of her mood was calm, maNtuli was chatty and lovable.

"What strange news is this you're telling me, father?" As maNtuli talked she simultaneously laid the table for her beloved husband. She had already taken out of the cupboard a tablecloth that was white in its heyday but was now a shadow of its former self. It had a hole on one edge. She put it on the table and folded it twice to hide the embarrassing hole.

"I swear by the heavens, this is indeed strange!" said Mkhwanazi as if he had not heard maNtuli's question. MaNtuli asked again: "What are you talking about, father, what strangeness?"

"This letter!"

"And where does this strange letter come from?"

"MaNtuli, have you ever heard of the name Ndebenkulu?"

"What name?" MaNtuli stopped what she was doing and looked at her husband with utter disbelief.

"Ndebenkulu?"

"Father, don't joke like that," said MaNtuli breaking into giggles, which she tried half-heartedly to hide. As she spoke she was preparing the table for her husband.

"Read here, if you think I'm taking you a for a ride." He showed her the name at the bottom of the letter.

MaNtuli had not been educated that much either. When she reached Standard Four, Mabhozomela, her father, had sworn it was enough, for fear that an educated girl might become a promiscuous drifter, and so she and her husband were equals as regards their levels of education. "My God! I never realised that you were telling the truth, Nkwali!" MaNtuli, her hands on her waist, addressed her husband by his clan name.

"Do you believe me now?"

"I do, since I've read it for myself. Staying at home too much can make one ignorant of so many things. I've sometimes heard of unusual names for people from well-off places like Durban and Johannesburg. Maybe Ndebenkulu could even be a surname from the southern parts of the province. What, then, is this writing at the very end?"

"How am I supposed to know what this strange signature is?" said Mkhwanazi.

"But then, Nkwali, why would Ndebenkulu write to you as if he's missing you, while you have never even heard of him?"

"Listen carefully, maNtuli. It's not because Ndebenkulu

misses me. He's just written to make the strangest request ever to plague my ears, a request I'm struggling to fathom. Kindly lend me your ears, Ntuli." Mkhwanazi read the letter again, aloud this time, from beginning to end.

"*Hhayi*, don't joke with me, *baba*, this man is talking woolly stuff. What kind of help does he want, that he's so mysterious?"

"That's precisely my gripe, mama kaThemba. Actually, I wonder about the identity of his purported friend, who has invited this man to Nyanyadu and even gave him my name as the local contact person. What's more, whoever he is, he lacked the courtesy to write me a letter and forewarn me about this unknown friend he would be sending to me unannounced. Where the hell does that friend of his know me from? I don't know anyone who lives in Pietermaritzburg!"

"You know what, *baba* kaThemba? I'm filled with so much pride," said maNtuli tenderly, flashing her snow-white teeth.

"Really? You find this something to be proud of?" Mkhwanazi echoed her words, trying to make sense of them.

"True's God, I'm so proud of you. Little did I realise, Nkwali, that you were such a famous person. You're known even in Pietermaritzburg where you've never even set foot. So why shouldn't I be as proud as a peacock?" maNtuli said with a laugh. "But look at me, now. I've been sidetracked by Ndebenkulu's letter and forgotten the *mielie pap* and a wooden spoon. Hey, Thoko! Kindly bring your father's *mielie pap* and a wooden spoon. While you're at it, please also call Themba for me."

As maNtuli said all this, she was shouting, trying to talk to Thoko who was not in the same room, but in the kitchen, and who now emerged with her father's *mielie pap* and a wooden spoon. Thoko was a daughter of the Mkhwanazi household. She was born after Themba. The two are the Mkhwanazis' only children.

Thoko shared her brother's light complexion but, unlike Themba, did not have a muscular body, and unlike her brother, who was already attending college, she was still at school in Nyanyadu.

15

"Food is ready, *baba*, please help yourself." Mkhwanazi immediately sat down at the table where a pot of sour milk and *mielie pap* had been placed. "Please say grace for us, Ntuli," he asked. They closed their eyes and maNtuli led them in prayer.

"Thoko said you asked for me, mother," Themba said.

"Since you're the educated one, Themba my child, just tell me what this is. Where is the letter, *baba* kaThemba?"

Mkhwanazi passed Ndebenkulu's letter to maNtuli. "What does this mean, Themba?" she asked, pointing to the word 'Esq'.

"Who is this person, mother?" Themba asked with a suspicious laugh.

"It's the letter with a Pietermaritzburg postal stamp that you brought home."

"Nde...be...nku...lu! Well, I must admit, I've never heard of this surname before."

"Do you mean that at your college no one has this surname?"

"Not at all, mother. I've never even heard of it in the newspapers. After all, there are so many surnames that even at the college I have encountered some we don't have here in the northern parts of the province. This one is also new to my ears."

"I asked you to explain what he wrote after his name."

"I've no idea either. It's normally on the postal address but never part of a person's signature."

"You must realise, maNtuli," Mkhwanazi interjected with a full mouth, "that Themba is still uneducated. Such things would only make sense to people who are highly educated. We, with our Standard Four, are much better than them doing Standard Seven. Our generation was blessed with the fortune of high-quality education." As he spoke he kept looking into his bowl, stirring his food as if his sour milk was not well mixed.

"Oh, *baba*! At times you can be arrogant over nothing, when the reality is that you're a true illiterate like me," said maNtuli.

"Not really, maNtuli. You see, maNtuli, I've heard men who work in the cities talking about whites who have risen to the social status of Esquires, filthy rich whites. What I didn't know until today was that even a black person could qualify for the Esquire rank. You see, Themba, it's written this way to denote his rank."

"Indeed, father, that's how it's written."

"It's okay, my son, you may go now, that's the only thing I had called you for," maNtuli told Themba. "Clearly, the Ndebenkulus are part of the upper class elite in Pietermaritzburg," she said, smiling.

"Even if you find this amusing, maNtuli, what you are saying is highly probable. You see, maNtuli, Themba doesn't understand the meaning of Esquire, but lacks the courage to admit it. As I was saying, this title is for elite whites. It's quite clear that this person must be a very special individual to enjoy this social status as well."

"And it means he wants to be hosted in my house?"

"Certainly," responded Mkhwanazi as he continued eating with enthusiasm.

"Why would he want to come to my house? Oh God! What would an ordinary country bumpkin like me do with such a modern individual from the big city? You said it yourself, *baba* kaThemba, that Esquires are high-flying white people. It takes a very important black person to rise to the Esquire rank. In all likelihood, since he's an Esquire, he must be fond of English. In that case, who will he be babbling with, in that nasal tongue, in this house? No, *baba* kaThemba, why make fun of me?"

"What do you mean, maNtuli, making fun of you? How could that be the case, when you're also a witness to this letter? Why would I be teasing you?" He speaks with his mouth full, now and then wiping remnants of sour milk from his moustache.

"No, *baba*, no. Let him go somewhere else. I simply can't bear it. *Hhawu*! Just imagine, having Esquires in my house! No!"

"Well, just explain this to me – how are you going to turn this person away when he's already on his way here? His letter is directly addressed to your house. I also doubt very much that he knows anyone else here."

"And so what, since he doesn't know us either! Let him pass through, and look for help somewhere else."

"Don't babble like a child, mama kaThemba. No one is going to welcome him. Everyone else will wash their hands of him, like you. In any case, to farm a stranger out to other people is unwise."

"To invite a total stranger into your home is equally unwise," maNtuli insisted. "What will he sleep on? I have nothing befitting his status. Not so long ago, a cow from the Nkosi household ate one of my decent sheets while it was hanging on the washing line. Just when I thought I could rescue it, the silly cow was already done with its dirty job, tearing my sheet into shreds. The only other sheet is yours. Whenever I ask for money to improve our household goods, you bluntly refuse. In this desperate state I'm in, how would I dare welcome a visitor into my house?"

"He'll have to make do with the flour-sack sheets. After all, he must realise that he's far away from home. When one is far away from home even mud may be offered as food. He's bound to know that hard reality quite well."

"Do you think someone who has risen to become an Esquire would know such things? After all, even his mission is vague. He's here to cause us grief and headaches," protested maNtuli.

"I must agree with you fully, Ntuli, when you say the purpose of his visit is unclear. I hardly know what to tell the local men when inviting them to the meeting this man is requesting. His claim that he's a good Samaritan is neither here nor there. It's unadulterated nonsense, a headless and tailless object. It will make people look at me as an utter fool." As Mkhwanazi spoke he was re-reading the letter in the hope of finding some information he might have missed at first.

"In all fairness, Nkwali, how are you going to break the

18

news? Where will you start your efforts to invite them to this meeting?"

"I've no idea how to do it, whether to visit each and every household or meet the people at the fields early in the morning. That's something one can only do tomorrow."

"As if it would be difficult to merely throw the letter away and relax, instead of bothering yourself with the dawn of such meaningless darkness! What is this man really up to, coming here to disturb our peace?"

"Throwing the letter away is certainly a possibility. But I'm concerned that he will have travelled a pretty long distance from Pietermaritzburg to Nyanyadu. That is a faraway place, really. It would be terrible if he arrived to find us not having bothered to make an effort on his behalf."

"My Lord! This man is thoroughly inconveniencing me. I wanted to finish planting my fields this week."

• •

The next morning, Mkhwanazi rode his dark brown horse to the *mielie* fields.

"Eh! *Siyabonana*, Nkabinde."

"Good morning, Mkhwanazi. Take a breather, boy."

Whistles filled the air as the ox-drawn plough came to a halt for Nkabinde to hear the urgent news that had prompted Mkhwanazi to defer his farming while other men were busy in the fields. The sun was scorching, and Nkabinde was sweating, wiping his perspiring face now and then with a dirty handkerchief. Silently attentive, he digested Mkhwanazi's narrative.

"I hear you well, Mkhwanazi, although what you're telling me sounds absurd. Worse still, I'm very much behind with my farming schedule, due to recent troubles with the gauge for the plough. The day before yesterday I had to go to Dannhauser to get a new one. I'm concerned this will delay me even more, when I'm already far behind."

"I can't agree with you more, Nkabinde. Unfortunately, as

I've already tried explaining, this matter puzzles me as well. My troubles started with the puzzling letter that arrived unannounced from a total stranger, someone I've never met. I admitted as much to maNtuli, and shared my anxiety about telling people about something when the details are also unclear to me."

"I hear you well, Mkhwanazi. You're not to blame. As you say, you knew nothing about this affair either."

"Indeed, Nkabinde."

"Well, Mkhwanazi, you've said it all. We now simply have to wait for the arrival of this mysterious man."

"Thanks for your reassurance, Nkabinde. Till then – let me move on and spread the news to other men."

"Goodbye. Shalbek! Sphahlan! Jamlud! Come on! Move!"

Nkabinde's oxen obliged at once. He was only too glad to continue with his farming.

"Eh! Good morning, Buthelezi of the Shenge clan!"

"Same to you, Mkhwanazi. Hold on ... just give the oxen a break, boy. What brings you our way in such blistering heat? D'you mean you're done with your farming, now that you're up and down on your horse, whereas we are still at it?" Buthelezi asked, chuckling, as he extended his hand to Mkhwanazi.

The two stood for some time, as Mkhwanazi gave the news contained in Ndebenkulu's letter.

"Well, Mkhwanazi, as you can see for yourself, it's difficult to commit oneself."

"Please bear with me, Buthelezi. I fully appreciate that you're busy, but nevertheless it would be advisable for you to attend and hear for yourself what this man has to say. One can't deny that his timing is terrible, since it's the sowing season. It would have been a different matter if we had already placed some seeds in the ground. I urge you to come, mainly because this is someone from a faraway place. Let me leave you, Shenge, and continue spreading the news."

"Farewell, Mkhwanazi. Get to your feet, boy. *Hhe...yi bo!*" It was back to work for Shenge's oxen.

"*Sanibona*, Shozi."

"Stop the oxen for a while, boy, and let me hear what Mkhwanazi has to say."

"Greetings," Mkhwanazi said.

"Greetings to you as well, Mkhwanazi. Pardon me, but I couldn't hear you well because of this boy who's driving the oxen."

"Are you well, Shozi?"

"We are, Mkhwanazi, save for the worry of being behind with our cultivation. Are you perhaps done with yours, that you find time to inspect other fields on horseback?"

"Not at all, Shozi. I'm just troubled at having to go back and forth, by a strange man I've never even heard of." Mkhwanazi began telling Shozi about the Ndebenkulu fellow.

"You're so right, Mkhwanazi, to describe this matter as a daylight fairy tale. What's worse, the man wrote his letter when he was already on his way – clearly, he intended not to give you any choice in the matter."

"You have a point, Shozi. I simply hadn't made much of the late arrival of the letter, but now that you mention it, it makes perfect sense. He insists he has no other day except this one."

"You see, Mkhwanazi, one must be vigilant nowadays – the world is full of wolves dressed in sheep's clothing."

"I doubt this man harbours such sinister intentions. He wouldn't gather all the men at once if he intended to rob them. Instead he would hit at them one by one, so that they wouldn't be able to warn each other about his wickedness. Overall, it would appear that this is a man one can trust."

"I take your point, Mkhwanazi. I shouldn't be saying so much about someone I haven't even met. By the way, when again did you say he would be arriving?"

"On Saturday morning. Themba will be there to fetch him."

"Does that mean he will alight at Tayside station?"

"That's what he says in his letter."

"All is well, Mkhwanazi. We look forward to meeting this Ndebenkulu and hearing at first hand what news he brings us. We, too, would like to hear more about his benevolence scheme. Let's move, boy!"

Promptly, the oxen went back to work.

By sunset, Mkhwanazi had spoken to almost every man in Nyanyadu, Mzinyathi and even in Willis. In households where the men were away, as in the case of Shandu, he left the message with their wives. Mkhwanazi also urged the men to spread the news, so that everyone would be in the know and, if interested, would attend the meeting.

At the Mkhwanazi household, spring-cleaning began in earnest, for it was important to ensure that when the visitor arrived the home was clean and the yard perfect. After realising that she couldn't pass the stranger on to anyone else, maNtuli had resigned herself to the situation and had begun preparing for his arrival.

What troubled maNtuli most was that, as a rural person whose smoke-filled kitchen was a way of life, she had no clue as to what to cook for someone from the big city of Pietermaritzburg. She was concerned that, too often, city dwellers find typical Zulu food unappetising.

"I have an idea, my child," said maNtuli to her daughter Thoko in the middle of the preparations, "I will ask maShezi's help since she used to work as a domestic helper for white people."

"Are you saying that because you've just seen her, mother?" Thoko asked, looking out of the window.

"Seen who?"

"Aunt maShezi."

"Where is she?" maNtuli raised her head and also looked out of the window.

"There she is, going down the road. I wonder if she's coming here or just passing by."

"I'm so relieved she has virtually delivered herself to my doorstep. The Lord has sent her my way. In fact I hadn't seen her at all. I meant to visit her house as soon as we were done here."

"She's passing by, mother, not coming here."

"She's passing? Let me call her." MaNtuli went outside. "Kindly come this way, maShezi. Apologies for the inconvenience."

"It's you with your sharp eyes again. How did you notice me when I was deliberately trying to hide?" she said with a laugh, immediately coming towards the back gate where maNtuli was waiting for her. "True's God, I didn't want you to see me since I knew you'd hold me back, although I'm in a hurry."

"So when did I ever hold you back?"

MaShezi was a tall, strong woman with breasts that shelter almost her entire chest. She liked to fasten a tight belt around her waist, resulting in an artificially big stomach. When she laughed, the stomach wobbled up and down like a person on a trampoline. But she was an agile person, and her body didn't burden her at all.

"Where are you rushing to today? You're always in a hurry," maNtuli said as she grasped her friend's hand.

"Who else if not the children? True's God, Mpisekhaya's departure for work, which left me alone with that impolite and stone-headed son of his, was the beginning of all my miseries."

She spoke at full volume, as if she wanted the whole village to hear her story.

"Aren't you being unduly harsh on the child, maShezi? What has Mpisekhaya done to upset you?"

"Harsh? Do you know Mpisekhaya well, maNtuli? If I could, I'd farm him out to you for a week, your blood pressure would shoot up."

"Don't tell me you're really not coming in!"

"I swear to God, I can't come in, I have to go and put out the fires started by the very same Mpisekhaya you believe I'm being unjustly harsh towards. This silly boy let loose the cattle into Ndawonde's plantation. What a disaster! You know, these boys like to let cattle graze near meadows and then swim in the Mzinyathi River with careless abandon. Even worse, maNtuli, when their crop was so promising. Really, Mpisekhaya irks me."

23

"You mean the Ndawondes were so far ahead that their crop was high enough to be devoured by cows?"

"The Ndawondes are early birds. You have no idea, maNtuli, how much harm the cows have caused. Now Ndawonde is livid and won't take anything for an explanation. I swear to God, he's angry enough to brave a raging fire, and insists he wants his crop back. I'm going there to apologise and find out what they plan to do to us for ruining their crop."

"Children!"

"Worse still, maNtuli, my husband is poor. Until recently he had no job. Just when he has started working, this happens. Dear Lord, what is our sin, to be on the receiving end of such cruel and recurring misfortune?"

"I hear you, maShezi, and don't mean to delay you. I was intending to pay you a visit regarding a letter we have just received." MaNtuli told her friend about Ndebenkulu's letter.

"What did you say this stranger's name was, maNtuli?"

"He is Ndebenkulu."

"Don't tell me tales," said maShezi, laughing, her stomach jiggling. "You want to tell me there's someone with the surname Ndebenkulu?"

"I'm telling you the truth. This strange man will be arriving this very Saturday morning. As you know, I'm an absolute idiot when it comes to white men's food – Thoko is much better since they're taught this at school."

"Do you mean that this Ndebenkulu character is white?"

'Don't ask me, maShezi. We hear that urban people sometimes graduate and become white people. Even his letter indicates that he is someone who has adopted the white man's way of life, because he even describes himself as an Esquire."

MaShezi burst out laughing and her stomach did a jig in approval.

"Since you once worked in white people's kitchens," maNtuli continued, "I thought it right to ask for your help. Just when you came this way, I was already preparing to visit you."

"You're really making fun of me. Until now I didn't realise you could be this rude," maShezi said with a laugh.

"I'm dead serious. Do come, I beg you."

"Is this high-flyer a blood relative of this family?"

"Oh no! I've already told you that we have no idea who he is either. We first heard of him when we received his letter asking us to play host when he arrives. He says he wants to meet the men. I can't even tell you who in Nyanyadu gave him our name and address since he doesn't say who. As I speak, *baba* kaThemba is not in the fields, instead he's going up and down informing the men about this."

"I saw him riding a horse, and wondered where he was going so early in the morning when it's the planting season. Let me go now, maNtuli, in case I get delayed. I hope to find Ndawonde at home."

"I really beg you to come, maShezi. I'll be waiting for you on Saturday morning. I really mean it. Please don't disappoint me."

"We will see. Maybe it would be a good idea if I come tomorrow since I remember very little of what I learnt from white people when I worked as a domestic servant. It's so long since I last worked for whites."

"That would be a great idea. I look forward to seeing you tomorrow."

MaShezi turned and walked away quickly, her clothes dancing this way and that to the rhythm of her gigantic body, on the road to Ndawonde's home.

• •

"I'm relying on you, Themba, to wake up early tomorrow morning and shoot straight to Tayside to fetch this person," said Mkhwanazi to his son.

"It's a tough job, father. I've no clue how I will recognise him, since I don't know him."

"Themba, do you want to tell me that a grown-up person like you, who even wears long trousers and is a college student, would fail to find a person alighting from a train? When I thought I was educating a man, little did I realise that I was wasting my money." Mkhwanazi uttered these words jovially, with a broad smile. "In any case, very few people alight at Tayside, something that should make your search much easier. I suggest you ensure that the horse sleeps in the yard tonight. It will make it easier for you in the morning to simply harness it for your trip."

"I'll ask mother to wake me in the morning since I know the Vryheid train comes early."

"What the hell happens to you, Themba, at college? Since you went there you've suddenly become lazy."

"Not really, father, it's just that we wake up at dawn every day except Sundays. When I'm home I do my best to relax."

"I will personally wake you up because I'm anxious to work the fields early in the morning."

Early the next morning, when a kaleidoscope of branches resembled horns against the rising sun, Themba was woken by the footsteps of someone entering his bedroom. His father had already come to wake him up. "The morning has broken, Themba. You have to promptly harness the horse and get going. By the time the train leaves Glencoe station, you must have long been gone."

"I'm waking up now, father," said Themba kicking his blankets away. He sat on the edge of the bed. Next to the bed was a chair on which he usually put the lamp when going to bed.

He lit a match and the candle, as the room was still dark. He was only wearing a shirt as nightclothes. His trousers were hanging on the chair next to his bed. He put them on. Because his socks had holes he had to pull them carefully forward a bit before folding them beneath his toes to get some comfort. He wore a jersey against the early morning chill. He took his coat that hung from a nail on the wall and put it on. He put the lamp out and tip-toed out of the house so as not to disturb those who were still asleep.

He started at the kitchen, to get water. The kitchen had a small and very old coal stove. Some of the handles were missing. Sometimes it emitted awful fumes. When the fire was made of dried cow dung, the smoke was unbearable. Some of its legs were wobbly and stones were a permanent feature of its support system.

The kitchen table was now pitch-black, thanks to the smoke. Inside the table's crevices, resident cockroaches ruled the roost, their flickering tentacles suggesting mischief-filled revelry. In front of the table was a huge water jug. Smoke had changed the colour of the tiny old kitchen cupboard to sooty brown. It was also a favourite hangout for cockroaches.

Cow dung was the only form of polish the floor knew, but by now the floor was crying out for more than just cow dung – to restore its former glory, the slab full of cracks needed a fresh round of polishing. The corrugated iron roof had begun showing signs of wear, it had become almost black and would often leak on winter mornings so that if one wasn't careful one's belongings would get wet, with irritating black stains. The window was tiny, with an equally tiny and faded curtain that hung on a string also almost black with dirt. The nails on which the string hung were loose, since the mud walls could not hold them firmly.

Themba poured water into a jam tin and went outside to wash his face, splashing the water repeatedly from one hand to the other. He used the remaining water to brush his teeth. As his father had advised, he had brought the horse in the previous night. While he was hitching the horse to the cart, the idea that he had had to wake up so early, to interrupt his sleep at its height and at the hour of sweetest dreams, for a complete stranger, was simply too irritating for words. What incensed him the most was that he couldn't even get a coffee at the station, to enhance his alertness. When he thought of this strange name, Ndebenkulu, curiosity overtook his outrage – he was indeed anxious to meet a man with such an odd surname. He chuckled as he mumbled the surname to himself. After he had prepared the horse, he took his whip, opened the big gate, and left.

It's quite a distance from Nyanyadu to Tayside. To be on

time he had to really rush, since the morning express to Vryheid usually arrived very early at Tayside. Fortunately for him, Mkhwanazi's horses were big and well-fed. For them, the distance to Tayside was nothing.

As he travelled through the meadows and valleys along the way, he was constantly painting a picture of this Ndebenkulu fellow in his head. He imagined an old man with big lips and a bulging stomach. This image suddenly fell apart and he pictured an impressively tall man. He then looked at this man closely, smiling, developing a liking for him. Again the image crumbled, and was replaced by that of a scruffy tramp with ricketty legs and shoes so worn-out that his feet were almost begging for corns. Then, ruminations of Ndebenkulu were replaced by other trivial thoughts. He was determined to arrive early at the station. Indeed, when he looked at his wristwatch he realised that he was ahead of the train, as he had hoped to be. After dismounting, he parked the wagon next to the store. The train would be arriving at any minute now. He went into the waiting room for a moment. Save for an old woman, and a little girl in an oversized coat, the waiting room was empty. The tiny girl had pulled the coat tightly around her – she was feeling cold. She kept on toying with annoying mucus that was peeping through her nose. Judging from their luggage, tucked away next to them, the two looked like they were waiting to board the train. Themba greeted them and they exchanged pleasantries. He confirmed that the elderly woman was the one who was going away. The little girl was her grandchild. She was on her way back home to Ncome. They were also waiting for the Vryheid Express. Themba left them and went outside.

In no time the rails hummed as an indication that the train was coming. He was certain it was on its way. Suddenly the train's whistle sounded, deafening. The old woman and her tiny grandchild arose, took their modest luggage and stood in the open air waiting for the train. "Where are we supposed to go, my child?" the grandmother asked, visibly afraid.

"Don't worry, grandma, I will help you. Today the journey

is short because the train is not going to Piet Retief but only as far as Vryheid."

"Help me, my child. People like me don't know much about these white men's things. Come nearer me!" she said, as she roughly pulled her grandchild closer, absorbed by the approaching train. "By the way, on Saturdays does it only go as far as Vryheid?"

"Yes, grandma, it only goes as far as Vryheid on Saturdays."

Since it was early, and cold, very few heads dared show themselves outside the windows, and it seemed that most people were still fast asleep. In any event, Tayside was barren, with hardly anything to satisfy a curious eye.

In the second carriage, a man wearing a hat looked all set to disembark. This turned out to be so. When the train came to a halt, Themba helped the elderly woman and her grandchild aboard, then walked towards the man. When he reached him, the man had already alighted and was receiving his suitcase, saying "Thank you kindly" to the one who had just given him the case, throwing in some English words to embellish his speech.

When Themba heard the man speaking English it dawned on him that at last he had met C.C. Ndebenkulu in the flesh. This must be the Esquire. He went up to him, saying that he had come to receive a Mr Ndebenkulu from Pietermaritzburg. Mr Mkhwanazi had sent him, he explained.

"I am the one," the man said as he shook Themba's hand. "I am the one. Are you well, Mr Mkhwanazi?"

"We are well, sir."

"Thank you graciously, Mr Mkhwanazi, thank you graciously," said the man.

"Is this the only luggage you have, sir?"

"That's the one, Mr Mkhwanazi, that's the one. It's all here. I don't travel like someone who takes everything with him as if he'll never set foot back home."

They both burst out laughing. Themba picked up his luggage, saying: "We can go now, sir. It's a pleasure to have you as our guest, sir." Themba was only saying this for the sake of starting a polite conversation with the man, who, at first glance, looked like a Very Important Person.

"I'm also quite pleased to visit your area, Mr Mkhwanazi, I have long heard about it from others and am really most pleased to be here. Your area must count itself lucky, as I don't often visit small places. It's a big stroke of luck. From what people who know the place have said, I used to imagine Nyanyadu as a bigger place than what I'm seeing. That's what I used to think. However, this station amazes me. Since I can barely see any houses, tell me really, Mr Mkhwanazi, where exactly is Nyanyadu?"

As Ndebenkulu is speaking, his hands are tightly tucked inside his coat. Now and then they come out, to gently twirl his moustache. His speech is peppered with English – a language he is undoubtedly quite comfortable with.

Themba found his remarks off-putting. It was hard to fathom that someone who had just arrived in a place could be so disparaging about it.

He said: "You can't see our house from here. This is Tayside. We'll only see it once we have reached Nyanyadu, after having passed the Italian area."

"Oh I see, Mr Mkhwanazi, I see. As I was saying earlier, someone of my status doesn't visit any insignificant place," said the very important Ndebenkulu, his hands safely placed in his pockets. "I'm a very busy man, Mr Mkhwanazi, a very busy man."

Such talk surprised Themba. He began asking himself what kind of person this character he'd come to fetch was. He looked at the man piercingly, but just as the urge to breathe fire started to get the better of him, he softened, and merely said: "That's why, sir, I'm also saying that we're happy to have someone as important as you visiting us in these rural backwaters. By the way, sir, what is your profession?"

Ndebenkulu smiled, gently twirling his moustache, as if he found Themba's question amusing. "It's quite evident that in this area you don't read prestigious newspapers. If you did, that question would not arise. I'm not someone you can think of as an employee, I have no white man who calls himself my boss. I'm an independent person, Mr Mkhwanazi, indeed, Mr Mkhwanazi, an independent person. It's all thanks to my superior education, certainly, my superior education."

Themba sneaked a glance at the man as he sang praises in his own honour, and was convinced this was really someone with a superior education.

Mr Ndebenkulu was a tall man; he looked down on the ground from quite a distance. His had a dark complexion. His face was rough. He liked to gently twirl his moustache whenever his hands were not in his pockets. He pushed his lips forward when he spoke. One tooth was long and hung over his lower lip. He was immaculately and expensively dressed from his hat right down to his shoes.

"The wagon is there," Themba said.

From the sudden clearing of his throat, Ndebenkulu was clearly a bit uneasy about the prospect of riding in an animal-drawn wagon. He said: "*Hhawu*, goodness gracious, Mr Mkhwanazi, in this place you still ride makeshift carts? Where are the buses?"

"We don't have buses in this area."

"Tch...tch...," Ndebenkulu said shaking his head in disbelief. He looked at Themba patronisingly, feeling sorry for this boy who lived in such a backward place. "It has now become patently clear to me why people from urban areas refuse to come to rural backwaters like these, indeed, now I see why. They hate the very idea of travelling on makeshift carts."

"No, sir, it's not a makeshift cart, it's a wagon."

"It's all the same, Mr Mkhwanazi. What's the difference?" He was visibly irritated by this countryside upstart who had the audacity to argue with him, C.C. Ndebenkulu Esq. "It's all the same for city people like us, we see no difference between this thing and a makeshift cart," said Ndebenkulu condescendingly, pointing at the wagon with his foot.

This thing. Themba was hurt to hear his family's wagon called 'this thing'. It dawned on him that today was the day

31

he might get hot under the collar. For the first time, he was stuck with someone who didn't just loathe the idea of riding in a wagon, but also couldn't distinguish between a wagon and a makeshift cart.

"I'm very sorry, sir, if you are not satisfied," Themba said calmly. "Here at Nyanyadu we use wagons. We don't have money in bucketloads. We're not rich people. Perhaps you in big cities are rich. We are poor people here. This is the best mode of transport for us, it's convenient for us."

"I have seen at first-hand, Mr Mkhwanazi, that you are poor. You don't have to tell me, I have seen it myself."

Those words pierced Themba's heart deeply. He was bewildered, and battled to find words in case he spoke out of turn. He said: "Those who use makeshift carts are still better off, as most people simply walk."

"It really never occurred to me that this place was so backward ... no, it never occurred. I thought highly of this place."

"What kind of transport does sir usually use in Pietermaritzburg, where he comes from?"

Ndebenkulu laughed loudly, as if feeling sorry for this silly rural boy. He said: "You see, had I known in advance that I was coming to such a place, I would have come in my car. I didn't imagine that in such a famous place people still use makeshift carts. It shocks me to find a place without a bus, I'm really shocked. Buses are common in even the most rural of rural areas."

Although Themba had started to be annoyed with Ndebenkulu, he was suddenly respectful, and in awe of him. He really was a tycoon – he even had a car. No wonder he spoke carelessly, and so insultingly.

"You have a car, sir!" Themba said, amazed.

Ndebenkulu simply smiled, relishing the gullibility of this countryside nincompoop. He started to gently caress his whiskers and said: "I don't have a car, my dear son, I have cars. You see, I don't like my wife to keep on nagging me, I simply don't like it. Since she is an enlightened person, involved in so many projects, she is hardly at home. When she wants to get around she simply takes her car and doesn't bother me. When I have a trip I simply do likewise. I find it too bothersome to have to wait for my wife whenever I have to go somewhere. It is inordinately bothersome."

For a moment they were quiet, Ndebenkulu stroking his moustache and Themba silently digesting Ndebenkulu's words. Then Ndebenkulu continued: "You see, Mr Mkhwanazi, it is unfortunate I didn't know better. Had I known, I wouldn't have worried you, I would have taken my car. The result is that now I have to make do with makeshift carts."

These constant references to his family's wagon as a makeshift cart revived Themba's anoyance. Although he was fully aware that this was a very important person who commanded respect, he was so annoyed that he was unable to regard the man highly. Realising that the tycoon had suffered by not coming by car, he apologised for the wagon and tried to explain that the alternative to this mode of transport would have been on foot. "So it means, sir, that you have never travelled by wagon?"

"I thought I had long told you, Mr Mkhwanazi, that I am not a rural bumpkin, I had thought I had made it very clear. I don't mean to insult your place by saying it in so many words. Don't get me wrong. Also, when I speak like this, Mkhwanazi, don't mistake it for arrogance. It is not. I am merely trying to tell things as they are. You see, for us people from big cities it's hard to notice any difference between this place and the rural countryside. I have never sat on a makeshift cart."

"Indeed, this place is rural."

"At least you agree."

As they were speaking, Themba was not standing still. He was loading Ndebenkulu's luggage on to the wagon. There was no room for luggage in front, and belongings were usually put at the back and fastened with rope or a strap. As Themba was loading the luggage, Ndebenkulu kept on gently twirling his moustache. His pointed tooth stuck out.

Ndebenkulu's gaze made Themba uneasy – he sensed that there was something the man was unhappy about. And he was damn right.

"Ignorance is problematic, Mr Mkhwanazi."

Themba turned to look at the man.

"Why is it problematic, sir?" asked Themba.

"You see, Mr Mkhwanazi, as I had said, I should have come with my car. You see, I paid 20 pounds for that suitcase, 20 pounds," repeating himself in English to emphasise the suitcase's price tag. "I paid two green notes and got no change back. I doubt very much that there is even a single person in this area who has this type of suitcase. Even white people, very few have this type of suitcase, very few really."

"One can see, sir, that yours is an expensive suitcase," Themba said, with a mixture of sarcasm and annoyance.

"Certainly," said Ndebenkulu, "it shows. It cost two fresh green notes! Now you see, Mr Mkhwanazi, if you fasten my exclusive suitcase with a cowhide strap, you press it hard and you risk damaging it."

For a while Themba stood, bewildered, his hands on his waist. What was the best way to handle a situation like this? Had he woken up in the dead of night and sacrificed his sleep for this kind of annoyance? If he left this person at the station, his father would be enraged. It was becoming increasingly clear that if this man continued with his waywardness, chances were that he would be left to his own devices at the station, even though he was rich, highly educated and with many cars. When he looked at that moustache that was always being stroked, and the overhanging tooth, he was infuriated. But he controlled himself, and refused to let his rage get the better of him.

"You hear well, my boy? I put 20 pounds down. This is a real suitcase. It's not something that is bitten by rain once and immediately turns into porridge, not at all. Therefore your fury – as I see you cheaply frowning – doesn't bother me, not even a bit."

Being called a boy and being provoked in this manner made

Themba even more angry. He was fuming so much that he was shaking. This person was not just condescending, but downright rude.

"If I don't fasten it, it will fall off along the way and get damaged," he said angrily. Themba realised that if he kept on arguing they would not make it home. He was not used to this type of person, someone who, upon his arrival, exhibited an exaggerated sense of self-importance and looked down on others. Themba continued tightening the strap, deciding not to bother any longer with the disagreement that was resulting from every single question. The wagon seat was dusty. Themba realised that this arrogant man would refuse to sit on it. Instead, he would keep on being grumpy about the car he had left at home and the ordeal of visiting rural areas. Themba pulled out a piece of cloth and wiped the seat, then asked him to get aboard. Ndebenkulu didn't utter even a word of appreciation. When Themba invited him to mount, he merely moved closer to the wagon. His unhappiness was written all over his sulky face, and he was clearly displeased that a man of his social standing had to ride in this fashion. It was as if the Indians, who were witnessing the drama from a nearby shop, were making him even more wrathful.

For him, riding in a wagon was demeaning. He finally climbed up, after asking Themba how to "ride on this thing", and sat there as if telling the world he was of royal stock. He pulled his trousers up a bit, revealing his socks in the process. He sat with his legs apart and his hands on his knees, but they quickly returned to the comfort of his pockets, since the morning winds were biting. Even then, one kept going back to his moustache. Because of the way Ndebenkulu sat, Themba sat uncomfortably, but was reluctant to ask him to be more considerate.

From the station they took the road from Dundee to Vryheid. When they had left the station far behind they turned and, leaving the Vryheid road behind, took the road to Nyanyadu. Even if the road was not regularly maintained, it was passable. For a long stretch there was silence on the wagon. Themba's blood was boiling, he was furious with this impolite man who was forever complaining about visiting such a backward community, enraged by travelling on a wagon with his suitcase – which cost him 20 pounds – strapped by cowhide. Themba battled to make up his mind as to the nature of the beast that had come to pay his family a visit. He recalled that in his letter the man had signed off as an Esquire. He was wondering how they would react at home, when the two of them arrived.

As they were travelling, one horse lifted its tail and, bang, it farted, comfortably unaware of the tension around it. Immediately, Ndebenkulu protested. "What the hell is this horse doing?" Surprised, Themba turned to look at him. What on earth is wrong with this person, Themba thought.

"What do you mean?" asked Themba.

"How will we be by the time we reach our destination, if horses keep on raising their tails in the air?"

Themba didn't say a word, there was no way he could respond to this nonsense. It was beginning to dawn on him that perhaps the man was crazy. The thought that he might have a madman aboard was disquieting. Worse, there was no way one could predict the moves of a mental case. The possibility that the man might be a madman grew stronger when Themba thought about the letter he had written to his father and the kinds of things they had discussed since he had met him at the station. For the better part of the trip they travelled in silence, neither dared initiate a conversation. Themba's anger had made him forget that he was hungry. They travelled along the smooth part of the road, and passed the Italian place. Ahead, the road was long and steep. Suddenly they were descending towards rocky plains, leaving Nyanyadu Mountain behind. As the rocky and gravelly road repeatedly unsettled the wagon, Ndebenkulu grew unsettled too. One hand was now firmly holding on to the side. It could no longer be comfortably fixed inside his pocket. The road was now terrible, hard hit by erosion. At times the wagon would rock as if about to capsize, and the rich man of

Pietermaritzburg would open his eyes wide, terrified. These roads were not pleasing to people from urban areas, where roads were regularly maintained and upgraded. As you drove, you saw the contours of the old road where, after destructive torrential rainfall, people had shaped a new road alongside the old one.

"When, exactly, are we going to arrive where we are going?" asked Ndebenkulu, looking at his wristwatch.

"We're almost there. In a while, there, we'll see some new houses. Just below, in the valley."

The road was really bad. There was no road at times, they were basically in the heart of thick grasslands. The wagon kept on rocking. Finally, the descent was over.

"We're now at the new housing development. We're going just there," Themba said, indicating his house, already visible in the distance. Ndebenkulu was silent.

After parking the wagon in the yard, Themba said: "We're at home now, sir, you may get down." Then he jumped down. Ndebenkulu stood up. As he was trying to get down from the wagon, his heel was trapped on the steps and he fell. A bumbling fool. His hat flew off and hit the ground. Themba's eyes opened wide in alarm and instantly he took the man's hand to help him up. Fortunately, that day Themba had opted for obedient horses for the wagon, for, had they been skittish, tragedy could have struck.

Ndebenkulu's face was beyond description. Sand was sticking to the protruding tooth. Ndebenkulu touched it momentarily, as if to confirm that it was not loose. He kept on spitting the sand out of his mouth. His clothes were covered in dust. His trousers were torn at the knee.

All at the Mkhwanazi household, Themba's mother maNtuli and his sister Thoko, stood in awe as the impromptu circus unfolded. They just couldn't believe that a visitor could arrive at their household only to be injured.

"Themba, what's wrong with you, almost killing someone?" MaNtuli asked.

"Not at all, mother, it's not my fault. I was getting down on this side and Mr Ndebenkulu was doing the same on his side. As he was getting down his shoe must have got trapped on the step. Do you think I would deliberately arrange someone's fall?"

"You see, madam," Ndebenkulu said, as he continued to spit sand, and brush the dust off his trousers, "you are the lady of the house, is that not so?"

MaNtuli nodded.

"As I was saying, madam, this is the very matter I raised repeatedly along the way."

As he said these words he was looking at Themba like an angry snake – straight in the eye. When he paused to take a breath his odd tooth trembled a bit. He was livid and shaking. His face was fiery and you dared not look at him now. His eyes were ablaze. Themba was simply astounded at this anger, since he was not responsible for the accident. After all, Ndebenkulu was the one who climbed down carelessly and got his shoe wedged. How could that be his fault?

Themba felt a sudden bolt of fury and defiance, sensing that this man was going to continue being just as rude as he had been all the way. Ndebenkulu was unrelenting, giving Themba a devil's gaze all the time he was speaking to maNtuli.

"You see, madam, I did tell your son... this is your son, is it not, maNtuli?"

MaNtuli nodded.

"It is the way I had imagined it. You see, maNtuli, I did tell your son that had I known better I would have driven myself to this place. I am not a commoner who can be driven on these makeshift carts you call wagons. Not at all. Just look at me now, just take a good look at me now!"

"Forgive us, sir, it was a terrible mistake," maNtuli said, apologetically.

"Madam, I am someone whose friends include prominent white people. I even correspond with them. Whenever they write to me they never forget to add at the end my title of Esquire." As he spoke he kept tapping his chest and peppering his speech with English.

"Then I get driven on makeshift carts that some people have the audacity of referring to as wagons. That is a terrible mistake. People were never equal, madam. There are people who can be transported on makeshift carts. I am not one of them. Not at all, me."

MaNtuli realised that the man was discourteous because he was angry. He could no longer sift his words with caution. The pain in his heart was now doing the talking. She resolved to express regret once more.

"Really, sir, your fall was an accident, as my son Themba has been trying to explain. We often transport city dwellers, and they never fall. Maybe it's because as an Esquire you are not used to such things. By the way, you said that's what white people call you?"

"Get me very well, madam, I really mean it."

"Wo! I really heard you very well. I was growing worried in case I missed something."

"I wonder what kind of an animal an Esquire is, daughter of Mphemba!" MaNtuli whispered to herself, addressing herself by her maiden clan name.

"You must bear with us, we're not used to these titles you people have, in your big civilised cities. We are mere rural dwellers. Do forgive us when we fail to pronounce the title with which whites address you. I'm sure you will get used to the wagon, and even develop a liking for it. Unless, of course, your stay here is short. If you were to stay here for a few more days, you would have got used to it by the time you left."

Themba is battling to suppress an insistent guffaw. His wrath has vanished and the fury that could have thrown his manners out of the window has lost its fangs. His mother's sarcastic reference to the title of Esquire is just too amusing to go unnoticed. Thoko was also suppressing her laughter but was still alarmed by the visitor's near accident.

"You see, Madam Mkhwanazi," said a still visibly enraged Ndebenkulu (he has not stopped spicing his speech with English — undoubtedly he is at home in this language), "it's quite clear that you are getting old now and your brain is beginning to fail you. Maybe it is due to the fact that you are a rural person. You have said as much already."

MaNtuli was dumbfounded, hardly believing that a stranger could speak to her so condescendingly. Both Themba and Thoko were stunned – if the man continued his tirade he would be unwelcome at the Mkhwanazi household. They knew that their mother was spontaneous wildfire. Fortunately, maNtuli simply kept quiet, though her heart was pounding.

Then Ndebenkulu went on: "Since you have lost your marbles..."

"What is this man up to, really, how can he talk to me in this way?" said maNtuli with her hands on her hips. "Can anyone confirm that I'm really hearing this man properly? What nonsense is this strange man talking, straight to my face? What kind of tomfoolery is this for you, daughter of Mphemba?"

"Take it easy, mother, please," Themba said looking for the best way to douse this growing fire.

"Get out of my way, Themba," said maNtuli, pushing him aside. "You keep telling me to calm down while this person is hurling abuse at me!"

"Please stay calm, mother, stay calm, beautiful Mphemba," pleaded Themba. Although he also thought the man obnoxious, he felt it would be improper for him to leave Nyanyadu on a sour note. Worse still, his father had not yet returned from the fields. Themba's sense that Ndebenkulu was a nutcase increased now. No sane person would act so strangely.

"Allow me to make my point, madam," Ndebenkulu said.

"To make your point and go on insulting me?" said maNtuli, livid.

"Let me finish, madam. Where I come from, in big places, even big white people listen when I speak and don't interrupt me until I'm done. I'm not used to being interrupted when I'm speaking, I'm not, simply not, used to that. Well, to a point I understand because maybe people in rural areas are not familiar with civilised etiquette."

"*Yehheni*, good gracious me! Oh! Themba, my child, what have we done, for you to bring us such a pompous big shot!" MaNtuli clapped her hands in mid-air in disbelief. "I just wonder – where are you, *baba* kaThemba, to help me witness this?" MaNtuli put her hands on her hips again and looked at this incredible man from Pietermaritzburg.

Ndebenkulu continued, not even slightly affected by maNtuli's anger. "I put down five pounds for this hat of mine that is now, as you see, dusty all over, madam." As Ndebenkulu spoke his eyes were bulging and his long tooth did not stop quivering. "You have never seen a hat like this, you never have. I'm certain that not even one person in this area has one, not even the local whites – if there are any here. Five pounds down! Not to mention my clothes. Just look at my torn trousers. Do you have any idea how much I paid for these clothes? How much? I'm asking you!"

"Goodness gracious me! What the hell is the matter with this strange many-lipped Ndebeningi fellow? No one was responsible for your fall, it was completely your own doing! What the hell is wrong with you? Why do you annoy me in broad daylight? What terrible omen are you bringing upon me?"

While maNtuli was talking, Themba went behind the wagon and began to loosen the long cord so that he could offload the luggage.

"Where is the luggage you're offloading going, Themba?" asked maNtuli abrasively.

Themba realised that his worst fears had come true.

"You want to tell me that you are offloading luggage because you think this fellow can be accommodated in my house? I would turn in my grave. Not in my house. Transport him on this box, because for him a wagon is a box, carry him on this box back to Tayside where he comes from. Not in my house. What nonsense is this? Am I someone that strange fellows should take for a fool?"

"Mother, do you mean me to take him back before father meets him?" asked Themba.

"Why does your father have to meet this man, I ask you? For what good reason does your father have to meet him? Oh, alright, let him wait outside, then, with his lousy luggage. But once your father has met him, I don't want him to set his foot inside my house."

"Hold on, madam, I think there is some misunderstanding. I don't mean to fight with you," said Ndebenkulu more gently, perhaps regretting his bad manners. "Even though you're refusing me entry into your house, when I'm already in your yard, do understand that my aim was not to start a fight. I was simply trying to show you that I was injured and also to make you aware of my social status, since you don't know me. You couldn't have known about my social status unless I had enlightened you about this very important fact."

MaNtuli, who was about to disappear into her house, answered carelessly: "As if I cared about your social status!" Then she was silent for a moment, before saying: "Themba, let him inside," as she turned and vanished into the house. Her angry words could be heard from inside; she got louder as her anger increased. "I've no idea where this high-flyer is going to stay, since we're poor people here, we have no cars and rely on boxes for transport. We don't have hats that cost five pounds here. We had no idea we were going to host a white man. Had we known, we wouldn't have allowed this fellow to stay with us. Even now I feel like showing him the door."

When maNtuli was done with her outburst, she came out of the house.

"I assure you, madam, don't worry much about where I will stay, don't worry, really. Even though I am used to a red carpet lifestyle, I will make do with what you have here. You see, the test of being a very important person is exactly one's ability to be humble. When I speak like this, madam, I don't mean to be as haughty as you think," then immediately began stroking his dusty whiskers. That tooth kept on asserting its presence. "I guess from your sharp tongue that when I try to explain all this you think I'm looking down on you and being arrogant. The fact is that I'm not trying to prove that I'm an important man, madam. No, that's not what I'm doing. I actually don't need to make myself look important. I'm already a very important man. I merely wanted you to know the truth about me since you've never seen me before. As I was saying, people who hail from the same area as me would also confirm my social status to you. When big white people write to me, they never forget to add the title of Esquire to my name."

MaNtuli did not believe a word of it. She had never met such a character in her life. She told herself that it was futile arguing with this fellow. Instead, she simply had to wait for Themba's father, who, in any event, was about to come home from the fields.

"Bring him in, Themba," said maNtuli, clapping her hands in the air as she returned to the house, and calling to Thoko to follow her.

•••••••••••••••••••••••••••••

As maNtuli was entering the household through the front door, Mkhwanazi was coming in from the fields, through the kitchen door at the back.

"You've come just in time to witness absurdity personified, courtesy of Themba's hospitality," said an enraged maNtuli.

"How come you welcome me with such absurdity?" Mkhwanazi said, alarmed to see maNtuli as angry as a raging sea.

"Don't tell me you aren't coming to meet this strange fellow Themba has brought us."

"Themba is back?"

"Hhe!" exclaimed maNtuli, clapping her hands in the air. "Only time will tell," she said as she sat down. After a momentary silence she said: "Themba is indeed back with this strange fellow."

"Get to the point, maNtuli, what's the matter?"

"Don't tell me you aren't going to see it for yourself. Lord have mercy on us! Themba has really brought us a problem man."

For a while Mkhwanazi stood in silence, looking at his wife. "What do you mean?" he enquired.

"I don't mean anything, *baba*, in no time you will see it for yourself."

Mkhwanazi was perplexed, and said nothing, but when he had gathered his thoughts, he said: "MaNtuli, the person you describe in such derogatory terms is a man of high social standing."

"You're not the first person to tell me that, baba kaThemba. Since the man arrived that's the monotonous song he's been singing without end."

"He's been monotonous? What do you mean, he's been monotonous?" Mkhwanazi is getting angry – what maNtuli is saying doesn't make sense.

"Nkwali, I am a fully grown adult now. Let's get that one straight," she said, punctuating her words with a clapping of hands.

"MaNtuli, just get to the point."

"Well, he fell off the wagon."

"What?"

"Yes, he fell off the wagon. In fact, in his wayward city wisdom this rich man calls it a makeshift cart, if not a box." MaNtuli immediately burst out laughing, shaking her head.

"If Ndebenkulu had an accident, what's funny about that? What the hell is wrong with Themba? How could he do that to such a big man? Where is Ndebenkulu? Was he hurt?" Mkhwanazi was suddenly nervous at the thought.

"Yehhe, it's just so funny to realise that you two actually speak the same language. He also keeps harping on his greatness."

"It's not a matter of him saying so. He is. He has a big name. How dare you speak of him this way, maNtuli!"

"*Baba* kaThemba, why are you staring at me like that? What gives you so much confidence in the truth of this man's greatness? Did you perhaps have a vision of the fellow when you were in the fields? Isn't it true that his letter fell into both our hands while you were at the table eating sour milk? Isn't it true that you didn't tell me then that you knew this man? For what good reason did you not say this? Because both of us were confused by the contents of the letter? Why didn't you tell me?"

"Who says I know him?"

"What's your point then? Why then, if you don't know him, do you insist that this is a big man?"

"The letter he wrote says it all."

"You've got to be joking. More is in store for you. Did he tell you in his letter that whenever white people write to him they never forget to address him as an Esquire? Did he tell you?"

"What caused him to say that, maNtuli?"

"I just told you that Ndebeningi fell off the wagon!"

"I have already heard that, maNtuli. Tell me more – what led to the accident?"

"He's not familiar with a horse-drawn wagon, he's an urban high-flyer. This was his first encounter with it. He regrets heavily that he didn't know he would be transported on a box, saying that had he known, he would have brought his car." MaNtuli sniggered sarcastically.

"He's never seen a wagon?"

"Yes, never. After all, white people call him an Esquire!"

"We already know that, maNtuli, since he signed his letter in that manner. There's nothing surprising about that."

"Well, unfortunately wagons don't give a damn about Esquires. Would you like to know how he actually fell off? He kissed the earth, I swear on my father's soul."

"MaNtuli, just explain this to me – what do you mean? Why are you wasting the whole day failing to make yourself understood when I still need to see this Ndebenkulu that you greeted by letting him fall off the wagon?"

"He says he had never travelled by wagon before today."

"That may well be true. There are no horse-drawn wagons where Ndebenkulu comes from. We hear that people there are better off. They have cars."

"He also tells us so."

"Why, maNtuli, do you keep on saying 'he also tells us so', as if you think Ndebenkulu is telling lies?"

"You seem to know all about how great he is, so I had better believe him as well," she said mockingly.

"Really. Really," said Mkhwanazi repeating himself in English, "I know it by the simple fact that I know in the cities some people are well-off. In fact, they are so well-off that they have essentially become white people."

"Oh! *Baba* kaThemba, it's so funny to hear you speaking exactly like Ndebenkulu," said maNtuli as she got up from her chair.

Mkhwanazi looked at his wife, bewildered by her words. She continued: "To this fellow, English is God. No dialogue is complete for him until there is an English word to enhance it. To my surprise, you've started doing the same."

Mkhwanazi said nothing. Then he went to greet his visitor. He had initially intended to ask for water, to wash his hands, but after maNtuli had annoyed him, he had forgotten.

When he went to the room, Ndebenkulu was moving around nonchalantly, looking at the pictures on the wall, smoking a cigarette. He was still wearing the same clothes he had been wearing in the morning. When he heard someone entering the room, he turned at once.

"It's a pleasure to meet you, sir," said Mkhwanazi.

"It's also my pleasure to meet you, sir. You must be Mr Mkhwanazi, the head of this household," said Ndebenkulu, extending his hand to shake Mkhwanazi's. He looked much better, since he had dusted off his clothes after the accident. One hand went straight to his moustache. Immediately, the tooth protruded.

"Indeed, I am Mr Mkhwanazi. You may take a seat, sir," Mkhwanazi said, as he sat down.

"Thank you very much, Mr Mkhwanazi," said Ndebenkulu, sitting.

Mkhwanazi looked at the man intently, trying to assess the extent of his injuries. He had entered the room quite anxious in case they were serious. When he had tried to get maNtuli to explain, she had typically been like most women, simply kept beating about the bush. Mkhwanazi was relieved to find the man looking at pictures and smoking a cigarette. It looked like he was fine, after all.

"I hear that you almost had a terrible accident."

"It is so, Mr Mkhwanazi, indeed it is so. Those who told you so were telling the truth."

"These things happen, Ndebenkulu, more so if one isn't used to this type of transport." Mkhwanazi said, lighting his pipe. After a few puffs, he said: "You people in big cities like Pietermaritzburg aren't used to travelling by horse-drawn wagons. You're used to better modes of transport that are also good for one's health, such as cars."

Ndebenkulu smiled a little and pulled out another cigarette from an elegant silver case. He then pulled out a cigarette lighter.

"It's wonderful, Mr Mkhwanazi, indeed it's just wonderful to meet someone with a sharp mind, someone who is quick to understand things. It's just wonderful. Look, I don't have to tell you that, as someone who comes from a big city, a horse-drawn cart is a strange animal to me."

As the two puffed, smoke filled the air. Both men were relaxed in armchairs, each man with one leg crossed over the other.

The armchairs had been top quality in their day, but since Mkhwanazi had bought them second-hand, from a Nyanyadu priest who had been transferred to another mission station, signs of wear and tear were evident. Their colour had begun to fade and they had a terrible smell – it was quite possible that mice had found a home and a toilet inside these tired chairs. Interestingly, though, at Nyanyadu these chairs were the favourites of the people who had seen and sat on them. They were also the pride of the Mkhwanazi household. In this room there were these two armchairs and two tall chairs, also thoroughly bitten by age. They were originally brownish – but one could no longer vouch for this colour with any certainty. When you sat on them, the legs were unsteady. You would sit with a great deal of anxiety, waiting for the chair to take you down at any minute. There was also an old cupboard. It was once brown but with time had turned black. The drawers were stiff and even when opened, after great difficulty, would often be crooked. Holes had become prominent where there were once handles. To open the drawers, you would insert a finger, or a stick or nail. This was a very old type of cupboard. In the cupboards, maNtuli kept her crockery and other household things. On the wobbly legged dining table, empty jam jars served as decorations. One contained flowers – once decorative but long dead and dried out.

Cow dung was used to polish the floor. This was Thoko's job virtually every Saturday. A few goatskins were scattered on the floor. There was only one window, and it was rather too small for such a big room.

"Here in these farmlands we rely on horse-drawn wagons – it's our form of transport," Mkhwanazi said with a laugh.

"I realise this, but you see, Mr Mkhwanazi, it is also important that you are wary of things that may cause you accidents and lawsuits."

Ndebenkulu paused, and Mkhwanazi gripped his pipe tighly as he tried to digest these words.

"You see, Mr Mkhwanazi," Ndebenkulu said, "a person of my stature isn't familiar with a makeshift cart. Since I was born, I have never had a cart ride. Never! Now I pay you a visit and you impose your cart on me as my transport. Because I'm not familiar with a cart, I will make a mistake, and get hurt. If I'm injured by your cart, driven by you, I'll simply take the matter to the police."

"I hear you well, sir," Mkhwanazi said, pulling his pipe out of his mouth. He pressed the tobacco hard with a matchbox, as if he had not packed it in properly. It was soon back in his mouth.

"It's such a pleasant surprise for me to find such a wise man in the countryside. I just can't emphasise it enough, it's such a pleasure, really," said Ndebenkulu. "Too often, we assume that all countryside people are fools, only to be proven wrong," he said with a smile, looking at Mkhwanazi as if to assess how he was absorbing these words. He kept puffing cigarette smoke until it drifted throughout the room. Mkhwanazi found the compliment flattering. He felt immensely proud to receive praise from such an esteemed person as Ndebenkulu, a person who came from high places.

"You see, now, my trousers are damaged. My shirt is damaged. My coat is damaged. And so is my hat. I paid a lot of money for these items, Mr Mkhwanazi, yes, a lot of money. You see, this hat alone cost me five pounds. I dare not say anything more about the rest of my clothes." While Ndebenkulu is saying all this, he is looking Mkhwanazi straight in the eye, to be sure that what he is saying is well understood. Mkhwanazi hurriedly blew smoke from his pipe, as if to shield himself from his guest's piercing eyes. He looked at the clothes Ndebenkulu was talking about. He looked at the moustache and the tooth. He understood that this was no ordinary fellow.

"You see, Mr Mkhwanazi, at this stage I'm only talking about the clothes," said Ndebenkulu. "I'm also injured. I'm supposed to be compensated for the injury. It depends on the social stature of the person in question. In my case, you must know that not even one white person who knows me writes to me without addressing me as an Esquire. Not even one."

For a while, Ndebenkulu was silent, smoking his cigarette and blowing thick smoke into the air. He looked Mkhwanazi in the eye. Mkhwanazi was at a loss for words, and could only ask: "By the way, what type of person is an Esquire?"

Ndebenkulu looked a bit disappointed. He had thought highly of Mkhwanazi. Little did it occur to him that Mkhwanazi's question was the desperate measure of someone as flood waters swept him away.

"I don't know how best to explain this, Mr Mkhwanazi. Only important whites have this title. You will never hear an average white person addressed with this title. When I was trying to explain this to the lady of the house, I noticed that she didn't take it seriously."

Ndebenkulu lit another cigarette. Mkhwanazi was disturbed that MaNtuli had been rude to such a distinguished person.

"Oh yes, I observed that she took it lightly. You see, Mkhwanazi, were I to take the matter to court, I would deplete your entire cattle stock."

By then, his moustache had grown two pointed horns. His weird tooth looked as if it had suddenly grown even longer. He was seated as if about to disembark from the chair, one hand on his leg and the other on his knee to hide the hole in his trousers. He was looking straight at Mkhwanazi. Mkhwanazi pulled out his khaki handkerchief and wiped the sweat from his face.

Ndebenkulu smiled, and said: "Fortunately I am not that type of man, Mr Mkhwanazi, not at all. I must say, though, that I almost lost my temper when I saw the lady of the house making fun of my misfortune and showing no sympathy after the cart had caused me to be injured. At that time it came to my mind that I should let the law take its course and show her the real world. But now I realise that what was at work was the typically dull mind of a woman, a mind that's incapable of guarding against accidents."

"Indeed, sir," Mkhwanazi said. By now he was so overwhelmed with sweat that the handkerchief hardly left his face.

Ndebenkulu smiled as he carried on smoking.

"Oh yes, I know women very well, Mr Mkhwanazi. Unlike us men, they aren't wise. Yes, they aren't wise. Women in the city are better. Rural women are dangerous. They can cause a man a great deal of trouble without realising it."

"It's sheer ignorance, Mr Ndebenkulu. At least you city people know everything. You even know the law. You even know that when someone has fallen off a wagon he can go to court and get money in return. People like us have fallen off wagons many times and have never been paid even a penny." As Mkhwanazi said all this, he was lighting his pipe. It often troubled him by going out by itself. For a while he remained silent, as if considering this unique way of making money.

"You see, in the city the law is our cash cow. Oh yes, it's our cash cow," Ndebenkulu said. "You see, Mr Mkhwanazi, you won't survive city life if you don't understand the law. Oh yes, you will not survive. You can become easy meat for the cunning types, I tell you. You see, in my case, not even one person, not even a white man, can take me for a ride. I've got volumes of legal books, huge volumes, I tell you. By the way, Mr Mkhwanazi, how far did you go with your formal education?"

Mkhwanazi laughed. "Oh, Mr Ndebenkulu, there is no education to speak of in our case. We only went as far as Standard Four, and couldn't afford to go any further."

"I was asking, Mr Mkhwanazi, so that I could perhaps tell you the names of the books I have, but now I realise it wouldn't be of any use. You see, I have these law books. That's one of the reasons whites call me an Esquire. Oh yes, that's one of the reasons. Mr Mkhwanazi, when you hear me talking like this don't get the wrong impression – that Mr Ndebenkulu is arrogant. It's not so. I'm not at all arrogant. I'm definitely not the arrogant type. I'm saying all this to lay bare real facts that people in the countryside don't know. Even more, Mr Mkhwanazi, it disturbed me to see that the lady of the house had no idea who she was speaking to. But since I have noted that you are a different and intelligent person, I have calmed down. What's done is done."

Mkhwanazi was getting increasingly irritated at his silly wife maNtuli for her failure to know who she was dealing with. Now she is going for high people like Ndebenkulu, people who know a lot about the law and even have big books to show for it. No wonder she had avoided being clear when Mkhwanazi was enquiring about the circumstances surrounding Ndebenkulu's accident. Obviously, she was hiding her shame. MaNtuli's shortcoming is her short fuse. Had Ndebenkulu not been the kind and peaceful man he is, his entire livestock would have been depleted in one day, all thanks to a woman's stupidity. As he thought about his cattle, a rush of anger overwhelmed him and made him breathe heavily. He was wet with sweat and his pipe had gone out.

Mkhwanazi could not hide his fear from this fellow. He was battling to sit still and face the man's piercing eyes. He had to find an excuse to go outside for some fresh air. "I think, sir, you might want to change your clothes," he said.

"I would be most grateful, Mr Mkhwanazi, oh yes, I would be most grateful. Really, it won't be a good idea for me to find myself in the company of other people whilst wearing a pair of trousers that reveal my knees," he said with a smile, looking at where his trousers were torn.

"I'll give you some privacy so that you can change into other clothes. No one will disturb you in this room, I'll just close the door."

Still sweating, Mkhwanazi left the room and went straight to the kitchen with his pipe. As he entered he was greeted by raucous laughter. Themba was saying: "...five pounds down," and kept on repeating the statement in English. Mkhwanazi almost lost his temper, rushed at Themba and narrowly missed hitting him in the face. This shocked everyone in the household, since Themba was already an adult and no longer subjected to corporal punishment. Mkhwanazi's lips were quivering with rage and when he tried to speak his voice refused to come out. When he regained his composure he shouted: "What the hell is this? Is everyone in this household mad, or what?" He looked behind him and suddenly closed the door so that his loud voice would not be heard in the rest of the house. "I'm busy that side trying to douse the fires that almost burned my house down while you here in the kitchen are busy playing silly games."

Stammering in his rage, his eyes were menacing – he looked at this one, then that one and then all of them. Themba was still standing near the door. He was afraid, angry and confused. They were all shocked into silence at their father's sudden fury, and had no idea what caused it. What kind of fire was he extinguishing? What was he talking about?

He then addressed maNtuli. "Even you, maNtuli, an adult, are busy encouraging children to be rude to important people instead of calling them to order."

MaNtuli felt she had to speak out. She was also getting annoyed. "*Baba* kaThemba, what on earth is wrong with you, butting in and almost eating everyone alive, what's the matter? What kind of bad luck are you courting? How have the children been rude to important people?"

"Have you no shame to even ask me about it, when my entire livestock was almost confiscated?" He moved closer to maNtuli, as if about to hit her as well. MaNtuli didn't move an inch. Mkhwanazi continued: "What's this mischief Themba is up to, mimicking Ndebenkulu?"

"Good heavens! What do you mean? Is there anyone who is above mimicry? Even a king can be mimicked!"

"A king can be mimicked! I'm asking you, is a king mimicked? Did you ever mimic a king, maNtuli, you tell me? In any event, I'm not taking about a king, I'm talking about Mr Ndebenkulu. He had an accident that you told me about. However, you chose not to tell me about your crazy behaviour afterwards."

"What the hell is wrong with you, *baba* kaThemba? What's the matter with you?"

"What is wrong with me? Is that the correct way for a wife to speak to her husband and ask what the hell is wrong with him? What's the matter with me? Who are you asking that silly question? Don't you realise that you are the source of it all, now that you want to leave me as poor as a church mouse? MaNtuli, it astonishes me that an adult like you chooses to take Ndebenkulu's accident lightly. I almost lost all my livestock because of your behaviour!"

As his temper was rising, he started sweating heavily again. The fireplace was lit, and the heat in the kitchen made it worse.

He continued, now speaking to himself. "I have my ancestors to thank that I left the fields early and returned home. Little did I realise that my ancestors were bringing me home so early to douse the fire that maNtuli had made, thanks to her childishness."

He looked at maNtuli. "Ndebenkulu was fuming about his

clothes. Perhaps you didn't notice his anger, since important people have the knack of concealing their feelings. When we were speaking a few minutes back, he made it clear that, had he wanted to, he could have taken us to a court of law and taken away all my cattle."

"How would he take away your livestock, father?" asked Themba.

"Shut up! Shut up! Nx! You have the nerve to ask me such a question when you're the source of it all!" He moved closer to Themba as if to hit him. Themba realised that the situation was tense, and said nothing more.

"I'd forgotten about your type. Your little exposure to college life makes you think you're better off and that you can do as you please. What's worse is that your mother is sniggering along instead of reprimanding you. Meanwhile, it's left to me to douse the fire. Oh, my entire herd of cattle!"

"Well, we don't know, *baba*," MaNtuli said, trying not to prolong the quarrel. She was baffled. Her husband had turned into a man she didn't know.

"What is it you don't know, MaNtuli? Just tell me what is it you don't know? Ndebenkulu showed me something I always suspected, that rural women are stupid and their brains move slowly like a wagon wheel. Someone from a civilised city life was quick to realise that your behaviour, maNtuli, was the result of your countryside upbringing. It's a surprise for me, that he could be so spot on. This is a really bright fellow. No wonder white people respect him! Despite all that, maNtuli decides to be impolite to him!"

"I swear to God you are not well, *baba ka* Themba. How dare you talk like that when someone has just insulted me? Do you know that this fellow insulted me and said I was a mental case? And now you also repeat that kind of nonsense!"

"You see, father..."

"Sh! You better keep your mouth shut, Themba, right away! Shut up! Don't think of uttering even a word!"

"Let my child speak. Come rain, come sunshine, what the hell is wrong here that a strange man comes and sows confu-

54

sion in my household? You even attempt to smack my children, a habit you long abandoned. You're even using swear-words when talking to me. Have you lost your mind, *baba ka* Themba? Do you realise that I can leave you and disappear, right away, so that you and your Ndebeningi can be left to your own devices? I won't stand for such nonsense. Are all you men are like that? You respond to respect by treating another person like filth!" MaNtuli was really livid, and suddenly her short temper seemed to bring Mkhwanazi back to his senses.

"I'm just objecting to being interrupted by children while in the middle of saying something. That is not proper behaviour, maNtuli."

"What do you mean, he's interrupting you, when you didn't even give him an ear? Do you want to tell me that Themba is a crawling baby, or what? Why don't you give him a chance to make his point?"

Mkhwanazi was at a loss for words, not knowing whether to leave or to let Themba speak his mind. He simply stood still, silent and confused.

"Speak, Themba, this nonsense of being silenced in our own house, because of some strange fellow, can't be tolerated anymore."

After her mother had reassured him that he could speak, Themba said, "It's now clear to me that this person is not who he claims he is."

"It's this kind of drivel that you want me to listen to, MaNtuli? You want me to let children mistake my head for a stadium on which to play their silly games?" said Mkhwanazi, touching his head to make his point. "Since when have children interjected with their silly ideas when I'm speaking? Is this what they teach at the college? What do you mean, you don't believe this man's story?"

"I don't know, but ..."

"You don't know! So why then do you open your mouth, when you don't know what you're talking about?"

"What the hell is wrong, *baba ka* Themba? Why don't you

let the child finish making his point before you interrupt him? What were you saying, Themba?"

"I was saying there is something amiss about Ndebenkulu."

"I'm not surprised since you also have your mother's stubbornness. A person may see your long trousers and think you have grown up, not realising that like a fowl it's only your legs that have grown, your mind hasn't grown at all! I send you to receive Ndebenkulu at the station and you decide to make him fall from the wagon. Is this your scheme to see the end of my cattle stock?"

"Father, he fell off the wagon on his own."

"Themba, you better shut up! Just shut up! Where do you get the audacity from, to argue with me? Who says I have time for such hot air? Your wayward mother, who makes you mistake my head for your playground, has spoiled you. Do you think it's a small matter to have my entire livestock impounded because of your stupidity?"

"I curse the arrival of this strange man who from the moment he got here has caused so much quarrelling in my household. By the way, do we call him an Esquire?" MaNtuli asked innocently.

Had they not feared their livid father, the children would have burst out laughing at this stage. He was looking at them as if daring them to slip up, laugh and face the music. Foremost in his mind was a nagging conviction that maNtuli was trying to make fun of him. He was silent for quite some time, unable to utter a single word.

At last he said, "MaNtuli, as an adult you are the last person I would expect to do this. You're conniving with children to make fun of an adult and a very important person. What's wrong if he tells you he's an Esquire? Didn't he say that even when white people write to him that's how they address him? Do you want to tell me that he's lying? You tell me, is he lying?"

"The fact that he calls himself an Esquire doesn't mean much, father," said Themba in a measured tone. "They can also write to me ..."

"They call him an Esquire!" Mkhwanazi interjected abrupt-ly. "You better keep quiet and stop talking nonsense! What kind of an Esquire are you? An Esquire that ensures people fall from wagons? Little did I realise that you have suddenly become so rude because you consider yourself an Esquire. I noticed a long time ago that your head, Themba, is messed-up – it's like your mother's. Now I see. You caused Ndebenkulu an accident because you considered yourself an Esquire as well!" As he finished the sentence he looked as if the thought of slapping Themba again had just crossed his mind. Themba stepped back.

"Just stop this, maNtuli. It makes me so angry, I'm afraid I could end up injuring someone."

Mkhwanazi opened the door to the other room. As he did so, his and Ndebenkulu's chests almost hit each another. While Mkhwanazi was visibly embarrassed, Ndebenkulu was at ease.

He said: "I was looking for you, Mr Mkhwanazi. I hope I'm not interrupting anything. Now that I have changed my clothes, I was wondering if you have a newspaper. Do you have it by any chance? I missed today's newspapers since when we passed Dundee the stores hadn't yet opened. For city people like us, a newspaper is our daily bread. Indeed, it's our daily bread. Pardon me, Mr Mkhwanazi, if I have troubled you."

Mkhwanazi was stunned. He wondered for how long Ndebenkulu had been eavesdropping. If he had been listening for quite some time, he had heard the whole quarrel. This annoyed him – how could a man of Ndebenkulu's stature do such a low thing?

"My newspaper will only arrive on Monday," said Mkhwanazi, walking out. He was followed by Ndebenkulu, who could see that Mkhwanazi was unhappy and obviously did not believe his excuse about coming to get a newspaper.

He said: "Really, Mr Mkhwanazi, don't let your mind wan-der too far. Believe me when I say I was coming to ask for a newspaper and the door opened just as I was about to knock.

I'm really worried that you found me at the door just when I was about to knock. Something like this can be wrongly interpreted — how can a man of my stature be caught tip-toeing in another man's house? The reality is that I wouldn't be seen dead doing such a low thing. Such deeds are the deeds of low-class people."

Mkhwanazi calmed down and began to believe that Ndebenkulu was telling the truth. Considering that this man had just been so kind to his family by not taking the matter of his accident to court, Mkhwanazi had a lot to be grateful for. A man with such a heart was definitely not the tip-toeing type.

• •

"You know, mother, I really don't understand why father is so upset," said Themba. MaNtuli was quiet for a while, as if she had not heard. Then she said: "My child, the source of his anger is obvious. Your father believes he was almost left without any livestock, all because of me. He says this fellow says that if he had gone to court about the accident we would have been left with nothing. I think that's the only reason your father got so upset. After all, you know how much your father values cattle. In fact he possibly values cattle more than anyone I know. Themba, in his mind the fact that a stranger insulted me in my house is nothing. What matters a lot to him is that he almost lost his entire livestock."

"I'm sorry, mother, but I don't believe all that," Thoko said. "If it was someone else's fault that he fell off the wagon it would be a different story altogether. Since he did it all by himself, why would this lead to taking away all the livestock?"

"I agree with Thoko," added Themba. "There's something wrong about him, constantly telling us he's an Esquire."

"What use are your misgivings, since your father takes what this fellow says as gospel truth? Worse still, if he hears you talking the way you do, he will be mad. You'd better come to terms with the situation and not unduly frustrate your-selves."

"Well, it's hard to tell, mother," Themba said. "I never knew that some people have become so in love with white people to a point where they can't even ride on a wagon. In any case, other whites still ride wagons. I just think there's more than meets the eye about this Ndebenkulu fellow."

"By the way, mother, what brings this fellow here?" asked Thoko.

"How am I supposed to know? In his letter he merely asked that a meeting be called on his behalf with the community's men. He claims he wants to bring progress to the people of Nyanyadu. Apart from that, there's nothing else I know about his visit. Now I regret agreeing to host him in my house. Even now I'm considering asking him to leave."

"No, mother, that wouldn't be a good idea," pleaded Themba.

"Themba, did he tell you along the way what brought him here?"

"No. We hardly had a real conversation. We were fighting all the way. He was unhappy that I had put him on a horse-drawn wagon, in fact he called it a box. I've never known such a rude person in my entire life. Tell me, mother, do you think this story of helping people is genuine? Why would such a selfish person bother about helping others?"

"How would I know, since the little I know is what he wrote in his letter? I'm battling to understand why he chose our house in the whole of Nyanyadu. Maybe your father will put us in the picture once this man has explained things to him."

"Mother, given father's irritation with us, I doubt he'll give us more information. What's foremost in his mind now is the livestock he almost lost," Themba said.

"I still can't understand why your father would side with someone who insulted me in my own house, and even agree with him that I'm insane."

"Father can't find fault with anything this Ndebenkulu says," added Thoko, laughing.

"It's not so much that he's protecting Ndebenkulu. He's thinking about his cattle. Did you see how the matter of his livestock makes him perspire with anger?"

"What would you say, mother, if father asked for a sheep to be slaughtered for Ndebenkulu's welcome ceremony?" asked Thoko.

"You may well joke. The truth is that your father would do just that if he thought the gesture would save his livestock. It wouldn't surprise me at all. Themba, just check who the dog is barking at, it could be maShezi."

• •

"Apologies, I'm late," said maShezi with a laugh.

"*Sawubona*, good day, maShezi. You really don't have to apologise – you came just in time. How are you?"

"We're well. How are things going with you? You don't look happy at all. Has your guest arrived?"

"We're well. It's just that this strange fellow who is our guest has caused us so much grief." MaNtuli went into the kitchen, followed by maShezi.

"Really!" MaShezi was surprised.

"What a burden we have here, my sister! It's a real white man, I swear!"

"What do you mean, he's white? Didn't you say he's Ndebe...Ndebe who?"

"Indeed, he's Ndebeningi, who happens to be a black person who behaves as if he was white. The first thing he does when he opens his mouth is to speak in English." As maNtuli was saying this she was mimicking Ndebenkulu, even bobbing her head in the same way.

MaShezi burst out laughing, then suddenly felt uneasy and restrained herself.

"What's even worse, this person is damn impolite."

"It's hard to believe that, maNtuli. What on earth would give a visitor the courage?"

"Just sit down, so that I can tell you more." MaShezi sat down

next to maNtuli who then told her about Ndebenkulu's melo-
dramatic arrival after Themba had fetched him, as well as his
fall from the wagon. When she mentioned the wagon accident,
maShezi couldn't control her laughter, but then felt slightly
guilty, and said: "I should behave now, how can I take this misfortune as a laughing matter when someone could have died?"

"Maybe death is what he deserved."

"Don't talk like that, maNtuli," maShezi said with an
uneasy laugh.

"I'm completely aware of what I'm saying, and I mean it."
Then maNtuli told her friend how Mkhwanazi had suddenly
turned into an angry lion, ready to devour anyone alive who
dared ridicule Ndebenkulu.

"It's quite strange to associate Themba's father with that
kind of behaviour."

"I agree with you, but unfortunately that's exactly the situation we are in."

"I feel really sorry for you, " said maShezi.

"He must thank Themba for the fact that he's still here. If
I had things my way, he would not be in this house as we
speak."

"How could you do something like that? Indeed, Themba
did the right thing. You must be proud, your son is now a real
man, maNtuli. Anyway, where is this fellow who's caused you
so much grief?"

"I suppose he's in the house, where he continues to intimi-
date baba kaThemba."

This remark made maShezi burst out laughing again.

"Did you perhaps want to see him?" asked maNtuli.

"Not really, I just felt it polite to greet him as our visitor."

"You may go there if you so wish."

"Don't tell me you won't accompany me!"

"Not at all, me! Mabhozomela would rise from the dead!"

"*Yehheni!* That's very strange behaviour! Why, then, did
you invite me to your house?"

"Bear with me, Shezi. Just go and greet him, I'm still not in
the mood to see such a rude fellow."

Since maShezi was a regular guest at the Mkhwanazi household, she went off to meet Ndebenkulu. She was back in the kitchen in a few minutes. "Well, my friend, it seems there's a lot you could have told me." She was whispering to maNtuli, trying to contain her laughter.

"Please don't tell me anything more about this irritating man. I wish he was already on his way back to where he came from."

Giggling, maShezi said: "My friend, what on earth is cooking with that tooth?" She sat down. "Now I'm beginning to appreciate the source of your anxiety. Anyway, are the arrangements we spoke about yesterday still fine?"

"I've no idea. It's up to you."

"Please don't say that. You simply can't be so cold when you have a visitor in your household."

"My heart's no longer in it. After all that's happened, I'd rather be seen dead than find myself running around for this man. Anyway, he has Themba's father to do all that for him now, not me."

"You can't talk like that. How can you make a visitor go hungry in your household?"

"Do you think it's my problem if he's hungry?"

"Please don't act like a child, maNtuli, and stop being heartless. Where have you ever seen this kind of behaviour? Just tell me what to do, so that we can start cooking before sunset."

"I thank you for everything, maShezi. Don't bother yourself about cooking. Thoko will do it."

"MaNtuli, how dare you treat me like that? Make me leave my domestic duties to come and help you, then behave like a child! What you're doing is completely unacceptable. Even if this man has angered you, he's still your guest and you owe it to yourself to do the right thing. Despite everything that has happened, common courtesy demands that you must be friendly to him."

"Forgive me, Shezi. You know I wouldn't lie to you. I really intended to be warm to this important city man, and you're also aware of that. But now I have no interest whatsoever. I plead for your forgiveness. You remember that we both worked hard till sunset yesterday, but if I'd known better I wouldn't have bothered to allow the man into my house."

"Since there's nothing that needs to be done here, my friend, I might as well go home and attend to the chores that need my undivided attention."

"Please wait a bit, so that you can take your sheets before you leave. Thoko!"

"MaNtuli, please come to your senses. What's your visitor going to sleep on?"

"Like us, he'll have to make do with flour sacks. Thoko!"

"Thoko, don't listen to your mother. Really, maNtuli, I'm most disappointed with you – never allow anger to make you behave in such a manner. I'm certainly not taking the sheets with me. "

"It seems you have a soft spot for this man."

"Not at all. I'm just trying to show you the proper behaviour, maNtuli. In this world it's important to do the right thing."

"The trouble with you, maShezi, is that you're too kind."

"To be honest with you, I'd rather be too kind-hearted than have a heart as hard as stone like yours."

"I never thought that even you, maShezi, would turn against me."

"I'd be making a terrible mistake to support you when you're truly at fault. Simply treat the visitor well and stop being childish. I'm on my way."

"Forgive me, really, I was so upset I even forgot to send either Themba or Thoko to let you know you didn't have to bother any more."

• •

"Indeed, sir, now it's becoming clear to me that what brings you here is really an important job. Your job is really important, it's about uplifting your own people." Mkhwanazi said these words while loading his pipe. "The letter hardly explained anything. This was a problem, as I couldn't explain myself well to the local men when I was trying to invite them to a meeting with you."

"A letter couldn't have explained much. A matter like this is best explained in person. Oh yes, it's better explained in person. Helping my people is my first love," he said as he lit a cigarette. "You see, Mr Mkhwanazi, this requires deep love since our people are blind and stubborn to such a point that when you, as an enlightened person, try to make them see the light, they still insist on resisting your help. So much so that when you try to help them they're quick to think that your main purpose is to steal from them and bring them trouble."

"What you're saying is true. On the other hand, Mr Ndebenkulu, people are not to blame since there are so many crooks around nowadays, they even target helpless widows. It's understandable for most people to be cautious."

"You have a point, Mr Mkhwanazi, you have a point. It's just that someone like me, who believes in helping people, can be easily discouraged when people are negative. It's even worse since what I do is not driven by material gain. I don't get even a penny from what I do."

"Someone who works for people has to learn to be understanding and not be easily irritated with people. If you're short-tempered you will achieve nothing."

"I guess that's the reason I'm still doing my job. I'm also able to control my temper. I think my patience has a lot do with it," said Ndebenkulu, taking a puff of his cigarette. "My point earlier, Mr Mkhwanazi, is that this job is my calling. The challenges that come with this are nothing to me since I have my own material things. A person who is in trouble is one who can't do much because he is employed and can't do as he pleases for fear of losing his job. Such a person is in trouble. On the other hand, with me," he said as he crossed one leg over the other and put his hand to his moustache, "I'm an independent person. Even though some people think I'm rich, it's not true. What is true is that I'm not poor. Also, I don't need to be employed." He did not speak for a while, but pulled on his cigarette and released smoke through his mouth and nose. There was no doubt that this was a proud man, the Esquire of Pietermaritzburg.

"Mr Ndebenkulu, I would be pleased if you could expand a bit about how you help people."

Ndebenkulu looked at Mkhwanazi, then said: "Clearly you don't read newspapers in this area – I'm always in the newspapers." He searched in his pocket for a card. "This is my name."

Mkhwanazi studied the card and concluded that indeed he was in the company of an important man. He had seen business cards at Dundee, but only carried by doctors and lawyers – very important white people, in fact. It was the first time he had seen a black person carrying a business card. On it was is written C.C. Ndebenkulu Esq., 2a Blue Seal Arcade. It means that this man is telling the truth when he says he is an Esquire. He is really telling the truth. Even his business card confirms this fact. It is unlikely that white people would print something that was untrue. He felt the need to show the business card to his stubborn wife maNtuli, and her equally stubborn children, so that they might realise the wrongfulness of their attitudes. When Mkhwanazi had satisfied himself studying the business card, he handed it back to Ndebenkulu.

"Don't worry, Mr Mkhwanazi, you may keep it. I have many of them."

"Thank you." Mkhwanazi pulled out a box of matches, since his pipe had been doused. As he began smoking again, he said: "I'm still listening, sir."

"It's true, Mkhwanazi. Oh yes, it's true. However, since it has become clear that there are so many of our people who are blind, the few of us who have seen the light have a duty not to forget the blind. There are so many people who are still blind in their minds."

Ndebenkulu was smoking as he spoke. He also kept on shifting his legs, the left on top of the right, and vice versa.

Now and then he fiddled with his moustache.

"I fully agree with you. Most people like us, who are like the blind, often feel neglected by our people who have made it in life. Often, they see themselves better off and up there, while we are down here and worthless. It's the right thing to throw a rope down to us so that we may use it to climb to your level."

"That is why, as I have said before, Mr Mkhwanazi, our efforts are often undermined by people who think ill of our intentions. They would say we're crooks and intent on squandering their money. This mistrust makes me very angry and makes me even consider leaving everything to have a good time with my wife and children, because in any event I'm not poor. Whatever I do is solely inspired by my love of our nation."

"That's how we are as people. We hardly see what will bring us fortune until it's too late."

"You're right, Mr Mkhwanazi. When one is about to give up, letters like this one are very encouraging," Ndebenkulu said as he pulled a letter from a stack in his bag and gave it to Mkhwanazi. "Read it, Mr Mkhwanazi, it's written in Zulu."

Mkhwanazi took it and read it.

Esinadini School
P O Edendale

Dear Sir,
I am writing to you Mr Ndebenkulu to thank you for what you have done for me. I actually do not know what on earth would make me forget you. I know I will forget because that's how a human being is. Whenever he is out of a problem, he usually forgets those who helped him out. In fact, happy are those people who know your mother in person. I still insist that there is only one way to explain the reason for you to visit our area when we were having the hardest of all times. I think you were a messenger of God. The money which you helped me with came at the right time for my children, and me more so since I am a widow. I chased away jackals that were after my blood and that of my children day in and day out. What on earth can make me forget

you? What would be so wrong with me as to make me forget you for you became my father and mother when I was in dire need? I never get tired to pray for your blessings and that your work continues to prosper so that you may continue to help our poor black people. I never forget to pray for you and your family so that you may all be blessed. May you never stop doing your great work. May your heart forever be touched whenever you see poor and helpless people.

I am the one you freed from the chains of pain and poverty. I am the one who will never forget you – the one who forever wishes you well and long life.

Ndiletha Hlongwane.

Mkhwanazi was speechless for some time after having read this letter, and it was clear that it had deeply touched him. He looked at it for a long time, then folded it and gave it back to Ndebenkulu.

"As I was saying, Mr Mkhwanazi, these letters encourage me a lot even when certain situations threaten to dampen my spirit."

"It's a good letter, sir. Your work can only succeed when you have letters from widows you have helped, who wish you well."

"I would like to emphasise that I'm a man of means, Mr Mkhwanazi. I've got enough money for my family and me. I've got properties I bought through my own sweat. I have my own livestock. I have two cars, one for me and another for my wife. I'm not trying to show off about my material possessions, no, it's not the case. I'm merely showing you that for someone who is as successful and self-sufficient as I am, it's truly disappointing when people doubt your good intentions. It's truly disappointing."

"I hear you well, sir. I hear you, and also fully agree with you. We have also observed that, here in the countryside. As I said, one shouldn't stop doing good because of that attitude. Also, the letter you just showed me is evidence that not all people are ungrateful. You shouldn't stop doing good simply because of those few people who don't appreciate your deeds."

"I can't agree with you more, Mr Mkhwanazi, you are very right. The reason I still bother is that my heart aches when I see that our people are in need. I can see that they need help."

"Also, Mr Ndebenkulu, God gave us different gifts. It's becoming clear to me that perhaps your gift is helping your own people. God brought you to this earth for that mission. Allowing negative people to discourage you is like falling into temptation."

"You know, Mr Mkhwanazi, I've never seen it quite like that. You're so right. You're actually giving me a new way of looking at it. I really get your point."

"Regarding the meeting, Mr Ndebenkulu, you will be pleased to know that the notice is out. I personally took care of it and I went on horseback to speak to all the men. But when people asked me to explain the purpose of the meeting, I couldn't tell them anything since your letter was vague."

"You're right, Mr Mkhwanazi," he said as he crossed one leg on top of the other. "I often make the mistake of assuming that everyone knows about my service to my own people. It's a job that hardly gives me an opportunity to be at home with my family as other men are. You know, Mr Mkhwanazi, at times I worry that one day I'll arrive at home and my children will mistake me for a stranger."

They both laughed heartily. Ndebenkulu puffed on his cigarette, twirled his moustache and let his long tooth show. It was clear to Mkhwanazi that no matter what his social status was, this man was good humoured. He felt honoured to share a light moment with such an important man.

"As I was saying, Mr Mkhwanazi, I had thought that many people know my work by now. However, I now appreciate that there are others who have never heard of my job. I usually explain my work in newspapers – but I realise that it's been a mistake for me to use English newspapers just because I know them to be read by most people. It's not everyone who reads English newspapers." He went to his briefcase, searched for a while, and said: "My apologies, Mr Mkhwanazi, I thought I'd brought one of these newspapers but now see that I left it behind. It has to do with the fact that I was in a hurry when I left home and had to rely on my wife to pack my newspapers for me."

"In any case, Mr Ndebenkulu, even the Zulu newspapers are not widely read. I often read important news in the Zulu newspapers since it's the only one I read. I don't get the English one. When I share the news with local people they're surprised, in most cases, as they don't read the newspaper. This disappoints me, since a lot of these people are even more educated than I am, yet they don't consider reading a newspaper something to bother about, and have to rely on us."

"It makes sense, Mr Mkhwanazi, that you have never heard about my work because you only read a Zulu newspaper. In future I must bear that in mind. I must remember to write to Zulu newspapers. At the meeting I will share my vision about the future of black people and how they can better their lives. For now, I can tell you that my aim is for our people to have enough money and be independent. I'm talking from experience, Mr Mkhwanazi. Oh yes, I'm talking from experience. Had I not been independent I would also not be here. I really mean it, as I've also realised that for the black person to rise, earn respect and power, he has to get economic independence. The rest of the things will follow. I'm just giving you a summary at this stage. Yes, it's just a summary, I'll say more about my vision at the meeting on Monday, when the entire community is in attendance. Fortunately I won't be taking chances when I outline my plan. I'm not a chancer. I'm speaking from experience and know that what I'm talking about does work and many people have benefited from it. You personally heard it from Mrs Hlongwane's letter. Do you think, Mr Mkhwanazi, that people here will attend a meeting addressed by a total stranger?"

"I must admit that your timing is inconvenient as we're busy cultivating the soil. Some people are very far behind and haven't even planted their seeds. I found this to be the concern of many people. I'm confident however, that they will come, since the meeting was announced far and wide. I also urged them to attend because it will only take one day. Fortunately, since visitors are rare at Nyanyadu, most people will be curious to meet a person from far away, especially someone who brings us good news like you do. So I'm optimistic that they'll come in their numbers. Others will come because we have a proverb that says those who always remain behind and do not seize the moment will never achieve much in life."

"I'm very happy to hear that, Mr Mkhwanazi. Indeed, I'm very happy. It's encouraging to know that my visit won't be in vain. It would also hurt me to achieve nothing after having travelled this far at my own expense, only to find that the men I've come all the way for are unable to meet me."

• •

"Mr Ndebenkulu, I think it would be better if we took a walk, we've been in the house for quite some time now. You need to stretch your legs a bit."

They went outside. One hand was tucked inside the pocket and another was holding a cigarette. Mkhwanazi had taken off his coat and was busy filling his pipe. It kept going out, and his matches were soon finished.

As they walked past the kitchen window, maNtuli noticed that they were going to the cattle kraal. Thoko also saw them and said: "Didn't I tell you, mother, that father intends slaughtering a beast for this man? I guess that's the reason they're going towards the kraal."

When Thoko burst out laughing, the sound reached Mkhwanazi and Ndebenkulu. Mkhwanazi was immediately annoyed, afraid that this might revive Ndebenkulu's ire, which had subsided by then, and in fact Ndebenkulu did not take kindly to the laughter. He thought it was sarcastic and was convinced that he was the subject of ridicule. He looked up and saw Thoko looking out through the window in their direction. When Thoko caught sight of Ndebenkulu she disappeared immediately. Seeing this simply confirmed Ndebenkulu's suspicions. Mkhwanazi glanced at him and saw him frowning, but soon he appeared to calm down, fortunately. It seemed inevitable to Mkhwanazi that eventually he would be on the receiving end of the man's wrath. Had Thoko been close by, who knows, that very laugh might have suddenly turned into tears.

"Were you to stay much longer, sir, I would have taken you on a tour of this district since I know you're unfamiliar with it. You see, down there, that's the Umzinyathi River, a famous river, I must add."

"Yes, Umzinyathi is a well known river. I didn't realise that it runs through this area. I remember learning about it at school. If I'm not mistaken, in our geography class it was called the Buffalo River."

"That's correct, this is the famous Buffalo River. If you look further down the valley, you'll see some houses. That area is called Basuthwini – the place of the Sothos. Only black people live in Nyanyadu. We live all around this area and the place you passed with Themba, where people have built four-cornered houses. Can you still see there, where you came from, in that direction? Down there are cultivated fields. The area where people have built four-cornered houses is called Clones. There, far away, is the Wesleyan Mission Station. Not far away from the Wesleyan church is the school, and that's where we will hold our meeting. Across there is a government-owned farm called Milifothwe. The road you see there passes a place called Stini, somewhere near the bushes. If you proceed straight on that road, they say, you can end up in Newcastle."

"I can't believe you just said that Mr Mkhwanazi! Why do you say 'they say'?"

"I'm simply telling the truth because I've never been there. I only go as far as Spookmill."

"I didn't know there was a place called Spookmill," said Ndebenkulu with a superior smile. "Tell me, Mr Mkhwanazi, where is Dannhauser from here?"

"It's this way," said Mkhwanazi, turning to show the direction.

"If I fell in love with this place, Mr Mkhwanazi, I might consider returning and spending more time appreciating it. I think, though, it would be a good idea to use my car next time because I'm not comfortable taking a ride on a cart. No, I'm not comfortable on it."

Mkhwanazi's heart momentarily beat faster as he was reminded about something he wished could be forgotten.

"You are most welcome, sir, to bring your car next time, so long as you remember that our roads are not the best. You saw it for yourself on your way from the train station. I'm concerned that bringing your car might damage it."

Mkhwanazi then called Themba, who turned up straight away from the direction of the horse paddock.

"Themba! Please ask those boys to bring the sheep much closer."

Themba immediately recalled Thoko's words but did as his father had instructed him. He was very unhappy about what his father was doing. The presence of this stranger annoyed him even more when he remembered that his father had even tried to hit him, something he had not done for a long time. Despite his dissatisfaction, he had to accept that the sheep were not his but his father's. There was simply nothing he could do to change that.

"What did I tell you, mother? You've just seen it for yourself," said Thoko softly. "Father has just asked Themba to ask the boys to bring the sheep home."

"Just don't tell me about your father and his Ndebeningi. He wants to earn his forgiveness so that he doesn't seize his entire livestock. I've now realised that you can never really be sure you know a person well. Your father disappointed me so much by allowing a total stranger to disturb his family's harmony. In any case, he's his own man. The sheep are his and he can do as he pleases with them."

"Father is really overwhelmed by this fellow."

"Overwhelmed, Thoko? Not at all — he's afraid. Fear best

explains his actions. Listen to me when I say he's bending over backwards for this man so that he forgives him and doesn't seize his livestock. Do you think I don't know your father that well? There's just no other away to explain his behaviour. Now he's only hearing the trumpet this arrogant man is blowing. There's nothing else your father's ears can hear. I'm just amazed your father behaves as if he never saw a big man constantly boasting, whereas this arrogance simply astonishes me. Nx! What irritates me the most is his cheap English."

In no time the boys emerged with the sheep. After he had inspected them, Mkhwanazi chose one.

"Forgive me, my guest," said Mkhwanazi. "A strange disease has killed the sheep recently. They're also thin, since it's been dry for some time. That's the reason we are now busy cultivating because only now are we seeing signs of rain. Even if it's only a lamb, it will help you defeat hunger. I hope that one day you'll find us in a much better position than this."

Ndebenkulu's happiness was written all over his face, and he was clearly moved by the gesture. He conveyed his heartfelt appreciation, adding that the animal's size did not matter. Expressing his gratitude, he even forgot to use English. He could not stop twirling his moustache now and his long tooth looked as if it, too, was craving the feast.

"Boys, remove its skin!" Mkhwanazi ordered.

Mkhwanazi left Ndebenkulu with the boys and walked towards the house. He entered through the kitchen door.

"You and the Esquire are madly in love," remarked maNtuli as Mkhwanazi passed by. "You're even slaughtering a sheep for him!" MaNtuli does not look at her husband as she speaks, she is up and down in the kitchen although one can hardly tell what, exactly, she is up to.

Mkhwanazi was so taken aback that he stood as if shocked by electricity. "Still busy with your rude tricks, maNtuli? Why are you doing this to me? Why do you drive me into doing something I don't want to do, beat you, more so when we have a visitor?"

"Beat me," maNtuli said lazily. "You must be joking, baba kaThemba. I don't think you can hear what you've just said. You have no shame. When I'm already this old and wrinkled, you still talk of beating me, all because of a fellow you barely know! Where d'you know this Ndebeningi of yours from, who you're now slaughtering my children's sheep for?"

"Your children's sheep? Where did they get them from? What makes you talk such nonsense, maNtuli, when you're this old? What disease has attacked your mind? When I left for the fields in the morning you were well – only to find you insane on my return!"

"*Hhabe*! Again repeating the same insulting remarks made by your Esquire? I'm surprised, *baba* kaThemba, that today you're slaughtering a sheep when not so long ago you refused to do likewise for my sister's child, saying that drought had greatly reduced your livestock – and I backed you up because I knew you were telling the truth. Much to my disbelief, a sheep has been slaughtered today. This has happened all because of this thing you don't even know, a thing with a hanging ugly tooth and a thing that keeps boasting in his cheap English about the fact that it's an Esquire."

Mkhwanazi was a bit frightened because maNtuli was so loud. He was afraid that Ndebenkulu might hear, and re-start the inferno that had been extinguished. He closed the kitchen door and spoke softly, trying to conceal his fury.

"MaNtuli, what on earth makes you so rude? Calling someone a thing, a thing with a hanging thing and a thing that is busy annoying everyone with its cheap English? Do you have any idea how Ndebenkulu would react if he heard you talk like this?"

"As if I cared about him! You'd better not bother about me, *baba* kaThemba. Am I telling a lie? You can also see that this fellow's tooth is hanging."

"The cause of this, maNtuli, is this raw head of yours. It didn't cook. Themba has the misfortune of having taken after you. You're doing this because you refuse to accept that Ndebenkulu is a big man. Take this, it's his card. Read it for yourself. For someone who only went as far as Standard Four it is odd, maNtuli, that you say Ndebenkulu is irritating you with his cheap English."

"Hhe! If you only realised, *baba* kaThemba, just how ridiculous you are!" She is not even looking at him, but studying the card he has given her. "So I'm a thing that went only as far as Standard Four! What about you, *baba*, which college did you study at, by the way? So this fellow of yours gave you this?" She thrusts the card at Thoko. "Take this, Thoko, and give him the card for his Esquire."

"I hope for the end to the rudeness that's being brewed in this kitchen, before someone gets hurt. I don't want to do something that will embarrass me and my household in front of our guest, as if there are no rules in this house." Mkhwanazi turned and went out of the kitchen.

"There you go, Nkwali, you might as well do that in case you catch your Esquire tip-toeing around, looking for you in the kitchen," maNtuli added.

The words cut into Mkhwanazi's heart like a sharp blade. Although he was so provoked that he felt the urge to say something more, he decided against it. He took out his handkerchief and wiped away the sweat.

•••••••••••••••••••••••••••••

The following day was a Sunday. As was the tradition in the Mkhwanazi household, on that day everyone woke up early to get ready for the church service. The animosity that had arisen since Ndebenkulu's arrival was still evident, and the lady of the house would not budge. When it was breakfast time she refused to join the rest of the family at the table, despite her husband's pleading. Mkhwanazi chose not to continue begging her, as this would be too humiliating. As a man, he had to pretend that maNtuli's stubbornness did not bother him at all — deep down, though, Mkhwanazi was remorseful about the way he had addressed his wife and children the previous day. Since, however, they were the ones who, from the beginning, were so determined to be impolite to Ndebenkulu, he soon consoled himself and concluded that after all he was not the one who had started it. What had angered him the most was the serious threat to his livestock, thanks to the wagon accident Themba had caused. Worse still, instead of being sorry they had poked fun at the man's English and his long tooth.

When Mkhwanazi thought Ndebenkulu was dressed, he went to him. Ndebenkulu had been accommodated in Themba's bedroom, much to Themba's displeasure. "Would you accept an invitation to join us at church, Mr Ndebenkulu?" he asked.

"Is the church something taken seriously in rural areas?"

As a staunch Christian, Mkhwanazi felt uneasy about this question. He did not take kindly to people who were disparaging towards God's house. Despite his slight discomfort, he knew that he had to play it easy since Ndebenkulu understood his rights and could promptly invoke the long arm of the law. The man has volumes and volumes of law books – he had to be cautious lest he court trouble. To say he was afraid of the man would be an understatement. He was in awe of him, his social status, knowledge and even, perhaps, his shadow. He could only say: "Do you mean that where you come from people don't go to church?"

At this point Ndebenkulu wished he could take back what he had said. "Please don't get me wrong, Mr Mkhwanazi, what I meant is that in the city there are just too many things to do, and at the end one forgets that it's a Sunday."

Mkhwanazi said that at Nyanyadu churchgoing was both a morning and an afternoon affair. "If you still feel tired, you might as well stay behind," he told Ndebenkulu.

"In actual fact, Mkhwanazi, I would love to attend and to see your church. The truth is that although I'm not a churchgoer myself, my parents are. In fact, my father used to be a Lutheran preacher."

"*Awu*! It's wonderful to hear that you're a son of a preacher. Now I see why you're so committed to the social uplifment of your people."

Ndebenkulu found this amusing. He took out a cigarette, lit it, and smoked.

"I'd be happy if you come along for the church service. There you'll meet many of the men and this would put them at ease about tomorrow's meeting, since they'll realise that you have already arrived."

"I couldn't agree with you more, Mkhwanazi. At what time does the service start?"

"Although it's supposed to start at 11 often this isn't the case as many people come from far away. We're still on time, the first round of bells hasn't rung yet."

• •

So when the first round of bells was heard, the household was locked up and everyone proceeded to church. Ndebenkulu and Mkhwanazi went together and took it easy, as the path was steep. Both were smoking, one a pipe and the other a cigarette. From Ndebenkulu's cautious walk it was clear he was concerned that the dust might make his suit dirty. It was evident that he was an immaculate dresser and someone to whom image was everything. Mkhwanazi kept on spitting on the ground, as if the nicotine was irritating his tongue. MaNtuli and the two children were following at a little distance.

In the church, everyone soon realised that a very important person was in their midst – when the rest of the congregation sang, he simply kept quiet, as if saving his energy for better things. Now and then he would clear his throat, his hand remaining firmly in his pocket. Even though he was not singing, the other hand was holding a hymnbook as if for effect. When the congregation sang the second hymn, he put the hymnbook down and took out a spotless white handkerchief. He gently wiped his glasses, clearly unperturbed by whatever was happening around him – if, at all, he still remembered where he was. As he did this, he glanced now and then at the congregants from the vantage point of the

front row – one befitting his status. When he was done, he put
the handkerchief back into his pocket and put the glasses on.
He took up the hymnbook again and enjoyed himself by show-
ering the bewildered congregants with occasional glances. His
left hand would leave his pocket only to play with his moustache, or so that he could look at his watch. His long tooth
also peeped out as it pleased. People kept glancing surreptitiously at this strange yet obviously important man. You did
not need anyone to tell you that, indeed, this was a man of
high social standing. Whenever their eyes met Ndebenkulu's,
they would immediately look down in awe. The children, that
morning, sang even louder than usual so that the man would
notice them. When it was time for the congregation to sit
down, he would take much longer to sit, as if he expected
applause. There are men, and then there is Ndebenkulu!

At the time of Ndebenkulu's visit to Nyanyadu, cow dung
was the only kind of floor polish the church could afford. This
was a poor church whose structure was made of mud.
Ndebenkulu found it uncomfortable to kneel, since it would
make his immaculate trousers dirty. Every time, before he
knelt, he laid his handkerchief down first, and made sure that
he knelt delicately so that his knee would derive some comfort, at least, from the hankie. As the kneeling became more
frequent, he simply sat, and ignored the call for all congregants to go down on their knees. By now, his handkerchief
was completely dirty – much to his displeasure.

When it was the time for announcements, Ndebenkulu was
introduced, and the congregation was told that this was the
man who would be addressing the community the following
day at the local school. Ndebenkulu was commended for
attending the church service, as was Mkhwanazi for bringing
such an important guest. This kind of recognition, and particularly being associated with a man of such high social standing, gave Mkhwanazi much pride. He took out his handkerchief and wiped his face. While the deacon of the church was
speaking, Ndebenkulu was quiet, but making all the subtle
gestures that underlined a great sense of self-importance. He

kept slightly pressing his long tooth against his pursed lips, as if busy contemplating something profound. For maNtuli, all this buffoonery was too irksome for words.

As was often the case in the countryside, after the sermon was over many people queued to greet Ndebenkulu and make him feel welcome. Many were rural women to the core. With blankets on their shoulders, as they went forward to greet him apprehension was written all over their faces. They would not look straight at the man, but would bow before him and laugh nervously, like little girls. Meeting the congregants, Ndebenkulu was adding some resonance to his voice and throwing in a few English words.

"I didn't realise you and your very important guest were still around," said maShezi mischievously, as she shook maNtuli's hand.

"Don't start it again, maShezi, just when I'm on my way back from church."

Then maShezi enquired how the mood had been at the Mkhwanazi house after she had left. "It was just fire all the way, Themba's father was just fire and nothing else."

"He's truly a man who would die for his livestock."

"Until now I hadn't realised that our family's livestock is life to him. You know, I'm not even speaking to this strange fellow. I've already had enough of him."

"On that, maNtuli, you're at fault. You must learn to manage your emotions maturely. You know quite well that in our culture one isn't allowed to be discourteous to a guest. As we say, there's no telling where your itchy foot will take you tomorrow."

"Well, that expression of our elders was definitely not coined for the kind of guests who insult their hosts and create disharmony in a family on their arrival."

"You were supposed to pray for God's wisdom in the church, maNtuli. You surely need his grace."

"Please go home past my house and fetch your bed linen."

"*Yehheni!* Will somebody tell me what is wrong with maNtuli? If I take the sheets what will this fellow sleep on?"

"I've already told you, he'll sleep on the flour sacks we all use."

"*Awu*! *Awu*! *Awu*!" said maShezi, clapping her hands mid-air in disbelief. "Your attitude, maNtuli, leaves me so astonished that it's as if you've defeated me in a boxing match we never had. Anyway, I'll fetch them later. I'm not going home yet because first I need to visit the Mdlaloses. The wife is apparently unwell."

They parted ways.

Ndebenkulu didn't attend the afternoon church service, saying that he wanted to rest and also to prepare for the community meeting the following day. "Don't worry about me, Mkhwanazi. I will remain behind and take care of the house. I can also ensure that your pots don't get burnt," he said with a smile. Mkhwanazi also laughed, then looked at maNtuli to gauge her reaction, but she found nothing humorous in it. Even Thoko, who was also laughing, had to cut it short when she realised that her mother's brow was creased. She found it embarrassing that Ndebenkulu had noticed that her mother did not welcome him.

"Don't worry about the pots. Thoko and I will take care of them," said maNtuli sulkily.

"So this means I'll have to go alone?" Mkhwanazi said, surprised that maNtuli was no longer prepared to go to church. "I might as well stay at home as well."

"It's entirely up to you, *baba*." MaNtuli put her hymnbook on the table and went outside.

Mkhwanazi and Ndebenkulu stayed behind in the lounge, while Thoko went to the kitchen to start cooking.

"He says he'll look after the pots when I doubt he even knows to cook simple *mielie pap*, for that matter," said maNtuli. "He's too arrogant, and so irritating."

"Don't you think, mother, that at times forgiveness is due?"

"Please, Thoko, don't even think of it. He could even be a crook, for all I know. Why do you think I decided not to go to church this afternoon?"

"You may be taking things too far, mother, accusing him of being a crook."

"Thoko, I'm surprised you think all is well with this man. You're just blind, like your father. In his case I understand, because his fear is the possible loss of his livestock – in your case it's just gullibility. Even his silly tooth is making me so angry I wish I could knock it out with a hammer."

"No, mother! Oh God! Your judgment is clouded by his insults. I think this is a decent man."

"Only time will tell, my child."

• •

The meeting was scheduled to take place at 10 o'clock at the local school, since the schools were on holiday. At the crack of dawn, some men started work in the fields before coming to the meeting, and as the heat of the morning sun grew stronger, men started to emerge from the fields, singly and in groups of two, three or more. Some came down from the Mzinyathi River, some from the valleys in which the Wills and Rutland farms were located. Some came from the near-by mountain, while others came from Malinga's direction. Some carried their traditional fighting sticks and knobkerries on their shoulders, and others wore heavy coats, despite the day's heat. Some were in many respects traditional countrymen, whereas others were clearly men with a certain degree of education and modern sophistication. Some were accompanied by their dogs, and others were on horseback. Even though they were already on their way to the meeting, some were seen shouting at herdboys, who seemed to be not doing their jobs properly, as the cattle were on the verge of invading the *mielie* fields. Most were not on time, and the few who were spent some time talking outside, and only entered the classroom when the heat of the sun became too much to bear.

Ndebenkulu came early and when it was time for the meeting to start he kept looking at his wristwatch, clearly a bit anxious. He said: "It's evident, Mr Mkhwanazi, that you are still true country folk with no sense of punctuality."

"That's mainly because many people here don't have watches," Mkhwanazi said. "People here rely on the position of the sun for time. Even in households with clocks, they're often not set correctly and people don't bother much about it. Let's be patient, they're on their way."

Ndebenkulu smiled sarcastically as if feeling sorry for these rural people for whom setting a clock was something they might do without making sure they knew the correct time. He said: "I hear you well, Mr Mkhwanazi. It's the same problem in the city, even there some people don't understand that punctuality is important. You know, Mkhwanazi, whether one is in the city or in the countryside, failure to be punctual is a sign that one is uncivilised. This is the reality all people have to face in the modern world. Indeed, a person who can't keep time is uncivilised."

"Good people," said Mkhwanazi, as he looked at his wristwatch, "it's long past the time that was set for this meeting. I think we must start the meeting so that we can all go back to the work that awaits us in the fields. Those who come late will have to catch up with us. We can't afford to waste the entire day here."

With his spectacles on, Ndebenkulu nodded his head in approval, and began to page through a pile of papers on the table in front of him. Then a group of men entered the classroom, among them a bearded young man who walked with a pronouced limp.

"My fellow men, since you haven't come here to listen to me, but to hear the words of this respectable man seated in front, Mr Ndebenkulu, let me not take up much of your time, but quickly allow him to address you."

The tall bearded man laughed a bit on hearing the name of their guest. Ndebenkulu heard the laugh and looked around to see where it came from.

"Who did he say this man is?" asked an old man who always showered you with his saliva when he spoke.

"He says he's Ndebenkulu," responded a young man impatiently.

"He says he's Ndebenkulu?" asked the old man.

"*Yebo*," said the young man.

"What ethnic group is he?" asked the old man.

"I've no idea," said the young man.

"What?" asked the old man.

"I'm telling you again, I don't know."

The old man fell silent as soon as he realised his questions were irritating the young man.

"Good people, Mr Ndebenkulu is a very important man. He is so important that it's still hard for me to understand why we in Nyanyadu came to be blessed with his visit today. Since I often make mistakes about who he really is, he will introduce himself properly when he rises to address us." Mkhwanazi paused. "Before he talks to us, let me say a few words about him and the purpose of his visit. Since he arrived at my house on Saturday I have had the opportunity of talking to him. Mr Ndebenkulu is a very wise and successful man, as you will soon find out. He has his own properties, two cars, and is without doubt no ordinary man, but a very important one in society. He believes in helping his people and today we have the rare good fortune of hearing him share the secrets of his achievements. What brings him here today must be highly commended by everyone."

Mkhwanazi's praise was echoed with murmurs by some men. Others, however, found his long-winded speech boring and could not wait to listen to the guest who, after all, was the reason they had come in the first place.

By then, Ndebenkulu seemed to be shuffling his papers even more and was heard clearing his throat repeatedly. With one hand, he kept adjusting his expensive spectacles. His other hand was doing what it did best, playing with his moustache. His long tooth did not move. Now and then, he would lift his eyes and look at the tall bearded man.

"Something that most of you here might fight exciting is the fact that Mr Ndebenkulu is the son of a preacher."

Although some attempted to clap hands, when they realised they were in the minority they quickly withdrew the gesture, slightly embarrassed.

"Well, let me not take up much of your time," said Mkhwanazi. "Before this respectable man speaks to us, I hope he will bear with me if I read a letter he read to me at home, which is proof that he is a man who helps his people."

Ndebenkulu was visibly pleased for Ndileta Hlongwane's letter to be read to the men of Nyanyadu. He was quite happy to pull it out for Mkhwanazi to read it. The classroom was dead silent as the letter was read. From the seriousness written all over their faces, it was pretty obvious they had absorbed its contents well.

"I will now hand over to Mr Ndebenkulu to explain his mission in detail," said Mkhwanazi.

At that stage the bearded young man burst out laughing but looked down as if to hide his behaviour. This irked Ndebenkulu but he nevertheless ignored it, shuffled his papers even more, removed his spectacles and cleared his throat. His hands were for the most part inside his pockets, except when he momentarily took one out to massage his moustache. He looked at the gathering.

"I am honoured today to be in this community of Nyanyadu, a place I have heard a lot about but did not have the opportunity to visit. Today it is my pleasure to come this far. I am really pleased, since I am someone who is usually quite busy. I am not someone who simply goes around visiting, without any clear purpose. I have much on my plate and have to plan my trips very carefully. Today I was supposed to be meeting with the mayor of our city to discuss matters relating to the social welfare of our people."

Tsi-tsi-tsi-tsi-tsi... the giggles of the young bearded man were testing Ndebenkulu's patience. As the young man took out his handkerchief to wipe his eyes, Ndebenkulu frowned, visibly irritated. But he continued: "With me is the letter from the mayor of my town. It is addressed to Mr C.C. Ndebenkulu." He held up the envelope for all to see. When he began reading it, the young man's laugh became louder and more brazen.

"Mr Chairman, I understand that in the countryside some

people might not know much about the most appropriate behaviour in a meeting. Indeed, I know that. However, how can I be expected to address you when some find what I am saying funny, and do not realise that their behaviour is barbaric?" Ndebenkulu was reaching the end of his tether.

He was not alone – some in the classroom were of the same view, after all, they had come there to listen to this important person and were not prepared to let a silly young man spoil such a serious occasion. People seated in the front started staring at the back, curious to know who was guffawing.

Mkhwanazi rose and called for calm and respect. "May we all behave, please, and not expose our rudeness. You may now continue addressing us, sir."

"As a city person, I am used to addressing gatherings attended by black and white people," said Ndebenkulu. "In such gatherings I usually use English because it is much easier to explain and simplify development concepts in that language."

Much to the chagrin of almost everyone in attendance, the bearded young man burst out laughing.

"You better get out now and not keep on giggling here. Do you think this is something to laugh at? What's the matter with you?"

At once the young man rose and left, sensing the rising wrath in the classroom. After a short silence there was order again, and everyone paid attention to Ndebenkulu.

"People of Nyanyadu, I really regret that after having sacrificed time to come here, someone of my high social standing is being reduced to something to laugh at. I truly regret this, people of Nyanyadu."

The men were genuinely embarrassed and wished a big hole would immediately swallow them up to save them from this humiliation.

Mkhwanazi again took the floor. "We don't mean to be disrespectful, sir. It's these wayward young men who have lost their manners and even dare defy their fathers. Please go ahead, Mr Ndebenkulu."

Ndebenkulu obliged. "I will do so, Mr Chairman, although I must say that I'm truly disappointed. As a visitor to Nyanyadu, it doesn't give me a good impression to see a young man misbehaving like this in the presence of old and grey men. No, this does not give me a good impression. Where I come from, such behaviour would simply not be tolerated."

A murmur of discontent was heard from the men, and some even looked outside as if getting ready to pounce on the young man who had caused them so much embarrassment.

"Respectable men of Nyanyadu, I am here to help develop your community. I am not here to benefit, nor to get a salary for my work. I would like to stress that. I'm a man of means. As the chairman said earlier, I own my own properties and am not a poor man at all. I'm highly respected where I come from and there is not even a single white person who writes to me without addressing me as an Esquire."

Again, laughter punctuated Ndebenkulu's speech. The culprit was the same – he was standing next to the wall and eavesdropping. One man went outside hurriedly, brandishing a stout stick, but the young man was ahead of the game. The man soon came back and sat down, huffing and puffing.

After waiting for the man to take his seat, Ndebenkulu spoke again. "I would like you to get this point quite clearly – not even a single white person writes to me without using the title Esquire after my name."

For a while Ndebenkulu was silent, as if to ensure that everyone had heard him well and had properly registered the significance of his statement.

"What did he say whites write after his name?" asked the old man who found it hard to control his saliva when he spoke.

"Sh-h-h-h!" A younger man quickly called the old man to order.

"Perhaps most of you have no idea what the word Esquire means. What I can tell you is that the title is only reserved for very important white people and no insignificant white person uses that title. That is why when a silly boy does what even whites don't do when I talk to them at very important gatherings, I am really annoyed." At this stage some men began showing signs of discomfort and boredom — Ndebenkulu had to get to the point.

"When is this man going to stop singing his praises and tell us why he called us here?" whispered one of the men.

"One wonders whether this is how Esquires do it. Anyway, let's pay attention man, he's now looking at us angrily, he might think we're like that boy."

"Truly, people of Nyanyadu, my relationship with important white people has enabled me to help our people. I am here to ensure that I do the same for you. My wish is to ensure that you also benefit from my good relations with important white people. I know some of you may think that I'm doing all this for profit. I would like everyone to be free at heart, I do not even expect a penny for my work."

After these words the men felt more comfortable with this philanthropic fellow. He was in Nyanyadu to help people and not to advance his interests at their expense. This was undoubtedly a man to be admired and a man to work with.

"My belief is that we have to start small. We must do something that will show returns for you and make you realise that I am not a thief. When I was talking with the honourable chairman on Saturday, he made me aware that people have become wary of people who promise to help the community when they actually want to rob people of their belongings. I agree with him and also fully share your anxiety. It is usually our people who end up losing, even when there is a genuine person who wants to help them. I also understand that it's not easy for you to simply trust a total stranger like me, who comes to Nyanyadu with promises of bringing development to the community."

For a moment Ndebenkulu was silent and took a deep breath as he thought to himself what to tell this captive and eager audience. He cleared his throat, picked up his spectacles, studied his pile of papers for a while and then put the spectacles down. One hand retreated to his pocket and the other, as usual, began to do what it did best to his moustache. His long tooth, on the other hand, did not move.

"My travels and interaction with many communities have taught me that needs differ a great deal. In some areas the people are unhappy with their low salaries and in others the problem is that people have to travel far before they can be seen by a surgeon. Sometimes the problem is that roads are bad and travelling is almost impossible on rainy days because there are no bridges. Having said all this, I now believe it is better to let the people speak first and be the ones who tell me about the most urgent needs in the community, so that we can collectively discuss possible ways for dealing with these challenges."

Ndebenkulu took a deep breath. "What brought me here in the first place is one local man who, after having heard about my work, said he would be very keen for me to come to Nyanyadu and help his people. This man, whose request I could not turn down, also told me that you were very concerned about your cattle." At that stage, the men became even more attentive — cattle meant life and death to them. "When this man mentioned the issue of cattle, I immediately felt his pain because I know that there is now this terrible law that forces people to reduce their cattle stock. I'm sure you also don't like that law, here in Nyanyadu."

A murmur of agreement reverberated throughout the building.

"People like us who live in the city do not care much about a cow with four legs, hair and horns. Our kind of cow stays in the bank. This kind of cow doesn't get cold and sick. This cow doesn't need to be taken to the dipping tank, it doesn't wreak havoc in other people's fields and cause unnecessary legal troubles, doesn't become a problem that requires one's *kraal* to be increased, because in our *kraal* there is no overcrowding. In short, I just want to tell those who still believe that a cow with hair is everything, to think again. They must also consider the cow that is mined down under the ground."

The disappointment of the men was overpowering. Some

uttered audible sounds of disgust. Some even concluded that perhaps the man was an agent of the state. Ndebenkulu continued. "Please don't get me wrong, dear people of Nyanyadu. I am the first to accept that a cow is very special to us black people. Indeed, it is very special. It is our wealth. It is therefore annoying to be told that we have to reduce our cattle stock. The reality we have to face, though, is that the law has been made already and there is no way to break it. I have been deeply concerned about this law as well, because I know that cows mean everything to our people. Indeed, this law has deeply troubled me. People like me who live in the city often battle to understand the attachment to a cow that rural people have. When this law came about, I was deeply hurt and realised that I had to do something to help our people reduce the burden of being forced to part with their cows. My hurt was caused by my understanding of the meaning of cows to black people. There is the reality to be faced, nevertheless, and I believe that a wise man should act now when he can make some profit, rather than wait for the long arm of the law to force things on him. Unfortunately, when that time comes, you will just be throwing your cows away and will get nothing of value from them. As I have said before, I am someone who is known by very important white people who own abattoirs and butcheries. When I learned about this matter, I realised that I must use my connections with important white people to help our people. I know good ways for cattle to bring a lot of money to their owners. My knowledge is yours, people of Nyanyadu. Indeed, it is yours. It would give me great pleasure to know that there is something I have done to help our people. At this stage, Mr Chairman, perhaps I should sit down and hear the views of the men gathered here today. I thank you all."

"Mr Chairman!" shouted a certain Mr Buthelezi, rising and fidgeting with his coat, then putting his hands behind his back. "We are grateful that the kind Mr Ndebenkulu so loved this tiny village of Nyanyadu that he left all behind to come here and help set us free from a life of misery and poverty. For

this we are eternally grateful. He is one of a kind, since most
people don't like coming to rural areas like ours because
transport here is a problem and this makes life difficult for an
outsider. I hope you will agree with me, Mr Chairman, that it
is rather unusual for people who live affluent lives to bother
about those who are poor like us. It's for that reason that I
hereby re-assert our deepest gratitude to you, sir. My only
concern is that perhaps Mr Ndebenkulu should have continued addressing us. It would be helpful if he could expand on
the ways for growing wealth that he is suggesting, and as
someone from the city and as someone who knows many
important white people, his advice on improving the living
conditions here would be most welcome. I believe, Mr
Chairman, that before we can get into lengthy discussions, if
our honourable guest gives us clarity on different options for
creating wealth, we would be better able to have an informed
meeting on what we can do."

"*Elethu!*" shouted a bunch of men, endorsing Buthelezi's
sentiments.

Ndebenkulu rose, and said he agreed with the speaker.
"However, the matter of the cows is one I think fully deserves
urgent attention. I'm saying so because I'm concerned about
your situation and know that you must cut down on the size
of your livestock."

"Mr Chairman!" Shandu stood up to make a point. "Mr
Chairman, let me say from the outset that I am not like the
silly boy who was busy making childish noises when the
meeting began. I just happen to be a frank person, and please,
Mr Chairman, the question I want to ask is asked with the
utmost respect for all the men gathered here today. By the
way, does this village of Nyanyadu no longer have its chief to
whom it pays respect?" After having dropped what might well
be described as a bombshell, Shandu stood silently for a
moment, letting his words sink in and looking out the window
as if indifferent to the gravity of his question.

"*Woshi!* We have a huge mess on our hands! Trust Shandu
to hit below the belt," old spitter man was heard saying to

himself. There was some commotion, and then utter silence.

Then Shandu continued. "It's possible, Mr Chairman, that perhaps you didn't understand me well. I'm simply asking if we have a chief here at Nyanyadu, or not." Each sentence was underlined by an emphatic slowness in his voice – he obviously wanted the seriousness of his question to be felt by all. He put his hands on his hips and looked through the window into the distance as if he was far away in thought.

"Shandu is asking a crucial question and he'd better get answers. After all, who called this meeting in the first place?" demanded someone.

Mkhwanazi arose in a flash and shouted: "You must sit down now so that I can answer you." Shandu responded to this order with typical defiance. "I won't take my seat because I'm not done yet. I would like a response, then I'll ask a second question."

"You better sit down, Mr Shandu, if you want a reply to your question. That's how meetings are conducted, we can't all stand at the same time, and I hope our guest, the knowledgeable Mr Ndebenkulu, agrees with me. That's a rule. Isn't it so, Mr Ndebenkulu?" Mkhwanazi looked at his guest, who nodded in agreement.

"Whose rule is it, Mkhwanazi?" asked Shandu.

"What's wrong with you, Mr Shandu? Why do you want to spoil this meeting when you're a grown man? First you refuse to sit down and now you're calling me by my name, Mkhwanazi, instead of addressing me as chairman. It's clear you want to disrupt this meeting. If you really want to get an answer, you must take your seat now and subject yourself to my rules as the chairman. I'm the reigning bull in this *kraal*."

The entire meeting almost cracked the roof with laughter at the words 'reigning bull'. Only Shandu didn't find it amusing. Then one man pulled him gently by his coat, saying: "Just sit down, Shandu, so that we may all hear what the reigning bull has to say." Reluctantly he took his seat, still visibly disgruntled.

"Good people, please try to show some decent manners,"

said Mkhwanazi as he stood up. "Today we have in our midst a guest from a place far away. He is a very important man and someone who is respected by even the most prominent white people. Despite all his achievements, some of you choose to behave in this manner! What impression do you think he will have of us? What's wrong with you black people?"

Cele could not take Mkhwanazi's tirade lying down. "Don't start preaching to us, Mkhwanazi. You said Shandu should sit down so that he could get an answer to his question, now please provide the answer and stop preaching to us as if we're in church. Some of us would also like to have our say."

"If this kind of behaviour continues, I might have no choice but to close the meeting." said Mkhwanazi, rattled.

"What? How dare you suggest that?" Cele was definitely losing his temper. "You're the one who was up and down on your horse inviting us to this meeting and now you have the audacity to threaten us, that you can close it! We all had to stop attending to very important matters only to be told that the meeting can be ended before we have heard and fully understood its purpose. You can't dare do that to us, Mkhwanazi! Are you out of your mind, Mkhwanazi?"

Shandu got up and, in a soft voice, urged Cele to sit down.

Cele obliged, and Shandu continued. "I'm asking again, Mkhwanazi, it's the third time now. Let us say, indeed, you are the reigning bull. I'm asking you to answer my question – and for a moment forget that you're the reigning bull. Don't we have a chief here at Nyanyadu, Mkhwanazi? Why can't you answer such a simple and straightforward question, Mkhwanazi? This time don't even try asking me to sit down, because I won't. Earlier you said I should sit down and you still didn't answer me."

"You keep on asking me but you know, and we all know, that we do have a chief here," said Mkhwanazi.

"Even though I'm offended by your answer, that was exactly our understanding, Mkhwanazi. What surprises me, though, is that when I look around I don't see the chief among us. I also don't know if anyone here is the eyes and ears of the chief." Shandu looked around, but no one stood up to indicate that he was the chief's envoy.

"I don't understand, Mr Shandu, why you bring the chief into this matter," Mkhwanazi said. "Is this the first time the people of Nyanyadu have held a meeting in the absence of the chief?"

The men laughed with their heads on their knees. Mkhwanazi was talking nonsense.

Shandu responded: "I wonder if you really mean what you just said, Mkhwanazi. What we knew was that there was only one chief at Nyanyadu. It's news to us to learn of another chief, the reigning bull, Mkhwanazi."

Again, the laughter was deafening. Even Ndebenkulu found it amusing but, since he was the VIP, he merely took out his handkerchief and pretended to be wiping his face. Mkhwanazi was mute, enraged.

Shandu continued: "In front of us is a total stranger. We're told that this person is very important where he comes from. We're also told that this man has many cars while we only have horse-drawn wagons. This man also tells us that important white people hold him in high esteem and even call him," he looks around at the rest of the men, "what do they call him?"

"An Esquire!" shouted the men.

"*Ehhe*! The name was escaping me for a while. This man says white people call him an Esquire. Since you, Mr Chairman, also live in Nyanyadu like the rest of us, it's surprising that you also endorse that white people call this man an Esquire. Were you ever with this man, even for a day, to witness white people addressing him as an Esquire?"

"It's clear, Mr Shandu, that you are here to disrupt this meeting," Mkhwanazi said, "and your constant reference to Mr Ndebenkulu as 'this man' is also proof that you simply mean to be offensive."

"I don't mean to be offensive, Mkhwanazi. I just want you to explain why the chief was not informed when such an important person, with many cars and who white people address as an Esquire, was visiting us. Secondly, since this honourable man – I apologise, sir, for earlier referring to you as 'this man' – is here to discuss such important matters as reducing our livestock, who else but the chief should take charge of an issue as serious as this? So, Mkhwanazi, you must explain to all of us, who has now made you the chief of Nyanyadu. When was Sisolengwe removed from the chieftaincy? Who did it, and at which *imbizo*? What are you trying to say, Mkhwanazi, when you invite visitors to our tribal authority to discuss issues that are so important that only the chief should preside over them?"

"You may sit down, Shandu, you've given him a good dressing down," said someone. "Let's now hear what he has to say in his defence."

Mkhwanazi rose meekly to take the floor, trying to control his temper. "You surprise me when you suddenly turn this meeting into a courtroom and I'm in the box defending myself. This really surprises me. As if you don't know how it came about for Mr Ndebenkulu to come here!"

Someone objected rudely. "Don't make assumptions! Who says we know how he came here?"

Mkhwanazi paused, trying to remain calm. Then he said: "Although you're now pleading ignorance, you all know that first I received his letter then I visited all of you to tell you about today's meeting."

"You never came to me," objected Shandu.

"In that case you must ask your children if I came to your house on Thursday," said Mkhwanazi. "You must all recall that when I informed you about this meeting no one ever suggested that we take this matter to the chief because of its seriousness. It really surprises me that the honourable Mr Ndebenkulu is now being thought of as mine. It also amazes me that people say I'm behaving as if I'm a chief. How am I trying to behave like a chief? If a mistake has been made today, we're all guilty, since we're all in attendance at a meeting that hasn't been called by our chief."

"It would appear that Shandu's point is extremely valid,"
said Lushozi. "I'm in full agreement with the sentiment that we
made a terrible mistake by attending a meeting in the jurisdic-
tion of our chief without his permission and knowledge. We're
all at fault, not just Mkhwanazi. I think, at this stage, since the
damage has already been done, we mustn't behave like children and call this meeting off prematurely. In any case, Mr
Ndebenkulu is already here. It would be better if he could
enlighten us on this matter of the reduction of our cattle stock.
This matter has been troubling us for some time and he has
already touched on it. Even though I'm not such a smart person, I think Shandu is making a mistake when he says we've
come here to reduce our cattle stock. This honourable man, our
guest today, isn't the one who says we should reduce our livestock. He is simply suggesting that we look at other ways for
making sure that when we're forced to reduce it, we don't lose
much. As I said earlier, I'm not a smart person, my understanding could be wrong. I heard Mr Ndebenkulu saying that
rich white people who own abattoirs and butcheries know him.
I think it would help if Mr Ndebenkulu could explain more,"
Lushozi said, and then sat down.

Throughout the argument between Mkhwanazi and
Shandu, Ndebenkulu had sat comfortably with one leg
crossed over the other, and had kept on twiddling with his
moustache, looking at his pile of papers and, now and then,
his wristwatch. His long tooth did not move and he did not
look particularly angry. But when his response was expected
he stood up and said: "Please understand me very well. I am
not telling you to get rid of your livestock. I'm just saying that
as you are being forced to reduce your livestock, here is a better way of doing it so that you don't do it at a loss. I am a
friend of important whites who own abattoirs and butcheries.
If they sell a cow that belongs to someone they don't know,
they reduce the price. On the other hand, because I am a well-
known person I have helped many people who wanted to sell
their cattle because, like you, they were faced with a similar
law to reduce their livestock. I'm really grateful to that man

seated over there for clarifying that I am not here to tell you to reduce your livestock. I'm responding to the law, and my main aim is to help you along so that you may do this wisely and not feel the pain on your pocket that much. If you personally take your cattle in order to sell them, you may be offered a stingy 20 pounds whereas for me if the offer was 60 pounds, that would be much too low."

"*Hhawu*! Sixty pounds – that's real money, man!" exclaimed Buthelezi and some others.

"Who among you ever got 60 pounds for a cow? Even the most fertile Nguni bull has never brought an owner so much money. We usually only get 40 pounds. Please clarify something," he said, rising, "what does one do for you to sell his cattle for him?"

Ndebenkulu paged through his pile of papers as if they held the answer to this question, and said: "It's easy and straightforward. What I need to know in advance is the date when you plan to put the cows on the train, so that I can wait for them. You also have to let me know their quantity so that I can arrange with the whites that run the abattoir. Because there is so much demand for meat in the city they are always expecting them in the abattoirs. You must realise that we city people eat a lot of meat," said Ndebenkulu with a smile.

"The only problem would be money for their transportation," mumbled Buthelezi, as if to himself.

"You don't have to worry yourself about that. It's something I can solve easily because white people know me very well. In any case, I can also pay it in advance since it would just be small change to me. You could then pay me later, once you have been paid for selling your cows."

"Clearly this man knows what he is talking about," said some men at the back.

"Not so long ago, before coming here, I had just sold 10 bulls for one man. For two of these he got paid 200 pounds each," he paused to let the gathering digest the amount. "Three were sold for 90 pounds each and the rest were sold for 80 pounds each. These were of a really high-quality breed."

The men were dumbfounded — they had never heard of bulls that fetched 200 pounds at the abattoir. Shandu, who had been angry that the meeting had been called without the permission of the chief, suddenly softened, and he too was eager to hear more about Ndebenkulu's miracles. Most men were not surprised at his unexpected interest — the whole of Nyanyadu knew that he liked money more than his chief.

"Your eyes tell me that what I'm saying surprises you. I wouldn't be surprised if some of you said this Ndebenkulu man has come all the way to tell us tales in broad daylight. I am not a man who lies. Not at all. Although now I'm doing what I'm not supposed to do, fortunately I still have one of this man's cheques." He pulled it out of his bag and showed to the men. "Here it is, whoever wants to come and see it may do so, this man got paid 910 pounds for 10 cows. I wonder if you want me to say more on this matter." Then Ndebenkulu sat down, and crossed his legs with a great deal of self-assurance.

The murmurs throughout the classroom were a clear indication that the men still could not believe their ears. They looked at one another, nodding their heads. Ndebenkulu had undoubtedly made a good impression, seemed to be the man they had always been waiting for, albeit with no idea whether or not he would actually arrive in their lifetimes. They felt as if they were in a sweet dream whose promise simply disappears at daybreak. Mkhwanazi took the cheque from Ndebenkulu, and said: "There you are, men. You're even afraid to touch this kind of money with your bare hands. Have you ever had this kind of money in your hands before?"

The men could not hide their changed views of Ndebenkulu — this was no ordinary man, indeed, this was a miracle-maker, and a man the whole of Nyanyadu had to hear.

A voice was heard at the back, mocking the men for their fear of touching the big cheque in their midst. As he said this, the man who spoke looked at Shandu with a smile, teasing him for having wanted to cause chaos at first, only to see the light when he realised that Ndebenkulu could take him to the promised land of honey and money.

Ndebenkulu arose. "As I was quiet, and looking at you, I was deeply concerned by the sad reality that we blacks are a cursed race. When opportunities present themselves, instead of taking them we keep on playing hide and seek, not realising that time is up. When I came here my aim was not to create disharmony among you. That was not my aim at all. Since I come from the city, I didn't realise that I should have contacted your chief first. Had I known, I would have addressed my letter to him. I'm really sorry about this and will write the chief a letter of apology. I will also enclose my business card so he will see that I'm not an impolite nobody but a man of high social standing in my own right."

These words embarrassed Shandu, who now felt an irresistible urge to go up to Ndebenkulu and Mkhwanazi and apologise in full view of everyone. Now he felt that he had been grossly unfair and harsh to Mkhwanazi. "I hear you well, Mr Ndebenkulu, you have really brought us good news. Although it would have been appropriate for you to apologise to the chief in person, the letter will now do. May I also apologise to you, Mr Mkhwanazi, for allowing my blood to boil prematurely? I do hope you won't bear a grudge against me. I truly ask for your forgiveness." Shandu took his seat.

Mkhwanazi got up, and said: "I've heard what Shandu had to say. Since he started it all, when he withdraws it, I forgive him. I must say, though, that it hurt me to see this kind of behaviour in front of a guest."

Ndebenkulu felt he also had to say a few words. "I'm a happy man, gentlemen, to see you making peace. It would have hurt me terribly to see this meeting turning ugly and ending on a sour note. To you, the gentleman who has just apologised, please be assured that, as someone who works hard to develop our people, I understand situations like these very well. I don't take things personally, and know that one has to be extremely tolerant."

The atmosphere was undoubtedly cheerful, and all the men seemed at ease. Mkhwanazi stood up and proposed closure, since it was almost lunchtime.

"We didn't conclude properly, Mr Chairman," interjected Lushozi. "What is Mr Ndebenkulu advising us to do?" Shandu got up and seconded Lushozi, adding: "What Mr Ndebenkulu has said is really tempting. Indeed, our people who have seen the light through education should lead us. After all, they don't go to school only for themselves but for the entire nation."

Ndebenkulu rose. "I agree with the chairman that time has run out. You are very right, Mr Chairman, we have been here for a long time now. I'm just saddened that I have not given you my entire plan for helping you but have only discussed what people can do to make money from their cattle. I would have loved to share my ideas about helping people to use land as mortgage when applying for bonds. Recently, I helped a widow from my city. She wanted to build a house on a site her husband had left her. I'm not talking about the Hlongwane widow whose letter the chairman read earlier. This one is somebody else and her financial situation was really bad. She desperately wanted me to help. But I don't want to just tell you about it – here is the photograph of the house she built, it tells the whole story."

The photograph moved from one hand to another like an object of communal wonder. The house was built in a modern architectural style – a far cry from the mud huts of most Nyanyadu dwellings. Outside the house stood a beautiful woman, obviously proud of her comfortable and brightly painted home. All this, and more, were cause for the men of Nyanyadu to look at this Pietermaritzburg man, C.C. Ndebenkulu, and realise that a great deal of good fortune lay ahead for them. It was all a matter of time before they too could milk their cash cows.

"That photograph gives me a great deal of joy. It hardly leaves my bag, and reassures me that all I do for our people is not in vain. Now, any man can do whatever he chooses. This should be entirely up to each man. I will leave my address so that once any one of you has decided to sell his cows, he can just write to me so that I can come back to help."

At the end of Ndebenkulu's words, Mkhwanazi gave a vote of thanks and officially closed the meeting.

●●●●●●●●●●●●●●●●●●●●●●●●●●●●

The men did not disperse at once. Some felt the urge to shake Ndebenkulu's hand personally and exchange pleasantries. Some were not sure whether they had really understood him and so had to clear up a few issues with others. Some could not wait to explore the Esquire's idea of cows to be sold for cash. Although the prospects of parting with their cattle disturbed them, they were increasingly convinced that, even if they resisted, soon they would lose them at no value at all. In general they felt that the arrival of Ndebenkulu was a big blessing for the people of Nyanyadu. This was their last chance to get rich pretty quickly. Shandu went over to shake Ndebenkulu's hand, apologise for his earlier behaviour, and ask to see the cheque that he had been too shy to go and look at when Ndebenkulu has asked the men to come forward. Ndebenkulu took out an envelope and gladly gave the cheque to Shandu. As Shandu looked at it, his hands shook as if he was unwell. Nine hundred and ten pounds! He shook his head in disbelief and handed it back to Ndebenkulu. Shandu's reaction brought a sense of personal satisfaction to Ndebenkulu, who was busy puffing on a cigarette.

Mkhwanazi and Ndebenkulu soon went home. On their way, they saw the bearded young man, who seemed to be amused as he looked at them. "That's the boy who kept on giggling at the meeting," Mkhwanazi said.

"You're right, it's him, where is he from?" said Ndebenkulu, annoyed.

"I've no idea. Nowadays many young boys who we don't know have come to live in the area, no wonder crime is on the rise."

"Mkhwanazi, do you mean that you also have criminals here at Nyanyadu? That surprises me a lot, since we usually think crime is confined to towns and cities."

"It's the opposite. After you give them a hard time in your cities, some run here and trouble us," Mkhwanazi said.

As they walked they reviewed the meeting and discussed Shandu. Then Mkhwanazi said: "I really didn't take kindly to Shandu's comments about the chief. All those men knew about the meeting and none advised us to inform the chief of it. First thing tomorrow morning, I have to visit the chief and apologise in person, since it's not enough that Shandu withdrew his remarks. It's even possible that if he doesn't get the whole story from me facts might be totally distorted. I also wouldn't be surprised if some others decided to inform the chief about the meeting, ahead of me."

"I agree with you, Mkhwanazi, certain people like to score points at the expense of others. Fortunately, that man who initially wanted to spoil our meeting gave in at the end."

"As soon as he heard about the money that whites pay for cattle, he changed his tune," said Mkhwanazi. "That's typical Shandu, we here all know that he's very fond of money. Well, I still think I can only visit the chief tomorrow." The two continued talking as they walked home.

On his way home, the young man with a beard decided to go past the school, and there he found Shandu and other men still talking about the meeting. He decided to join the conversation. "Do you really all believe that this man is telling the truth?" asked Shandu.

"That's difficult to tell, Shandu, since we've only just met him and even Mkhwanazi doesn't know him well," said Buthelezi.

"I must admit though, gentlemen, what this man has said is really hard to resist," said Shandu.

"I don't understand your confusion," said the old man who liked to spit in the air. "Didn't he say that he knows big white people, showed us the money and letters that praise him and even said that he sells land for people?" As he finished, the old man spat in the air, as was his habit.

"That man struck it big with his cattle – 900 pounds!" said Shandu clearly wishing such a large amount of money was his. "Since nowadays there are so many wolves in sheep's clothing, it's hard to tell if a man who says he's big is for real or a fraudster." Looking at his hands, Shandu said: "However, I must admit, I did touch the big cheque with my own hands."

"We even saw the widow's house," added Buthelezi.

"He also brought money with him, *baba*?" asked the young man with a beard.

"What do you think? I saw it with my own eyes!" Shandu said confidently, pointing at his eyes. "Nine hundred pounds! I even touched it with my hands! Nine hundred pounds!"

"What kind of money was it, *baba*?" continued the young man with a beard.

"What kind of money was it? What kind of question is that? What does money usually look like?" Shandu was annoyed at this line of questioning.

"My apologies, *baba*, I'm not trying to be rude. It's just that 900 pounds is a lot of money. Was it paper money or silver money?"

"Now I see. It was neither paper nor silver money. He had a green cheque, I swear by my older sister. Now that I've touched such a big amount of money, I really have seen it all." Shandu was shaking his head in a mixture of disbelief and pride. He said: "If one is prepared to listen carefully, his plan is definitely the one."

"What plan is that, *baba*?" asked the young man with a beard.

"Where the hell are you from, that you keep on pestering me with your endless questions? Why didn't you attend the meeting and hear everything for yourself?" Shandu was increasingly irritated.

"This is the same body who was hastily kicked out of the meeting because he kept laughing," responded Buthelezi. Then he addressed the young man. "You tell me, young man, what makes you so rude that you ignored the fact that we're as old as your father, and instead you chose to be disruptive at our meeting?"

"Pardon me, *baba*, I didn't mean to be rude, I just found that man amusing."

"What do you mean? The man made you laugh whereas the rest of us found nothing amusing?" asked Buthelezi.

The young man said: "Just listen to his surname, Nde...be...nku...lu! Have you ever heard a surname like that before?"

"What exactly is your point, boy? If that is his surname what should he do about it?" asked Shandu.

"I'm saying that since I've never heard of this surname before it may not be his real surname."

"*Hhabe*! What are you saying, boy?" asked Shandu.

"Now this boy is talking, gentlemen," said the old man, and he spat in the air.

"You mean that the man could come here and lie about his true identity?" Shandu was finding this too much to digest. He looked even more intently at the young man.

"No, *baba*, I can't say for sure that he's telling a lie. Maybe his surname is real. It's just that something about him seems unsatisfactory. Given that there are so many surnames, my discomfort could well be a result of the fact that I have never heard of his before."

"That's what I also wanted to say," said Buthelezi, adding that Mkhwanazi was a trustworthy man who would never invite a crook to rob the community.

"I agree with you, Buthelezi," said Shandu. "The problem, though, is that even Mkhwanazi doesn't know this man. Worse still, it's not clear who told him about Mkhwanazi. Ndebenkulu didn't reveal the name of the Nyanyadu person who advised him to visit this place."

"There's something else that worries me about this man," said the young man. "He's just too arrogant and I don't understand why. Do you think, *baba*, a respectable man would speak like Ndebenkulu? His constant boasting about being an Esquire is extremely unacceptable."

Shandu felt the young man was taking things too far, now. "It's the way he speaks. After all, he did tell us that he knows important white people and has to remind non-entities like us of this fact. I think you're being petty now."

"What does it mean, boy, to be an Esquire?" asked an old man with his stick balanced across his shoulders.

"It means nothing, *baba*. Even a simple man like me can receive a letter which addresses me as an Esquire."

"Don't talk nonsense, boy," said the old man as he spat in the air. "Who do you think you are, to be called Esquire?" The old man found the young man's assertion pretty amusing.

"Now that you're trying to show us that you're clever, where exactly do you come from, boy?" asked Buthelezi.

"I come from the Kheswa family."

"*Hhawu*! You're Kheswa's son!" Surprised, Shandu extended a hand to shake his. "We hardly know you since you're mostly away at work, we believe, and only come home occasionally."

"That is so, *baba*. I should have gone long ago but stayed because I expected a lot from the meeting. I'm now not sure what exactly to tell my father at home."

"There's not much to tell, boy," Shandu said. "This man is, basically, saying that our cattle will have to be reduced, and he suggests that we sell them. He knows important white people who own abattoirs and butcheries. Because of who he knows, he is able to sell big bulls for a 120 pounds."

"A hundred and twenty pounds!" The young man was surprised.

"At least that's what he says," added Buthelezi. "Mkhwanazi said his letter came from Pietermaritzburg. That's what he also said at the meeting."

"That's lies, *baba*," said the young man. "This man is telling tales."

"What the hell is wrong with you? What about us who not only saw the money but also touched it with our hands?" As he said this, Shandu threw his hands in the air. They were no longer ordinary hands – they had touched big money.

"It's just that, *baba*, this whole story doesn't make sense to me. Of course, if you say you saw the money, it's hard for me to dismiss your claims. Even then I would only be satisfied once I'd also seen the money."

"What do you suspect is wrong about the fellow, my son?" asked the old man of the spraying saliva.

"We also live in the city, *baba*, and have never heard of such big man, with links to big whites," said the bearded young man.

"This boy is really making a big mistake. There are such black people, we read about them in the newspapers," said Shandu.

"Even then, it's a myth that one can sell cattle at such a ridiculously high price."

For a while, in their silence, the men were clearly disappointed at the young man's attempt to destroy the hopes that had begun to simmer deep within them.

"Do you mean he might be lying to us with all these promises?" asked Buthelezi.

"I can't say so with absolute certainty, *baba*. Nevertheless, as someone who lives in the city, I'm familiar with smooth-talking crooks like him."

Shandu felt he had to intervene. "Be careful, boy! You must select your words carefully. Nowadays, talk like yours could land you in serious trouble. If you're wrong about this man, you could be sued, and you will deeply regret it."

"You're right, but I'm still not satisfied. Our family cattle will not go to that abattoir. Did he give you the addresses of the white people he sells to?"

"No. He insisted on being the one who does it because he's the one who's known," explained Buthelezi.

"*Hhawu*! What is he saying? That you send your cattle in his name? I didn't realise that you're allowing yourself to be fooled by a *tsotsi* in broad daylight! Let me rather leave you, my dear fathers." At once, the bearded young man walked away.

He left the men awfully confused. They watched him walk away, until he jumped over the school fence. Then, dumbfounded, they simply looked at one another. "We'd better go

now, gentlemen, we have no further matters to discuss," said
Buthelezi.

"Nowadays, young boys think they know everything just
because they've spent time in the cities," said Shandu.
"Ndebenkulu said important words that still echo in my ears.
He said that at times, when opportunity knocks, we don't
open our doors. It's very possible that we're doing that now.
This young man talks as if he has cows – meanwhile, they're
Kheswa's. Kheswa could still go ahead and send his cows
while ours remain, because we allowed a boy to deceive us."

Buthelezi saw things slightly differently, and proposed that
each man should do what he considered right. "No man
should blame another, just in case there are problems ahead.
I'd better leave you now, gentlemen."

That was how the small group of men standing next to the
school dispersed. The old man who spat saliva also walked
away to his homestead.

• •

When they arrived at home, Mkhwanazi left Ndebenkulu in
the lounge and went into the kitchen, hoping that maNtuli
had calmed down. Now that he was calm, he deeply regretted
their quarrel. He found her behind the house, relaxed and
talking to Thoko.

"You're back at last, *baba*." MaNtuli's words removed the
heaviness that weighed like a huge rock on Mkhwanazi's
shoulders.

"We were beginning to think that you would sleep there,"
said maNtuli with a warm laugh. Don't tell me! She had for-
given him! Mkhwanazi hadn't seen his wife laugh at all since
Saturday, the day Ndebenkulu had arrived.

"Please give me some cold water, I'm dying from this
unbearable heat," said Mkhwanazi.

"Thoko, my child, kindly give your father some water," said
maNtuli to her daughter. Thoko had already risen while she
was talking.

"Don't you perhaps also need a chair, so that you may rest a while, *baba?*" asked maNtuli.

"Thanks for the offer, Ntuli, but I have to go right away, as I left Ndebenkulu all by himself in the lounge."

Then maNtuli continued: "What took you so long? You left for the meeting quite early in the morning."

"You know very well that people here are never on time," said Mkhwanazi. "Instead of looking at their watches, they look at the movement of the sun. In any case, even when they do have watches, too often they don't give the right time."

MaNtuli asked him how the meeting had gone.

"I wonder how Ndebenkulu would describe the meeting," said Mkhwanazi. "At first there was a silly boy who kept on laughing, at nothing really, as if he was in a laughing competition."

"Where was the boy from?" asked maNtuli.

"I've no idea." Mkhwanazi drank the water Thoko had just brought, then wiped his mouth with his hand. "He has a beard along his jawline and he limps."

"Don't you know that's Kheswa's son?" asked maNtuli in surprise.

"What? That's Kheswa's son? I thought he was away at work," said Mkhwanazi, equally surprised.

"You're mistaken. Kheswa's son is at home. He's back. I'm sure that was him, he has a beard on his jaw, is light in complexion and limps. A few days ago he came to this house with Themba. They know each other well. Just wait a bit, I'll call Themba."

MaNtuli shouted for Themba and he came at once.

"Themba, tell me, this boy with a beard you came home with on... My God, why do I forget now?" Themba came immediately to his mother's rescue. "You mean on Friday, mother."

"Indeed, it was Friday. Please tell me – where was that boy from?"

Themba pressed his finger to his lips and looked down, mumbling: "On Friday... On Friday... You mean, you mean – oh, now I know, mother, you're talking about Diliza."

"I don't know his name," maNtuli said.

Before Themba could respond, they saw Ndebenkulu strolling towards them, his hands in his trouser pockets. When he lifted his eyes he realised that the entire Mkhwanazi family was deep in conversation. He decided not to go any closer. He was not comfortable with the lady of the house.

"We are here, *Mnumzane*," called Mkhwanazi. He said this with confidence, since maNtuli had calmed down. At once, Ndebenkulu accepted the invitation of the head of the Mkhwanazi household.

"Who did you say he was, Themba?" continued maNtuli, to finish what they had been discussing before Ndebenkulu joined them.

"It's Diliza, mother," said Themba. "Diliza Kheswa, the one I brought home on Friday."

"There you have it," said maNtuli.

"Where was I on Friday" asked Mkhwanazi. "As far I can recall, I was also here."

"Have you forgotten father, that on Friday morning you woke up early to take the cattle to the dipping pond?" said Themba, to jog his father's memory.

"Themba is right. I'm the one who is mistaken. I don't know that boy in person and today was the first time I saw him. We're talking about this boy with a beard, Ndebenkulu." Mkhwanazi was trying to help Ndebenkulu understand what they were discussing.

"I hear you, Mkhwanazi," Ndebenkulu said, with his hands in his trouser pockets.

Mkhwanazi continued. "What kind of person is your friend, Themba?"

Themba smiled and said: "Why do you ask?"

"I think he's rude," said Mkhwanazi. "Just imagine, there we were, the men of Nyanyadu, busy discussing serious matters, and a boy kept giggling endlessly like a madman. There was nothing to laugh at, really, even Ndebenkulu can bear me out."

"That boy is really rude, extremely rude, and I witnessed it," said Ndebenkulu spicing it with a few English words and adding: "He has no manners, he was lucky we didn't give him a serious hiding."

Themba felt very bad, hearing this about his friend. He was visibly uncomfortable and shifted around uneasily as if he wanted to disappear. In reality, he did want to leave, to avoid having to respond to such reports about his friend, but he merely said: "I never knew him to be like that."

"You're only a child, what would you know?" said Mkhwanazi. "You better listen to what Ndebenkulu and I are telling you. I didn't know that was Kheswa's son, I'll have to tell him about his son's behaviour when I next meet him."

"What bad thing did the boy do?"

As it turned out, there was no substantial response to maNtuli's question – the boy's biggest mistake was his solitary litany of giggles.

MaNtuli shifted the focus at once, and said: "I had asked how your meeting went and you decided to tell me about Kheswa's son instead."

"Perhaps, as a guest here, Ndebenkulu would be the best one to give you his impressions."

MaNtuli said nothing.

"What can one say, Mkhwanazi? I think the meeting went well." As he was saying this, Ndebenkulu did not forget to throw in a few English words. "I can't ignore the fact, though, that this was a rural meeting. There's no use expecting a rural meeting to be run the same way as a city meeting. Not at all, I wouldn't expect that. We started very late because people here have no sense of etiquette or time. Shandu's behaviour was a bit of a nuisance as well. You said he was Shandu, or am I mistaken?"

Although maNtuli was increasingly annoyed by Ndebenkulu's arrogance and his nauseating fondness for English, at the mention of Shandu she winked at Mkhwanazi so that he could tell her more about what Shandu had done at the meeting. Then Mkhwanazi explained how Shandu had at

first tried to disrupt the meeting, to which maNtuli responded: "It would be a good idea, *baba*, for you to pay the chief a
visit. Luckily, the horses are ready. What you've just told me
doesn't sit well with me. It would be good for the chief to hear
this matter from you first."

"That was on my mind, Ntuli, as well. I just feel it's better
that I do it in the morning, when I'm more likely to find the
chief at home."

"What's stopping you from going right away, *baba*
kaThemba, since it's still midday and you're not going there
on foot?" asked maNtuli. "If you go in the morning you might
be too late, and the chief might have already got the news —
and got it in a twisted manner. Going today would be the
right thing to do."

"I don't agree, Ntuli. Tomorrow is fine."

"What more can I say, since I know men only trust their
own thoughts. A woman's thoughts only matter afterwards,
once the damage is done."

"We'd better go inside, Ndebenkulu," said Mkhwanazi.

"Indeed," said his wife. "Please, Thoko, make the table
ready for your father and Mr Ndebenkulu."

Mkhwanazi and Ndebenkulu went indoors. Thoko followed,
and prepared lunch for them, while MaNtuli and Themba
remained behind.

"You know, mother, I'm struggling to understand what
father and Ndebenkulu are saying. What did they say Diliza
did?"

"But you were there when they explained it!" exclaimed
maNtuli. "They say he was a nuisance at the meeting, and
kept giggling like a fool. What else do you want me to say?"

Themba was quiet, looking down. He then said: "I don't like
this whole thing, mother. Diliza isn't a little boy, and
Ndebenkulu makes me cross when he says he deserved a hiding. If he dared do that, he'd rue the day he was born!"

"Do you think swanky city people have any idea of stick-
fighting?" asked maNtuli, jokingly.

"You know, mother, I pray for God's forgiveness, but I really don't like this man. I simply don't like him and I can't pretend otherwise. Look, he only arrived here the day before yesterday and already he's caused so much confusion in all of us. He's brought nothing good here, and I'm surprised that father is so close to him."

"You're reacting like this because you're still young and haven't seen much of this world," said maNtuli. "Sometimes people can be stomach-churning without having done anything. I suspect that it's the case with this man, who I don't like either. With me, though, it has to do with the fact that he insulted me without good reason."

"Rest assured, mother, I'll get to the root of the Diliza matter. I'm going to see him right now. The man simply annoys me."

"Themba, don't you think your father should have informed the chief about the meeting today? Don't you agree?"

"I agree with you fully, mother, especially because there was some misunderstanding at the meeting over a total stranger. But what else can we say about father? You know him, mother. When he's set his mind on something it's impossible to make him change it."

"You really know your father, my son. I just hope his delay won't cost him dearly. You'd better get going, my son, let me not delay you."

Just as Themba was about to go out of the gate, Thoko called him. Father wanted to see him. At once, he went to where his father and Ndebenkulu were seated.

"There's not much to tell you, Themba, except that I would prefer that the horses sleep at home tonight, since Mr Ndebenkulu has to leave very early in the morning."

• •

"Diliza, I understand you attended Ndebenkulu's meeting."

Diliza responded with a loud laugh. "Please don't make me laugh by mentioning that name. I did attend but couldn't stay that long."

"I also heard that," interjected Themba. "It was said that there was a small boy who giggled endlessly, like a fool, at the meeting."

"A small boy? How dare they call me a small boy! If you'd been there as well, Themba, you'd have also found the whole thing laughable."

"What were you laughing at?" asked Themba, straight-faced.

"The very name is funny. Nde...be...nku...lu! Just hear it for yourself, Themba, Nde ...be...nku...lu! You see, this man was seated up there in front and feeling so important. What made me unable to control myself, was his tooth." As soon as he said this, Diliza burst out laughing again.

"Is that the only thing that made you laugh?" asked Themba, surprised.

"Also, when he told the meeting who he was and kept on emphasising that even important white people call him an Esquire."

"He really is fond of being called an Esquire," said Themba, adding that Ndebenkulu had already told the Mkhwanazi household the same thing so many times it was getting on their nerves. "He also likes English too much. I must warn you though, Diliza, what you did could have caused you harm."

"Why? What could have harmed me?"

"Ndebenkulu."

"I thought you were serious."

"I am serious," Themba said. "Ndebenkulu said you are just something that deserved a serious beating with a stick."

"What?" asked the bearded Kheswa boy, with a frown.

"Indeed. He says you must be thoroughly beaten with a stick."

For a moment Diliza looked at Themba intently, then said: "I hope you're joking. Me! Does this man know who I really am? Am I a thing to be thrashed with a stick? I suppose he mistook my leaving the meeting as a sign that I was a coward and was running away!"

"Maybe," Themba said.

"For what sin should I be beaten?"

"Because you are so rude, it's unbearable."

"My friend, I don't like someone who doesn't know me to talk like that — as if I depend on his family's *mielie pap* for food. In any case, how come this man is staying in your household? How did you get to know him?"

"We have no idea who he really is either. We just received a letter asking for accommodation and in it he told us how important he was. I've no idea why he chose our family, he didn't know any of us."

"Has the old man told you about the man's plan to help the community?" asked Diliza.

"Not at all. Do you know about it?"

"I'd left when he explained his plan, and only got to hear about it from the men who got the information first-hand," said Diliza. "He wants men to send their cattle to him so that he can sell them on their behalf, because white people who own abattoirs and butcheries know him. He even says that when a cow is sold for 60 pounds, that's nothing if he's the one doing the selling."

Themba found this hard to believe. "He says 60 pounds is nothing?"

"He says he regularly sells a cow for 120. I think he's referring to big cows, like the ones you have at your family kraal, Themba."

"Diliza! He must think this is a land of fools where everyone has been blinded by the smoke that comes out of the fireplace when we cook. A hundred and twenty pounds! Who would believe that kind of fairytale in broad daylight!"

"Amazing!" Diliza said. "But the men out there are so impressed they simply can't wait to send their cattle to him. Who knows, maybe even your family livestock is on its way!"

"Ours! I'll have to die first, before ours go anywhere!"

Diliza laughed long and loud. "What's wrong with you, now? Why do you talk like a child? You say they'll only go if you're dead, but are they yours?"

"Do you think my father would take his cattle and give them to someone as easily as that?"

"What's to stop him, they're his after all? Or are they yours? Also, you mustn't forget that he was chairman at the meeting."

"You're right. I'm really only talking like this for its own sake," said Themba. "My father loves his cattle so much that only someone with supernatural powers would make him part with them."

"Do you think money doesn't matter to him?" asked Diliza. "Listen to me, Themba, I can see you're inexperienced. Ndebenkulu totally confused the men and even showed them a green cheque, saying he had to take it to a man he'd already sold cattle for at the kind of prices he was talking about. I think they were talking about 900 pounds and some change."

"Nine hundred? That's hard to believe!"

"You see, Themba, the men are now so excited and mixed up they don't know what to do. Tell me, Themba, have your hands ever touched that kind of money?"

"Never, Diliza. I'll ask him to show it to me as well."

"It would be good to ask for it, to satisfy yourself. The men who were at the meeting swear they saw the real thing. I wouldn't be surprised, Themba, if I heard that your family's cows are leaving early tomorrow morning with this Esquire." Then Diliza laughed again, snidely.

Themba said nothing. Even though he did not show it, deep within he found this disturbing. What Diliza was saying seemed fairly possible, since his father was so impressed with the man. His father was doing his best to make the man happy, so how far might he go? It struck him that, perhaps, while he was busy talking to Diliza, his family's cattle were being stolen.

"What you're saying, Diliza, is worrying me. I'd better go home now, and talk to the old lady. But she's quite angry!"

Themba then told his friend the details of what had tran-spired in the Mkhwanazi household since Ndebenkulu had arrived on Saturday. He also told him about their trip from Tayside. Diliza merely stood, open-mouthed.

"To me, Diliza, this man is in every respect a hooligan. It's a pity my father can't see it, and keeps dismissing me as if I was a child."

"When is the man going?" asked Diliza.

"Early in the morning. I'm the one who is supposed to take him to the station with the same farm wagon he looks down on and calls a box. I'm really unhappy about taking him there. Who knows, maybe I'll wake up sick tomorrow morning!"

"He's leaving tomorrow? My advice, Themba, is not to pretend to be sick. You'd better take him along, so that I'll go with you, and we can talk more along the way."

"That's a wonderful idea. The road to Tayside is very long and lonely. I'll fetch you in the morning, on the way."

"That's fine, Themba, I'll see you then."

Diliza escorted his friend outside but abruptly stood still and frowned, as something came to mind. He took his friend's hand, and said: "You know, Themba, I forgot to tell you that the men at the gate also said this man promised to help people who wanted to use their land as mortgage for cash loans."

"And so?"

"Just listen to me. As someone who lives in the city, I now recall that the police in Ladysmith are looking for a man who has taken people's money by promising them cash loans against their land. I don't know him, but I believe he's a real crook."

"Diliza, how could you be silent when you have such important information?"

"Is it possible this Ndebenkulu fellow could be linked to the one I'm talking about?" Diliza was deep in thought.

"It's hard to be certain," Themba said. "I must say, though, that if there are people as wicked as the man you're talking about, this one must be watched carefully as well. I also don't trust him, and I'm very worried about my father, because if this is a crook he'll be his first victim. I've given up trying to warn him. Maybe, Diliza, I must tell him about the person you're talking about. I really can't understand why he's so blind, and can't see Ndebenkulu's real intentions. Maybe I've already angered him so much that he won't hear even another word from me."

"I wouldn't like you to talk about Ndebenkulu, Themba, because if he's the culprit I'm talking about he'll vanish instantly. And if he isn't the man I'm talking about he could sue us, and we'd have no money for that. I'm going to enquire from some of my relatives who live in the city."

"That's fine, Diliza. I'll see you in the morning when I'm taking him to the station."

"Okay, see you in the morning, then, Themba."

• •

On his way home, Themba was very worried. Could his father get carried away and give his cattle to a total stranger? Could he? He walked fast, like a madman, as if he was flying. He was oblivious of the long distance and only too surprised when he arrived at home.

Ndebenkulu and his father were outside, inspecting the family's livestock. Where could the cattle be going at this time of the day? Fear gripped Themba.

"Here they are, Ndebenkulu," said Mkhwanazi. Themba could hear him clearly, since his voice was loud. "These are good breeds," said Ndebenkulu.

It occurred to Themba that his father had really been duped, and he moved closer so that he could hear more. Ndebenkulu was speaking. "I just can't begin to describe the quality of your breed, Mkhwanazi. I've never seen such wonderful cattle before. You see, Mkhwanazi," he said, pointing, "those five cows would sell for 160 pounds each."

"*Hhawu! Hhawu! Hhawu!*" shouted Mkhwanazi as he clapped his hands in the air like a woman. "A hundred and sixty pounds! I still can't believe it!"

'That's easy, just believe me, Mkhwanazi. I've seen many

fine looking cattle, but I've never seen something superior to this. These are first grade cattle. First grade, yes, first grade. My white friends will never forget me for bringing them such a quality breed of cattle. Yes, they will never forget me. Even the cows I was talking about at the meeting, that sold for 120 pounds each, were nowhere near yours. Really, they're nowhere near yours."

Mkhwanazi smiled a little, obviously flattered. A hundred and sixty pounds each for just five cows! He was proud that the bulls were offspring of his cows. He had not paid even a penny for them. A hundred and sixty pounds each! He felt as if he had that amount of money in his hands. Nine hundred pounds! The full meaning of it hit him and he pulled out a handkerchief and wiped his sweating face. Ndebenkulu looked at him discreetly and noticed that his friend found his offer irresistible.

"That's good money, Ndebenkulu," said Mkhwanazi as he wiped his face. He was silent for a while. Themba's heart was beating fast. But when he heard how much money Ndebenkulu was talking about, he was also confused. Could this be the luck his father had long been waiting for? Then he recalled how Ndebenkulu had looked deviously at his father earlier, and his suspicions resurfaced. He abruptly dismissed the thought that this could be his father's long-awaited jackpot.

"What about these?" asked Mkhwanazi, pointing at another herd of his bulls. His voice was squeaky with excitement.

Ndebenkulu looked at them for a while, smiling as he caressed his moustache.

"Don't ask, Mkhwanazi, what I think, because that means I'm giving you prices based on what I think. They're not based on what I think at all. I'm not doing guesswork at all. I know what I'm talking about, and that's the truth. I've been doing this job for far too long to do guesswork. I'm not guessing at all. Not at all. There are a lot of people who keep on thanking me for my help. As I was telling you, those big ones would sell for 60 pounds each. It's possible they could sell for more but I can guarantee that they would never sell for less. The ones you are pointing at would sell for 100 pounds each."

"You must be joking, *Mnumzane*. A hundred pounds for this size? I would have expected 60 pounds."

"Mkhwanazi," said Ndebenkulu, as if a bit annoyed. "Please don't make me feel like a liar. Had you been somebody else, I would just leave you at once, as you are, and forget about you. Really, I would simply forget about you. But I feel attached to you, my heart has warmed to you and I like you. So I'll simply ignore what you just said, making me look like a liar. Yes, I'll simply ignore it."

"Don't get me wrong, Ndebenkulu. Please forgive me. It was a mistake, you must understand that in this area we don't know that kind of money just for cattle. In most cases cunning buyers only give us 20 or 30 pounds per cow."

"That's the reason, Mkhwanazi, I decided to sacrifice my own personal happiness staying in the city and enjoying my wealth but instead came here to help our people. That's why I'm here. I've come to wake you up so that you don't become an easy harvest for the cunning." Ndebenkulu smiled and played gently with his moustache.

"You took the words out of my mouth, Ndebenkulu. I would have said the same about how our people are victims of their ignorance, to a point where they're robbed of their wealth."

Themba looked on without saying a word. Whenever he thought that he had organised his thoughts properly something frightened and confused him again. Fools are a harvest of the cunning! What on earth makes this man use such words? Does he mean that if his father was stupid enough to part with his cattle he wouldn't be the first to do it since he, Ndebenkulu, was cunning? Themba was worried.

"How much did you say they would fetch again, a hundred pounds each?" asked Mkhwanazi.

"You heard me well, Mkhwanazi. You heard me well, that's what I said. Even more, I'm confident about saying it. You can have your money as early as tomorrow. Such bulls! Unless

118

you're not serious!" That Ndebenkulu was in no doubt about what he was saying was written in his eyes.

A hundred pounds each! Ten bulls for a thousand pounds! Do you hear well? Mkhwanazi took out his handkerchief again, and wiped his face. His trousers were trembling. A thousand pounds for ten cows? Why is ignorance such a curse? Could he be sitting on so much instant wealth? Only last week he sold one of the smaller bulls to the Mdlaloses, who had wanted it for a ritual feast. He had sold it for a measly 30 pounds, whereas his bulls were worth 100 pounds each. Clearly, he'd just given that bull away. Mkhwanazi wiped his face again.

Themba could only stand and witness with amazement what was unfolding in front of his eyes. Even when it occurred to him to say something, he was at a loss for words. His fear of his father made it even harder for him to pluck up the courage to intervene. He was weak at the knees, and shaking. He saw the end of his family's livestock. Then he remembered what Diliza had said. Ndebenkulu's words about the cunning harvesting the wealth of the foolish were vivid in his memory. What did this man really mean, with such words?

"We'll talk later, Ndebenkulu," said Mkhwanazi in a strange voice, and proceeded into the house without saying another word. Ndebenkulu remained outside, admiring Mkhwanazi's cattle.

• •

Very worried, Themba went to his mother, who was sewing in her bedroom. As soon as maNtuli saw Themba's face she could tell that something was amiss – his anxiety was notice-able, and brought heaviness to the bedroom. Thoko, who saw Themba hurrying to her mother's bedroom, could also tell that her brother was deeply troubled. She decided to follow Themba and find out for herself what had disturbed her brother.

119

"What's the matter, Themba?" asked maNtuli. She stopped what she was doing.

"Mother, our livestock is gone."

MaNtuli opened her eyes wide, shocked. "Themba, what do you mean, our livestock is gone?"

"Don't panic, mother. Listen to what I have to say."

Thoko was also shocked, and immediately suspected that this whole fuss had something to do with Ndebenkulu.

"Themba, you'd better speak fast and explain to me what has happened to our livestock, and why." All maNtuli wanted was for Themba to cut to the chase. "Did father give you details of what happened at the meeting, mother?" asked Themba.

"He hasn't said much. In any case, what does that have to do with our livestock? What's wrong with you, Themba, why don't you get to the point?" Impatience had given MaNtuli's voice a harsher and more forceful pitch.

"Didn't he tell you about Ndebenkulu's plans to make people rich?" asked Themba.

"I don't care a damn about Ndebenkulu for now, just tell me about our livestock."

MaNtuli stood up and decided to go and see for herself what was going on between her husband and Ndebenkulu.

Hurriedly, Themba stopped her, and asked her to hear him out first. "Listen, mother, Diliza told me that Ndebenkulu has advised the local men to give him their cattle, claiming he could sell them on their behalf at huge prices."

MaNtuli said nothing, simply looked at her son.

"Do you hear me, mother?" asked an anxious Themba.

"I can hear you, Themba, I'm not deaf."

"Why, mother, does it look like you don't care at all about what I'm telling you?"

"Because, Themba, you haven't told me what will wipe out our livestock."

"You see, mother, on my way back from seeing Diliza I saw father and Ndebenkulu inspecting the cattle."

"We also noticed that, but we didn't think it worth worrying about," responded maNtuli. "You know very well that your father likes to show people his livestock, what was wrong with showing them to Ndebenkulu?"

Themba's anxiety deepened. As the arch enemy of Ndebenkulu, his mother should have been the first to help him expose this evil character's scheme before the possessions of fools became an easy harvest for the cunning. Themba sat down in silence. MaNtuli went back to her sewing. Thoko simply stood, not knowing how to save the situation.

"After what Diliza had told me about Ndebenkulu's intentions, I was very concerned when I saw him and my father looking at the cattle." Themba was trying to break the tension and also making another attempt at showing his mother how urgent it was.

"You had no reason to be worried, my son," said maNtuli indifferently. "You know your father well, he loves his cattle far too much for this fellow to trick him into giving them away just like that. Is that the main reason you entered the room in a rush, telling us our livestock is vanishing?" MaNtuli unconcernedly picked up the garment she had been working on, and continued sewing.

"I also thought about that, mother. But then listen to this – when I arrived I heard Ndebenkulu telling him that he can sell Falteni, Kwayimani, Blobhere, Sphahlanti and Kreyisimani for 160 pounds each." Themba looked his mother straight in the eye as he offered this piece of new information – maybe this time she would grasp the urgency of the crisis.

"What are you telling me, Themba?" MaNtuli could not believe her ears. "Who would want to pay that much money for cattle?"

"Furthermore, mother, he says he can sell a bull Vetfudi's size for a hundred pounds."

"I thought you'd come here to tell me something worth listening to, Themba. If I knew you'd come to tell me fables in broad daylight, I wouldn't have bothered stopping what I was doing." MaNtuli put her foot to the pedal of her sewing

121

machine as if completely oblivious to Themba's presence.

"Mother, this isn't a fable. Father is already keen and this could see the end of our livestock."

"Have you forgotten how protective your father is towards his cattle, Themba? He wouldn't let anyone put the wool over his eyes when it comes to that. Have you forgotten that when he was fighting with us on Saturday it all had to do with his panic about the possibility of seeing his cattle taken as Ndebenkulu's compensation. In any case, if he decided to give his cattle away he would investigate the matter properly first." MaNtuli continued to sew.

Themba gave up, realising that his mother would not be of help. He sat despondently, not saying a word, like someone who has just been handed a death sentence.

"Thoko, what's wrong with your brother? He almost made us panic over nothing. Instead of telling us that we're sitting on wealth, he's telling us we must get worried that our live-stock is under threat. Ignorance, what a curse!" MaNtuli looked at her son pityingly as she uttered those last words, as if bewildered that he was sad when the occasion called for cel-ebration.

"What's up, my dear mother? What's wrong with you, my dear Ntuli? Are you also easily deceived, like father?" Themba was battling tears as he spoke to his mother in desperation.

"If the man is lying and we don't get the money he's talking about, the police will deal with him."

"Mother, why do you even believe what he's saying? Not so long ago you said you were suspicious about his intentions. I think he's a crook and here to rob us. As to my father getting anything for his cattle, I swear on my ancestors, nothing of the sort will happen. The rascal is a wolf trying to entice a sheep."

"Themba, please stop wasting my time, pretending to be a wise man. Do you think a person would just mention a selling price out of nowhere?"

"It saddens me, mother, that you're ignoring what I'm say-ing just because I'm young. Unfortunately your child is right this time and you should believe him. Can't you see that he is mentioning all these inflated prices so that you get excited and think with your emotions? Don't you see that he keeps telling you how important he is so that you don't question him, and believe every lie he tells?"

"Not again, Themba. You speak as if you've suddenly seen the light, but you don't know what you're talking about. Thoko, is there anything wrong with your brother today?"

Themba looked at his sister as if to challenge her for being silent while he was fighting such an impossible war all by himself. Fortunately for him, Thoko responded as if she had heard his silent protest. "Actually, Themba is making a lot of sense and I fully agree with him."

"What's wrong with these children? What's your reason for agreeing with Themba?"

"I simply don't trust this person, mother, not at all. I don't know why."

"At least you admit that you don't know why you don't trust him." MaNtuli continued with her work.

"You see, mother, his eyes resemble a snake's," said Thoko with a smile.

"Now you're talking nonsense! Where did you see his snake-like eyes?"

"I really don't like him, mother, and I wish he was gone already. This man will bring us so many misfortunes."

"What's the matter with these children? You're talking about misfortunes, what do you know about misfortunes? Someone is bringing us fortunes and for you this means misfortunes! Has anyone ever told you about a bull being sold for 160 pounds? What about one that can sell for a hundred pounds?"

"If we'll even get that money, mother," said Themba.

"Let me speak as well. All along, you've been telling about the disappearance of our livestock. The bull taken by the Mdlaloses for only 30 pounds is Vetfudi's size. What's wrong with you?"

"Mother, I only came to talk you in the hope that you would

understand what's going on and save father and all of us from disaster. I've given up now and it saddens me."

"You've no reason to be worried, my son. Leave everything to your father. You see, he's got so many cattle today because of his intelligence. You simply must learn to trust your father's judgment, my child."

After maNtuli had finished speaking, she went over in her mind what Themba had said. Was it possible that, perhaps, the man's arrival was a blessing from the ancestors? Why did he choose their household, and not others? Well, she had to wait for Mkhwanazi to tell her more. As for Themba, even if he was now a college student wearing long trousers, his thinking remained that of a child. His skull was still not strong enough and his brains were still immature. Could this be a sign that the ancestors had not forgotten them? MaNtuli's thoughts were deep – it was hard to believe that there was so much wealth hidden in the family's kraal. She stopped sewing, as she realised she was no longer concentrating. A guilty thought hit her like a bolt of lightning when she remembered that she had almost chased the man away, on his arrival on Saturday.

• •

"Themba!"

"Father!"

"Please ignore my earlier request that you accompany Ndebenkulu in the morning. He's only going on Wednesday now – the two of us need to discuss outstanding matters."

Themba was terrified at the thought of them discussing outstanding matters – undoubtedly his father was set to give his cattle to the stranger. He couldn't think of any way to prevent it, since his mother seemed too tempted by the promises of money to give him an ear.

"Ask your mother to come over immediately," said Mkhwanazi.

Themba obliged. His mother was still preoccupied with the

imminent possibility of riches. She now understood the reason for her husband to stay close to Ndebenkulu, and was amazed at her son's foolishness. For a wise man like Mkhwanazi it was quite easy to understand that Ndebenkulu was an ancestral envoy. His mission was to bring fortune to the Mkhwanazi household and help the family make a fresh start in life. She regretted her earlier attitude towards him even more, now. She felt that her behaviour was as awful as Themba's who, in his childishness, behaved as if he was cleverer than his elders. She told herself to conduct herself well despite Ndebenkulu's insults earlier. In retrospect, it was clear that the devil had manipulated her to throw the family's luck away. So when maNtuli heard that her husband was calling her, perhaps for the big news, she was even more grateful that she had seen the light before things fell apart.

She entered the room with a warm smile and pulled out a chair. Both Ndebenkulu and Mkhwanazi were smoking and at ease. Now and then, Ndebenkulu would brush his moustache and surreptitiously show his long tooth. Mkhwanazi was relieved to see his wife smiling since he had been concerned she might completely oppose his plan. Ndebenkulu noted maNtuli's apparent change of attitude although he could not know the reason.

"The child says you have asked for me, *baba*," maNtuli said.

"That's right, Ntuli, I did ask for you," Mkhwanazi said. "We haven't had much time to talk more since my return from the meeting. I also wanted to let you know that I have asked Ndebenkulu not to go tomorrow but do so on Wednesday. It's only now that I have a better understanding of his job, and I felt it would be appropriate to discuss issues a bit more."

MaNtuli was momentarily uneasy as Themba's words suddenly came back. She looked at Ndebenkulu and simply said to Mkhwanazi: "I hear you well, *baba*."

"Thanks to his kindness, Ndebenkulu has agreed to stay a bit longer although this means some inconvenience for him," said Mkhwanazi.

"I agree with you, *baba*, it is really very kind of him to do this at his own inconvenience," added maNtuli.

Ndebenkulu acknowledged maNtuli. He was pleased to be talking with her in this friendly manner. "I was meant to meet a white man who usually buys cattle from me, but now I will simply make a telephone call and tell him I'll only see him on Thursday. I just hope he won't be disappointed – you know, Mkhwanazi, once you too are able to work with white people you will soon learn that they get annoyed when appointments are not kept. Oh yes, they hate it very much. Fortunately, because I've worked with him for a long time, he will understand that there must be a good reason for me to change my plans. He knows I'm a man of my word. Oh yes, he knows this fact. Is there a place where I can make a telephone call, Mkhwanazi?"

"Don't worry about that, Ndebenkulu, it's not a problem. Themba can ride a horse to Tayside early in the morning and make a call on your behalf. He might as well take the postal bag and fetch some mail, although today is only Tuesday."

"That's fine," said Ndebenkulu as he pulled out a new cigarette.

"Certainly we appreciate your kindness towards us, sir," maNtuli said softly.

Ndebenkulu was extremely pleased to hear such complimentary words. Mkhwanazi could not understand what had suddenly pacified his wife. He could only attribute it to the divine intervention of the Mkhwanazi ancestors.

"Another reason I called you," said a relaxed Mkhwanazi to his wife. "I wanted you to come and hear for yourself the miracles I have already heard."

He then went on to give her details of the meeting, and the amounts of money that one could get for selling cattle through this messenger of fortune. Throughout his speech, Mkhwanazi kept looking at his wife to ascertain how she was absorbing the financial aspects of his report. When he mentioned the payment of 900 pounds, Ndebenkulu got up, took out a cheque and showed it to maNtuli. "Mkhwanazi is right, madam. He's right. Have a look and satisfy yourself."

Since maNtuli knew next to nothing about cheques, she merely looked, noted the amount and could not grasp anything else. She knew that this paper was important and, because Mkhwanazi must have seen it already, she was confident that Ndebenkulu was telling the truth. "There isn't much I know about important people's money, dear visitor," she said with a sheepish laugh, which was echoed by the two men. "It's only the likes of *baba* kaThemba who are familiar with this type of money."

Ndebenkulu looked at Mkhwanazi condescendingly, as if to protest at being carelessly compared to a country bumpkin, whereas in reality he was the only one in the room used to handling cheques.

"That's why, maNtuli, I also felt you had to hear about the important work that has brought Ndebenkulu to our district." Then Mkhwanazi read his wife the a letter that he had read out at the meeting, the moving letter by the widow Ndiletha Hlongwane. He asked Ndebenkulu to show maNtuli a photograph of the Hlongwane house. MaNtuli studied the photograph intently and then gave it back to Ndebenkulu.

She said: "Thanks for the report about your meeting and for showing me all these items I've just seen. I was really dying to hear more about the meeting."

"My dear Ntuli, I must tell you right away that I'm sold on Ndebenkulu's ideas," said Mkhwanazi. "I'm convinced our ancestors have sent him so that our life could be improved. Knowing quite well that the two of us have travelled a long and difficult journey together, it's only right that I consult with you first. I'm afraid, though, that if we waste time, we could miss the last opportunity we ever have to better our lives, and defy the good wishes of our ancestors."

"What is there to say, *baba*, after all, livestock is the preserve of a man, for he heads the household. When one looks at how we've given our cattle almost for nothing, it's hard not find Ndebenkulu's talk tempting. Just look at the bull we gave to the Mdlaloses not so long ago."

"Don't even talk about that bull, Ntuli. It gives me pain to realise that we actually gave it away at 30 pounds when its real value is much more," said Mkhwanazi despondently.

"Don't you think it would be better, Mkhwanazi, if you both discussed this matter in my absence?" asked Ndebenkulu politely.

Mkhwanazi was against this idea for fear that he might fail to convince his wife all by himself. He was confident that, with Ndebenkulu looming over them while they discussed the matter, he could prevail over maNtuli. Already she appeared satisfied with the report of the meeting, perhaps because of Ndebenkulu's charm.

"The truth," he said, "is that I would be pleased if you were present since we're not discussing any confidential matters. After all, you're our advisor and it would be helpful to talk about this issue in your presence so that in case we err, you will quickly show us the way. What do you say, maNtuli?"

"That's fine with me, *baba*," said maNtuli. Ndebenkulu sat quietly, one leg crossed casually over the other, smoking his cigarette and clearly showing his satisfaction with the way things were turning out.

"By the way, what were you saying, Ntuli?" Mkhwanazi asked.

"I was saying, *baba*, that I find the gentleman's proposal extremely tempting. It's now up to you, really, to decide what should be done."

"Those words are encouraging, maNtuli, and I thank you dearly for your support. You see, Ndebenkulu, my wife gives me a great deal of pride – she's got clarity of mind when it comes to serious matters."

"Please, Themba's father, don't tell lies," said a flattered maNtuli, obviously finding the compliments as sweet as honey, especially since her beloved was singing such praises in the presence of an important visitor. "I hope, *baba*, you will soon release me so that I can continue with my household chores," she said.

"You may go back to your work, maNtuli. As I've already

said, Ndebenkulu will now leave on Wednesday — we have enough time for further talk either tonight or tomorrow."

When MaNtuli left, she left both men delighted. They had derived so much strength from her support, perhaps because it was such a complete surprise.

When Themba and Thoko prodded their mother to divulge what she had discussed with Mkhwanazi and Ndebenkulu, she simply avoided the subject. When they insisted, maNtuli suddenly became aggressive and told them that she was not obliged to discuss all serious family business with children, reprimanding them for not respecting their parents, and swearing to put an end to the nonsense pretty soon.

The two gave up all hope of a meaningful talk with their mother. It dawned on Themba that she was in full agreement with his father.

• •

After having a word with Themba, Diliza stood in front of the gate for a while, deep in thought and muttering to himself. Then he opened the gate and went down to a house not far away from that of the Mkhwanazis.

Although the dogs were growling, some young boys quickly shouted them to silence and they soon ran away. This was the Mpungose household — the home of a renowned criminal investigator. He was a close friend of Diliza's and although he was a few years older they shared a lot and worked in the same town of Ladysmith. Alert, Mpungose came out of the house just as the boys were calling the dogs to order. Whenever dogs were barking it was courteous to go outside and not let a human being become easy food. Mpungose was wearing a shirt, trousers and only one sock — he was just about to put his shoes on.

"*Sakubona* Mpungose! What more can a visitor ask of his host than to be grateful for whatever is provided." Diliza closed the gate behind him and shook Mpungose's hand with a smile. "Good day, Kheswa!" Mpungose was a gigantic, hand-

129

some and dark-skinned man. "Are you well, my brother? I thought you had already gone back to work!"

"I'm still around, brother, only for a few days, though," responded Diliza. "I'm going back next week."

"We're in the same position. Even when I asked for a few extra days they refused. Hey, boys, please bring two chairs here. We'll have to sit in the shade, Diliza. It's extremely hot and one can hardly manage indoors, I swear to God."

"It's terribly hot, I agree," Diliza said. "It's even worse for me, without a hat."

"Don't waste my time, Diliza, after all you're the type that thinks it's a crime to walk into a shop and buy a hat."

They both laughed.

"Don't make fun of me, Mpungose, please."

"I don't know what to do. My father had asked me to go to Mkhwanazi's meeting as he had to go to the fields. But sleep simply overwhelmed me last night, as if to defy him. It's as if I'm bewitched. My father will be disappointed when he returns to find that I didn't attend."

"Fortunately, I did," said Diliza.

"It's my lucky day. I did assure my mother that I would hear about it from someone, in time." Mpungose urged Diliza to tell him what had transpired at the meeting.

"I couldn't finish the meeting for fear the men would skin me alive," said Diliza with a laugh.

"Skin you alive, why would they do that?" Mpungose's face was serious and he looked Diliza straight in the eye.

"I wish you'd been there to see and hear everything yourself," said Diliza.

"What do you mean?" asked Mpungose. "What was happening there?"

"That's why I'm saying you should have been there to see for yourself that strange man who addressed the men. I bet you would have laughed fit to bust your gut! He even has a tooth that sticks out and this make him even funnier."

"He has a tooth that sticks out!" Mpungose was already in stitches. "You don't say, Diliza! All along I thought you had something important to tell me but it seems I was totally wrong. Now – please get to the point and stop behaving like a child."

"You think I'm not serious," said Diliza. "I must tell you this as well – when he started to speak he kept on telling everyone how important he is."

"What?" Mpungose seemed to be making a connection in his mind as Diliza was describing Ndebenkulu's mannerisms. "What did he do again?"

"There's more, just listen to me, Mpungose. He also told us that he has many cars and is friends with very important white people who, whenever they write to him, never forget to address him as an Esquire." Diliza laughed again. "It was that word which made me laugh so loudly, I had to get out of the meeting quickly before things could get bad for me."

"You left just as the meeting was starting?" Mpungose was disappointed by his friend's wayward behaviour.

"I had no choice and realised that the men were so angry they could have given me a serious beating. Why are looking at me like that?"

"I'm disappointed, Diliza, that you left the meeting too early. That was very unwise of you."

Mpungose sat on his chair looking the other way, without saying a word.

"Why? Why do you say that?" asked Diliza.

"Please describe this man in full for me," said Mpungose, ignoring his friend's question.

"I don't know what else to tell you about him except that I find him extremely funny. Of course the protruding tooth makes things worse. He's tall, and dark in complexion. His other outstanding feature is the moustache that he regularly strokes. That man really makes it a big deal to stroke his moustache."

"In that case, it's not the person I thought he was," said Mpungose, despondently.

"Who are you talking about, that this man isn't?" Diliza asked.

"I think it's not the person I had in mind because that person doesn't have a protruding tooth and a moustache."

"What about that person, Mpungose?"

"There's someone we're looking for in the city who is a hell of a crook. People can really be crooks, and only God knows why. Earlier, I told you I was refused extra leave days at work – the main reason is this man we're looking for. He's a real pimpernel, that one. It's just that he doesn't have a moustache and a protruding tooth."

"What criminal act did this man commit?" asked Diliza.

"It's even hard to know where to start. That man is a master thief. Fortunately for him, he's a smooth talker and by the time people wake up he is long gone and his victims are only left with his honeyed words to comfort them."

"What does that man do, Mpungose?"

"Where does one start? That man does almost everything. That's why when you said he calls himself an Esquire I almost jumped because the one I'm talking about is also pompous. The only difference is that he robs people of their land."

"You say this person is a land thief who makes empty promises to his unsuspecting victims?" It was Diliza's turn to be surprised.

"Indeed, that's what I'm saying. What's the matter, Diliza?"

"You know, this person told people at the meeting that they must sell their cattle and he will connect them with important white people who can offer him good prices."

"But you left the meeting quite early. Where did you get this information?"

"You're right to ask that, Mpungose. After leaving the meeting I visited the Mdunge household and stayed for a while. On my way home I met a group of men who were discussing among themselves some issues relating to the meeting. They also told me that this man had also spoken about selling land for them."

"Where is this man, Diliza?"

"Just relax, Mpungose. He's here, and only leaves tomorrow. The Mkhwanazis are his hosts."

"Are you sure he only leaves tomorrow?" asked Mpungose.

"Before coming here I was with Themba, Mkhwanazi's son, who told me that he's the one who will take Ndebenkulu to the station tomorrow morning. I'll be joining them as well."

Mpungose was silent. Then he said: "Indeed, Diliza, I would like to meet this man. Even if it's not him, it's possible he can give me information that may be useful for my investigation."

"Another problem, perhaps, is that you're looking for a criminal from Ladysmith, whereas this one is from Pietermaritzburg. I also heard that he had a cheque that he showed to the men."

"A cheque for what?"

"A real cheque, for 910 pounds, for someone he had sold cattle for. He told the meeting that cheque was on its way to its beneficiary."

"Are you serious, Diliza, or just whiling away time?"

"I'm merely giving you the information I got from the men who were at the meeting."

"Nine hundred pounds just for cows – clearly this is another crook you're talking about here," Mpungose said. "No one would be idling around with a cheque for such a huge amount. He knows very well that rural people would be easy to convince if he shows them a cheque to support his tales about his high social status. A cheque means nothing, because a person might have it without even a penny in the bank. People who don't know are easily deceived into thinking that a cheque is actual money whereas it's just a piece of paper. What did you say his name was again?"

"That's another reason I had to leave the meeting. When I heard his name was Ndebenkulu, I couldn't control myself."

"Ndebenkulu?"

"That's what we were told at the meeting."

"You must be joking, Diliza, there's no surname like that! Have you ever heard it before?"

"I've never heard about it before, but there are many surnames one doesn't know. What I do know is that Themba is

133

very worried because his father thinks this man is trustworthy."

"Do you mean Themba, Mkhwanazi's son?"

"That's the one."

"I know Mkhwanazi very well. He's a wise man and wouldn't easily be tricked."

"One can't say for sure," said Diliza. "What I know, though, is that Themba is deeply concerned."

"Diliza, you want to tell me that only Themba would see that this man is a criminal, and his father would not?"

"I get your point, but I must say I trust Themba's intelligence even though he is much younger than me."

"It's still quite likely that we're talking about the same smooth-talking culprit," said Mpungose.

"I almost forget to tell you that he also has letters," Diliza said.

"What kind of letters?"

"He has letters that he says were sent by grateful people in acknowledgement of his help. He also read these at the meeting."

"Undoubtedly this is a first-rate criminal. He clearly planned properly, and wrote letters to make his scheme look convincing. I wish I could see this man but I wouldn't want to alert him in case he vanishes. People like him might recognise me though I don't know them. What a pity I couldn't attend the meeting!"

"If you wait for us along the way tomorrow, wouldn't that work?"

"Maybe that's a good plan since you say he's leaving tomorrow morning," said Mpungose. "An even better plan would be to call another meeting so that he can get caught in full view of the men – and so that they'll also learn to be sceptical of strangers."

"This man seems too clever to get caught that easily. He's a really cunning man."

"Even then, Diliza, we must be sure he really is out to con people. After all, no mother has yet given birth to a man so smart that he can kiss his own back."

"I agree."

"Diliza, my heart is racing when I think about this. Criminals are now coming to the quiet, rural areas to con our elderly men, it's really disturbing to me, Diliza. I don't know what to do about it."

"Don't you think the chief might help?"

"The chief! The chief! That's a great idea! My boy, tell your mother you're going out and will be back quite soon."

• •

Although the chief was not around when Diliza and Mpungose arrived at his royal residence, they were assured of his imminent return. Fortunately he returned soon, and his aides immediately informed him about his two guests. This was a chief who had been to school, and whenever he had guests he believed in attending to them without delay, not letting them suffer under the scorching sun.

When he entered the traditional Zulu hut where Diliza and Mpungose were waiting for him, he politely shook their hands and welcomed them warmly. The two were standing, as was the custom. They paid their respects to the chief and said a few words in praise of his clan. He then sat, and asked them to do the same.

Without wasting a moment, Mpungose got straight to the matter that had brought them to the chief's residence. He explained to the chief the events of the day, and the meeting at the school, as Diliza had related them to him. Mpungose also told the chief about a criminal they were looking for in Ladysmith, after he had tricked people and left them empty-handed.

The chief did not say a word for some time, until he was satisfied Mpungose had finished. He then said: "I hear you well, Mpungose. Unfortunately I also have no idea about this man – I only heard rumours that he was coming but nothing official. My only relief was that I heard that Mkhwanazi, a man of integrity and wisdom, was the one who had called the meeting. It did worry me to learn that he had called a meeting in my tribe without my knowledge but, as is usually my approach, I decided against over-reacting and felt I had to pretend I had heard nothing, and wait to see what happened. I wanted to summon Mkhwanazi to my residence once the meeting had come and gone, so that he could explain his actions to me at length. Now that you are here, Mpungose, what do you want me to do?"

"I hear you well. My wish is that Ndebenkulu is called back to come and share his ideas with your excellency, in the presence of the men he addressed earlier today. Since I would like to verify the man's credentials, I will also attend but will hide so that he doesn't see me. It would be unfortunate, your excellency, if this quiet tribal authority of ours suddenly fell prey to hard-line criminals and city conmen. That's my suggestion in brief, your excellency."

"That's fine, Mpungose, although your idea is a departure from my initial plan. I would have preferred the visitor to leave first, so that Mkhwanazi has to come here in person to explain his actions. I'll change my plan now, and go along with your suggestion. When did you say he is leaving again?"

"Diliza, Kheswa's boy, told me he leaves early tomorrow morning," said Mpungose.

"Early in the morning?" asked the chief in surprise.

"That's so, your excellency."

"In that case I must immediately send word to Mkhwanazi requesting him to introduce his guest to me before he goes away. Son of Kheswa, just go outside and ask for Dlomo, my officer!"

At once Dlomo entered the hut, saluted the chief and sat down. The chief asked him to take a horse and hurry to invite Mkhwanazi to the royal residence that very afternoon, as a matter of urgency. He warned Dlomo not to mention that Mpungose was at the royal residence.

"I would prefer that you don't go until Mkhwanazi is here," the chief said after Dlomo had left. "I wouldn't want him to see you, though, Mpungose. It doesn't matter about Kheswa's son."

They then sat talking about different things – Mpungose even shared his adventures in Ladysmith, especially the daring and hard-to-believe acts of city criminals. It was almost sunset when Dlomo and Mkhwanazi arrived on horseback. Mpungose was taken to another hut within earshot – he had to hear every detail of the chief's conversation with Mkhwanazi.

When he entered, Mkhwanazi crouched in utter submission to the chief and was heard offering incoherent words of apology. "Why should his excellency be so hard on me? What else can I say now, since despite my intention to come in person tomorrow, his lordship was ahead of me?"

Although the chief had been angry at what Mkhwanazi had done, this sincere regret touched him and he quickly calmed down. He said: "Mkhwanazi, I understand you very well, and from what I know you are not an insubordinate person. That's why your action puzzled me, but then the best of us make mistakes."

"You make me so ashamed of myself, Ndabezitha! I deserve a serious punishment for my deed and it's true, Ndabezitha, that mistakes are made by the most well-meaning of us. Forgive me, for I didn't mean to be rude. It's just that I received a strange letter from a strange person and couldn't clearly understand his mission. I was completely in the dark, sir."

"Your apology is accepted, Mkhwanazi. I will not punish you at all and hope in future you will be more careful," said the chief gently.

"Words fail me, Ndabezitha!" Mkhwanazi said sighing in relief. "Good health, and may you live a long and blessed life, *Nkosi!*"

"Fortunately, Mkhwanazi, I have also heard about your guest and would be pleased to hear about his mission in person."

"That's in order, *Nkosi*. Even Ndebenkulu..." The chief interjected before Mkhwanazi could complete his sentence.

"Who?" asked the chief.

"He's Ndebenkulu, Ndabezitha. That's his name, Ndabezitha."

"Ndebenkulu?"

"*Yebo*, Ndabezitha."

"You must be joking, Mkhwanazi!" said the chief, laughing loudly. "What is his clan name?"

"I would be lying if I said I know it, Ndabezitha. Actually, I didn't ask him."

"Wo! Ndebenkulu! What a surname! Anyway, please continue, Mkhwanazi."

"Ndabezitha, I wanted to support your idea because I think Ndebenkulu would also be honoured to meet his lordship in person and tell him more about what brought him to Nyanyadu."

"Since you are hosting him, Mkhwanazi, tell me what exactly brought this man here?"

"What he says, Ndabezitha, is that since we are being asked to reduce our livestock he can help us to do so at a good profit. He's also interested to help people who want to use their land as mortgage when they want to borrow money from the bank."

"Is he talking about urban people who own their land?"

"I suppose so, Ndabezitha."

"He definitely must be referring to urban people, because here no one person can own tribal land. When is he leaving, Mkhwanazi?"

"He initially wanted to leave tomorrow morning, but has now decided to go on Wednesday."

"On Wednesday?" asked the chief, to confirm the day.

"It is so, Ndabezitha."

"I see...," said the chief, looking as if he was thinking about something.

"On what day would Ndabezitha want to see him?"

"Let me see... today is Monday and tomorrow is Tuesday, well... Wednesday would be fine except that you say he's supposed to leave on that day."

"In that case, Ndabezitha, one might need to talk to him in

the hope that he may change his plan on hearing that the *Nkosi* wants to see him."

"We don't have much choice, Mkhwanazi. It's too late to make it tomorrow, since we didn't inform the men. Even Dlomo won't be able to visit all households now, as it's almost dark already. We'd better settle for Wednesday and I trust that your guest will not feel inconvenienced, Mkhwanazi."

"I don't think he will mind, Ndabezitha."

"I hope you will also help spread the word about the meeting on Wednesday, Mkhwanazi."

"Without doubt, Nkosi. We'll make sure to let everyone know."

"That will be all, Mkhwanazi. You may go home now, it's getting late."

"*Ngiyabonga Nkosi*," Mkhwanazi said, with great humility. He again expressed gratitude to the Nkosi for letting him off the hook and ignoring the severity of his mistake.

"Don't worry yourself about that, Mkhwanazi."

"I also wish to express thanks on Ndebenkulu's behalf. Your kindness to host him together with the men of our tribe is a great honour indeed."

"Now I see, Mkhwanazi, that you want to embarrass us in front of guests and make us look like we're not hospitable," said the chief with a smile. "Anyway, go well Mkhwanazi."

"*Ndabezitha!*"

Mkhwanazi left, and mounted his horse feeling relieved that he had cleared things up with his chief.

"I thought all went well, Mpungose. What do you think?"

"Indeed, all went well, *Ndabezitha*. I heard everything."

"Is it possible I slipped up and said something that would make the man suspicious?"

"Not at all, *Ndabezitha*. Sometimes, though, criminals have a gift for sensing when something is wrong."

"That's normal, Mpungose. Even a cow becomes restless on the day of its slaughter. Let's just wait and see. You know we're meeting on Wednesday?"

"I heard, *Ndabezitha*. That day is perfect for me as well."

"By the way, you said it's this boy who brought you the news?"

"It's him, *Ndabezitha.*"

Then the chief shook Diliza's hand and said: "You're now a man Kheswa – when you suspect something is not going well, you alert other men without delay."

"*Ndabezitha!*" said Diliza, bowing before the chief.

"Young men, you may now go home. It's dark already."

"*Ndabezitha!*"

They both left.

•••••••••••••••••••••••••••••

"You're back, Mkhwanazi?

"I'm back, Ndebenkulu."

"Why do you come wearing a broad smile? You were quite fearful when you left? I was also very concerned."

"I must admit that when I saw Dlomo, the chief's officer, coming, my heart immediately started beating fast. I knew at once that some people had gone ahead to report me to the chief. At that stage maNtuli's words came back, but fortunately I found the chief as warm and gentle as ever."

"That's quite rare, Mkhwanazi. We often get news in the city that chiefs rule over their subjects with an iron fist. What this chief did is absolutely rare, I tell you."

"Ours is fortunately not like that," said Mkhwanazi. "I have no doubt that another chief would have asked for a cow as punishment because I called a meeting without his say-so."

"I believe you, Mkhwanazi, oh yes, I believe you. But then what's so urgent that he summons you at sunset?"

"You are the main cause for this, Ndebenkulu. He heard about you and would like to hear in person about your ideas, in the presence of all the men. He would like this meeting to be on Wednesday morning."

"You're lucky indeed, Mkhwanazi, to have an enlightened chief. Oh yes, you are. But what can I do, now that I'm supposed to leave on Wednesday?"

"You can't go, Ndebenkulu. The chief would like you to be at his royal residence on Wednesday."

"Which means I have to go on Thursday."

"That's so, it can't be changed now."

"That's a big inconvenience, Mkhwanazi. It means that all my work will have to wait. I also have to make a call and indicate that I'm now coming back on Thursday otherwise it won't be good for your relations with the chief."

"I'm glad you realise that your refusal would harm me. It's even worse because I started off on the wrong foot by calling a meeting without the chief's permission. You'll help me a lot, Ndebenkulu, if you wait for the Wednesday meeting. I also think that because we seldom have important people like you visiting us the chief thinks it's fit that he meets you in person."

"I believe you, Mkhwanazi. People like me hardly have time for paying courtesy visits. Who was with the chief when you arrived?"

"No one except Dlomo and that young Kheswa boy who kept on laughing like a fool at the meeting."

"You found him at the chief's residence?"

"Yes, I did."

"He must be the one who told the chief about the meeting," said Ndebenkulu.

"It must be him, unless of course someone had been there before him."

"That's fine, Mkhwanazi. I'm ready to meet the chief on Wednesday. I think I must only leave on Friday."

"Friday is better for me as well, Ndebenkulu."

• •

Early the next morning, Themba took a horse and went to Tayside to send a telegram to a Mr S. Southey of North Street, Pietermaritzburg. On his way, he passed by the Kheswa household to inform Diliza that, because of the chief's *imbizo*, Ndebenkulu would now only leave on Friday. But

Diliza told him that he already knew, since he had been present when Mkhwanazi spoke to the chief. Themba would have liked Diliza to accompany him but unfortunately he was also on his way, to Mbabane.

Although Tayside was quite far, Themba didn't notice the distance because he was preoccupied with the possible theft of his family's livestock, and disappointed about his mother's change of tune. On his way back he dropped the local postbag at Lushozi's house and went straight home. When he entered the main room, his father and mother were deep in discussion with Ndebenkulu. They stopped abruptly as he walked in, and he realised that negotiations must be at an advanced stage, and that he was not meant to hear their content. He put the family's mail on the table and asked if he could be the first to read the Zulu newspaper he had brought with him.

In the kitchen, there was Thoko, busy with the preparations for lunch, sweating heavily in the potentially lethal combination of the day's high temperature and the cooking fire. Now and then, she would pull out a facecloth and wipe off the sweat.

"I didn't realise you were back already, Themba!"

"I'm back, my sister, didn't you see me come into the house?" Themba sat down dejectedly.

"No, I didn't. That's why I'm surprised to see you in the kitchen."

"It's because you're busy. Why is it so hot in this kitchen, Thoko?"

"Can't you see I'm also wet with sweat? To be honest I'm now irritated with the whole thing."

"I'd better go outside," he said. "After being cooked almost to death by the vicious Tayside sun, I simply can't stand this heat."

"Don't leave me alone in here. You can sit next to the door, it's a bit better there."

"Thoko, you don't understand the hell I went through on my way. It was damn hot!" Themba pulled out a chair and sat next to the door as his sister had suggested. He opened the newspaper and started reading.

Thoko wondered if that was the day the newspaper usually arrived at their house.

"No, it's tomorrow," Themba answered.

"What's wrong with me? After all, it's only Tuesday, and not Wednesday. I'm so angry at the presence of that man that I'm even forgetting what day it is."

"What about me, who's so damn tired, all because I had to brave the heat to send telegrams for him?" Themba said. "I doubt he'll ever forget us after being treated like a king, like this. Maybe I'd better read the newspaper quickly in case father asks us to go the fields as soon as the sun has softened its sting. Perhaps I may see some coverage of the Mjiyako wedding."

"That's a better idea, Themba, there might even be some pictures of the wedding. I wonder how the bride's beautiful dress looks on paper. What a lovely dress it was!"

"Out of all the things you could think of, Thoko, you decide to focus on dresses. You never stop surprising me."

"Is there something else you suggest I think about?"

"In any case I doubt it would be covered in this edition – weddings usually take time before they appear in the paper. Tell me, Thoko, when did this meeting in the house start?"

"It's been going on for a long time, my brother, and it's hard to pick up a word because they're speaking so softly. When you enter the room, they suddenly go silent, for fear you might hear secrets that are too big for your young ears."

"That's what I felt as well, Thoko, and it made me very uneasy. When I came in to drop the mail, father looked at me with a snake's eyes – it was clear he saw me as a nuisance. D'you have any idea what they're discussing?"

"It's hard to tell since our mother has unexpectedly turned against us. You remember what she did yesterday afternoon. She's also become like a snake, waiting to pounce. But I'm convinced that it's still the same old story of the cattle."

"You're right, Thoko, I also think that's what's being dis-

cussed. What's your sense about all this, Thoko? Is it possible
that my suspicions about this man could be unfair?"

"I share your unease, my brother. What's been happening
here at home since his arrival on Saturday hurts me a lot. It's
also extremely disappointing to see adults so easily deceived.
They just see us as children whose views don't count. After
all, they own the livestock and we have none. That man must
definitely be enjoying himself for having been handed such a
gullible bunch on a platter."

"I couldn't agree with you more, Thoko. Remember, there's
a Zulu proverb that says no one can be refused to slaughter
his own cow. Our parents are doing exactly that, and who are
we to stop them? I'm just worried because I'm convinced the
man is a cheat. Yesterday he said something to father when
they were both looking at the livestock. What he said still
haunts me."

"What did he say?" asked Thoko.

"He told father that the possessions of fools are often an
easy harvest for the cunning. It's hard to know what those
words meant, and it makes me nervous."

"Themba, do you realise that money is a curse? Look at
father, he's a man who has everything, and his livestock
includes cattle, sheep and even horses. Now that this
stranger is dangling money in front of him, suddenly he
thinks he's a poor man, and this affects his sense of judgment."

"Worse still, Thoko, only yesterday mother was fiercely
opposed to the man and out of the blue she's in a meeting
about taking our cattle away."

Suddenly Themba was reading the newspaper with intense
concentration. Then he said: "Thoko, just listen to this and
tell me if I'm mad to be astonished."

Thoko couldn't wait to listen. She came close, to read the
newspaper headline next to her brother.

Zulus Beware!

*We feel it necessary to warn our people about a looming dan-
ger we have heard about in many places. As a newspaper of the*

nation, we see it as important to raise issues that disturb us, in the hope that we will help our readers in the process. A new wave of criminal activity has arisen and is affecting our people in different areas. There are con artists who promise people instant wealth by using their property for mortgage loans but never give the money to its intended beneficiaries. There is even a rumour that some of these people seize cattle from people under false pretences...

•••••••••••••••••••••••••••••••

"My God!" Thoko's shock came out in a whisper, as if she did not want anyone other than Themba to hear her. Themba rose from the chair and shivered as if from a sudden chill. For a moment, the two looked at each other without saying a word.

Then Themba said: "You see, Thoko, this is exactly what we've been talking about."

"My God!" said Thoko again.

"What should I do, Thoko?"

"I think you must take the newspaper right away, and show it to father," Thoko said nervously.

"How can I do that? You know father is going to shout at me."

"That shouldn't matter now, Themba. This is our last chance to save them from the inferno surrounding the household and threatening to destroy it. His rage doesn't matter — but what does matter is that he reads the newspaper."

"You might be right, Thoko."

Although Themba was doubtful he nevertheless went ahead. As he entered the room there was an abrupt silence. Ndebenkulu stared at the newspaper and for a moment he was tense, as if he suspected something.

"What's wrong with you, Themba? You keep disturbing us while we're busy discussing serious matters. What do you want that can't wait?" As Themba had predicted, Mkhwanazi was in a foul mood.

145

"Pardon me, father. I don't mean to disturb but just to show you something in the newspaper that I believe you must read." He gave the newspaper to his father and showed him the part he had to read.

"Is Themba mad, or what?" Mkhwanazi looked his son in the eye as if ready to attack him. Mkhwanazi could not believe that his son would have a nerve to disturb him merely because of a newspaper. "What do you want me to read that's so important that it can't wait for me to finish what I'm doing? You don't have any respect for Mr Ndebenkulu and instead you are busy embarrassing me in front of an important guest – like someone who was not properly brought up. What do they teach you at the college if they fail to teach you good manners?" Mkhwanazi snatched the newspaper from Themba and thrust it aside angrily.

"*Nx*! When is Themba going to grow up and learn good manners? Get out! Get out! MaNtuli, just see what your son is doing, it's unbelievable!"

"It's childishness, *baba*," responded maNtuli shamefacedly.

"I'm tired of hearing you defend Themba with the same argument. When will he grow up and behave properly?"

As Themba was closing the door, on his way out, he felt the callousness of these words. It hurt him that whenever he was attempting to alert his father about an imminent danger, Mkhwanazi merely became agitated and dismissed him like dirt. He had also not liked the way Mkhwanazi had snatched the newspaper and put it aside at once, as if he was ready to throw it away.

"Let's see what it is that's troubling your son, Mkhwanazi," said Ndebenkulu as he picked up the newspaper.

Mkhwanazi found this annoying – he would have preferred them to finalise the matter at hand before reading the newspaper. But since Ndebenkulu wanted it he simply had to manage, and hide his annoyance. Immediately, he felt cross that Themba had brought the newspaper and disrupted the flow of the discussion he was having with Ndebenkulu.

Ndebenkulu read the paper as if he had forgotten about the

cigarette in his mouth. MaNtuli, on the other hand, noticed that Ndebenkulu seemed to find what he was reading rather worrying. He read it once and then he re-read the same section, from beginning to end, without saying a word. After Ndebenkulu was done, he put the paper down and lit a fresh cigarette.

"What's in the newspaper? " asked maNtuli.

"MaNtuli, don't you think we should concentrate on what we're discussing, and finish it, before getting carried away with the newspaper?" Mkhwanazi was finding this whole newspaper business a big nuisance.

Ndebenkulu didn't respond immediately. He stopped brushing his moustache, and looked down in silence. Then he raised his head, and said: "Perhaps, Mkhwanazi, it would better if we read the newspaper your son has brought, and then continue with our conversation."

Mkhwanazi obliged grudgingly, shouting, "Where did this boy want me to read?"

"Here, Mkhwanazi," said Ndebenkulu, pointing with his finger.

"Please read aloud, *baba*, so that I can also hear," said maNtuli, not realising that this request intensified Mkhwanazi's fury.

After he had read a few lines, however, his trousers began to do a trembling dance underneath the table, and his voice suddenly became squeaky. His khaki handkerchief started to frequent his sweating face. Mkhwanazi was undoubtedly suffering pins and needles. MaNtuli, frightened, kept quiet at this unmistakeably delicate stage of the negotiations.

Ndebenkulu, on the other hand, merely looked at the two like an interrogating officer trying to extract the truth from a suspect merely by scrutinising their eyes. When he was done, Mkhwanazi was silent, one hand on his forehead, elbow balanced on the table, the other on top of the table while he did his best to end its uncontrollable trembling. His eyes were fixed on the table – he pulled out the newspaper and looked like he was about to attempt a second reading.

"Now you see, Mkhwanazi, why I was insisting that you read the newspaper before we finalise our matter. It must be clear why I was so adamant about that."

"Yes, I see," said Mkhwanazi, trying to pull himself together. His mind was all over, and he didn't know how to conduct himself under such circumstances.

"Now it's the time for me to speak, Mkhwanazi. I think that's perfectly in order," said Ndebenkulu. "Why I say that, Mkhwanazi, and you, madam, is all because of your son's actions. He rushed in here to make you read the newspaper for one reason only. He thinks the newspaper is talking about me. He thinks I'm the thief stealing money from people."

"It's not so, Ndebenkulu..."

"Please, Mkhwanazi, don't interrupt me, I genuinely beg you not to do that," Ndebenkulu held up his hands to underline the seriousness of his point. "Let me finish what I want to say. Clearly, that's what your son's behaviour means. Ehhe! That's what it means. Your son wants to tell me to my face that I'm a thief. He's come to wake up his parents to the possibility of being tricked by a crook." Ndebenkulu emphasised the last words – he was clearly beginning to fume. "Mkhwanazi, what you see today is a man who has seen it all before. I must say, though, that never even once did it occur to me that one day I would be called a thief. Never! A thief! A thief! Me, C.C. a thief! Never! What rubbish is this that's coming my way in your household, Mkhwanazi? Really, what rubbish is this? Could it be a bad omen? When I get home, will my house and my children be destroyed? Something really terrible must be coming my way!"

At that stage Ndebenkulu rose from his chair and moved about like a person possessed. Now Mkhwanazi was anxious, unsure as to what Ndebenkulu would do next.

"From the time I was fetched from the station by a farm cart, something wrong was unfolding. Me, C.C., travelling on a farm cart! I did suspect that this was a sign of something ominous ahead of me. Worse still, this silly boy of yours deliberately caused an accident that damaged my precious clothes.

148

As if that wasn't enough, he's now the one who calls me a thief!"

"*Mnumza...*"

"Please, Mkhwanazi," Ndebenkulu raised his hand again, to shut Mkhwanazi up.

"I'm not used to being interrupted whenever I speak. Really, I'm not used to that. Not even important white people interrupt me when I'm speaking."

Sheepishly, Mkhwanazi obliged. Ndebenkulu was moving up and down the room with immeasurable anger. Themba and Thoko were crouched behind the door, listening, after having heard the rise of temperature in the room. Ndebenkulu was as livid as a mamba under attack. His eyes were red with rage, the lips and the long tooth were trembling uncontrollably.

"You better sit down, *Mnumzane*, so that we can talk like men," said Mkhwanazi, starting to recover his composure.

"I refuse to sit down! I simply refuse to sit down! Why should I sit down? You tell me, Mkhwanazi, why should I sit down? There's no reason at all for me to sit down! None at all! How can I, a thief, sit down with people I'd come all the way to rob? How can I? In any case, your silly boy told you I'm a thief! I must be going now. I never knew that wanting to help people could bring so much pain. The ones you want to help turn against you and their children even hurl insults at you! How were these children brought up? Since I arrived these children have been behaving as if they know more than their parents. Indeed, that's what they think. I'd better go right away, Mkhwanazi – your children will help you, not me. C.C. is not the type to be made a monkey by silly rural children. Is it possible for you to take me to the station, Mkhwanazi?" Ndebenkulu looked at his wristwatch to show his intentions.

"Please take a seat, Ndebenkulu," Mkhwanazi tried again. "How are we going to talk when you behave like this?"

Ndebenkulu ignored him. "I realise, Mkhwanazi, no one is to blame. No one is to blame, really, because for a long time my wife has been warning me and asking me not to waste my time with people, people are never grateful she warned me long ago. She warned me long ago, but because I met so many people who praised my work, and received many letters of gratitude, and because of my determination to uplift my nation, I ignored her wise words. Those wise words have come back to haunt me today. Is this really happening to you, C.C.? Could you really be labelled a thief by a silly Nyanyadu boy? Important white people take their hats off to you, and yet a silly rural boy calls you a thief! Really now, Mkhwanazi, please tell me all this is happening in my dreams. Please do. Please just tell me all this is a nightmare. This can't be true. All this really can't be true!"

"Please, Mnumzane, take a seat so that we can finish our conversation."

"What is there to finish, Mkhwanazi? What? Are you ignoring the words of your trusted boy, who has alerted you to a thief? It's not my intention, Mkhwanazi, to see disunity in your house. I'm someone who serves the nation, not a person who creates disharmony in families. I came here in the hope that I would also help you, but to you I have now become a thief. Let this be the end of our relationship. You know, Mkhwanazi, for some people deprivation and misfortune are life's curse. Even when luck is knocking at the door, they resist and chase it away. Nothing matters now, Mkhwanazi. My wish to help you has been shattered like a clay pot, no one can put the pieces together again. It's been spilt like milk, and no one can bring it back."

"*Mnumzane*, I think you're making a terrible mistake to draw such conclusions when I haven't even said you are a thief."

"Mkhwanazi, you'd be making a big mistake if you talk to me as if you're talking to a child! I saw your reaction immediately after reading the newspaper. You saw this as a blessing from your ancestors – you thought they'd come to rescue you before you could fall into a bottomless pit. That's how you saw the whole thing!"

"It's not so!"

"That's why I'm saying let's forget everything we discussed. I'm no longer willing to help you! Not at all!"

"I assure you, Mr Ndebenkulu, that I'm going ahead with the plan we were discussing."

"What are you telling me, Mkhwanazi? Do you mean you're prepared to let a thief take your cattle? Do you hear what you're saying, Mkhwanazi." Ndebenkulu's sarcasm was intentional.

"I never called you thief – you must remember that."

"Mkhwanazi, you must think about this carefully now. You don't know me, and I'm trying to show you the way towards wealth creation, and this silly boy of yours decides to call me a thief. What on earth would make you go against the good advice of your son, your own blood, your own flesh, and trust me – a total stranger, someone who would rob you without any pity?"

As Ndebenkulu was giving this speech he looked Mkhwanazi straight in the eye. Mkhwanazi, on the other hand, was looking down at the table, unsure about the best thing to do.

"What if, Mkhwanazi, your son is telling the truth? What if it's so, Mkhwanazi?"

"Please, Ndebenkulu, let us finish our talks."

"Woman of the house, why are you quiet when a thief is about to finish off your family livestock? Why are you quiet?" asked Ndebenkulu sarcastically.

MaNtuli could not decide, in her mind, whether he was mocking her. Then she said, firmly: "I think there should be no further negotiations, we need to rethink this matter first. The truth is that Themba's father owns the cattle, and he has to make up his mind. As things stand, I'm withdrawing."

"I thought so from the very beginning. You believe the newspaper is talking about me. I saw it right away. Like your son, you also believe I'm a thief. You really have no sense of sympathy for me. When I had an accident in your house you simply dismissed it as a joke. It didn't end there. You also did your very best to show that I wasn't welcome in your house.

151

Today, your son insults me with an insult I can't even begin to describe, and there you go again, agreeing with him. You don't have even a word of rebuke for your wayward son. What do you think I should conclude about you, madam?"

MaNtuli found Ndebenkulu's words infuriating, but she tried to stay calm. Were the children, after all, on the right track? Was it possible that she and Mkhwanazi were being lured simply because of greed?

"*Baba ka* Themba, I insist we delay discussing this matter until we've had a private meeting," said maNtuli defiantly.

"Should I stop everything because of Themba? How can maNtuli say something like that? I'm not going to, otherwise this boy will make a habit of interfering in my affairs! Themba has no business in my affairs. Themba has no house and no cattle. If you are no longer interested in this matter, that's fine, we'll continue without you. I just can't allow Themba to dance on my head as he pleases!"

"Well, *baba*, this whole thing is over for me," said maNtuli calmly. "It's become too big for my brain and must now be discussed only by men. I have things to do in the house, in any case. In the end the cattle are yours, and you may do as you see fit."

MaNtuli got up and headed for the door. Themba and Thoko quickly ran away from the door, towards the kitchen. Now they were starting to hope that Ndebenkulu's tricks would fail.

•••••••••••••••••••••••••••••

Ndebenkulu and Mkhwanazi remained behind, and a momentary silence marked maNtuli's sudden exit. Mkhwanazi filled his pipe. "Mr Ndebenkulu, you must know that I'm not a man who beats about the bush. Once I have committed myself to something, I keep my word. If now I change my mind, it would mean I'm also pointing a finger at you and joining the chorus of those who think you're the one in the newspaper article." He broke off. "Ndebenkulu, I've asked you countless times to sit down."

Ndebenkulu had been standing, quietly, looking down at Mkhwanazi as if surprised by the kindness of his host. Finally, he gave in to Mkhwanazi's request and sat down, saying: "I apologise profusely, Mr Mkhwanazi, for drawing wrong conclusions about you, indeed, I apologise. I'm ashamed that anger made me forget who I am to the point of uttering words unbefitting my social status. In the short time I've been here you have shown yourself to be an intelligent and honourable man, you've really shown that many times. Let me be frank and admit that I really admire your intelligence, Mr Mkhwanazi. It's very unusual to meet someone with a great mind like yours, even in urban areas, indeed it's very unusual. I'm saying this with the full confidence of someone who has travelled this country a lot, indeed I've travelled this country a lot. I hope you forgive my mistake, Mr Mkhwanazi — you must surely understand how awkward I feel being associated with the kind of crooks mentioned in the newspaper. Clearly, your son believes I'm one of these horrible people. What pains me even more is that the behaviour of your wife shows that she also thinks I'm a thief."

Mkhwanazi received Ndebenkulu's compliments like butter melting into hot toast. He smoked his pipe with added relish and he regained his calm. He felt a bit annoyed with himself for having had bouts of doubt in the first place, and blamed Themba, concluding that his son was serious about chasing his ancestral luck away.

"Forget about Themba and maNtuli, Mr Ndebenkulu. Women and children are the same. One day you'll hear maNtuli saying the livestock belongs to her children and the next day you'll hear her saying it belongs to the patriarch of the family. Such people shouldn't be taken seriously, their minds are shallow and all over the place."

Mkhwanazi reflected on what he had just said to Ndebenkulu and concluded that his family was responsible for his misfortunes. Right at the beginning, Themba had caused the unfortunate accident that had greeted

Ndebenkulu's arrival – and to make matters worse maNtuli had shrugged it off. A childish and stupid act had almost cost him his entire livestock in compensation. Although this good and forgiving man had not acted against the Mkhwanazi household as he was entitled to do by his social status, Mkhwanazi was saddened to think that his family was still throwing insults at such a charitable man. Yet again, before he and Ndebenkulu could conclude the serious business that promised riches and happiness for the entire Mkhwanazi household, Themba was brewing more trouble, with the support of maNtuli. Undoubtedly his family was the source of his misfortune, he thought.

"Mkhwanazi, I must admit that my endless compassion for you is a surprise even to me. If you'd been someone else we would no longer be having a conversation at all – I would have shut you out completely. By now I'd be consulting with my lawyers and advising them to press libel charges and clear my name after it has been so besmirched. That I have not acted as my social status demands of me is because of my high regard for you, Mr Mkhwanazi. If truth be told, it's all because of you, Mr Mkhwanazi. So much has happened to me since I arrived in your house and it should have made my heart hard by now. Even when anger threatens to crush me, a new sun emerges between the dark clouds of rage and warms my heart to tenderness. This surprises me a lot, Mr Mkhwanazi. Oh yes, it does. It's clear your ancestors are determined to ensure that your good fortune is not lost."

These words were sweet to Mkhwanazi's ears. Unsure how to reciprocate the gesture, he merely said: "It would be wonderful if we could conclude our business, Mr Ndebenkulu."

They continued, and when they were finished they both appeared overjoyed by the milestone they had achieved, so much so that laughter filled the room as they agreed on almost everything. It seemed as if the two men were long-lost kindred spirits.

"That's fine, Mr Ndebenkulu. I also agree that we should

start with the ten small bulls. We'll use these as a sample, and afterwards I will decide which ones to send you as a second consignment."

"Indeed, Mr Mkhwanazi, that is my sincere proposal. Since you no longer have the full blessing of your family, it's advisable that you only send a few cows at this stage, to help minimise domestic discord. Equally important is that the first shipment must not be too big. No, that would be a terrible mistake. I'm quite confident that when they see the money reach the Mkhwanazi household they will change their minds instantly. It would be extremely unwise for you to be too stubborn at the expense of your dear family. Indeed, that would be unwise."

"You speak like a man, Mr Ndebenkulu. I've hardly ever met anyone as kind-hearted as you are. Clearly, son of Ndebenkulu, God must have moulded a unique and special heart for you – it's so different from the hearts of most people I've met in my whole life. Truly, you surprise me beyond any words I can find to capture my feelings. Someone else would have long abandoned the noble idea of helping people who caused him so much pain. I just don't know how, as a man, I can face the shame of knowing that my family has been so malicious towards you."

"You can forget that now, Mr Mkhwanazi, you can forget it," said Ndebenkulu. "Everything is in your hands now. I just have to wait for you. Even at this stage, if you are unsure about this big step, you are still at liberty to change your mind. I must reassure you – don't think that if you changed your mind I would lose anything, since there's absolutely nothing I stand to gain from your cows. All the money I collect goes straight back to the owner of the cattle. I'm therefore emphasising, Mr Mkhwanazi, once again, that you mustn't do anything you're unsure about just because you think it would make me happy. I really don't want you to make that kind of mistake. I would like you to do everything with a clean and clear conscience."

"Let's agree, Mr Ndebenkulu, that the boys will herd the

cows to Tayside station early on Friday morning, so that they will be on the same train with you."

"That would be wonderful, because there's a cattle sale on Monday. I would be very happy, Mr Mkhwanazi, if your livestock reached the cattle sale on time, before they suffer from hunger and thirst. I know this would please you a great deal. Oh yes, I know that. Like you, I would also not be pleased to see my guest feeling unwelcome in my household because of the wayward behaviour of my wife and my children. Oh yes, I wouldn't be pleased. I swear by the heavens and their godly angels that you will have your money before the end of next week. Oh yes. I even swear on the name of my eldest sister."

● ●

MaNtuli cut a lone figure in the kitchen. She was deep in thought, both worried and confused about the impending theft of her family's livestock. The children dared not interrupt her reverie since they knew her hot temper pretty well.

"Thoko, bring my shoes please!"

Thoko obliged at once. MaNtuli said that she was off to see maShezi. MaNtuli was still sombre as she set off for maShezi's house, the Zondi home. The Zondis were not that far away, it's just that the path was steep. Luckily, she arrived just as maShezi was returning from one of her errands. "You almost didn't find me, *iNkosi!*" said maShezi with a friendly laugh.

"I can see that I almost arrived only to be met by the walls of your house. Who were you visiting?"

"I wish it was a visit, maNtuli, but there's no time for that kind of luxury. I was just out to get some sugar and *mielie meal* at the shop. I resolved long ago to go to the shop in person because my son Mpisekhaya has to look after the cattle. The problem, though, is that often the cows invade other people's fields in broad daylight while he's busy catching flies. That one is a useless daydreamer!"

"*Hhawu*, maShezi! You end up going to the shops in this

heat while Themba is around and could have helped? Why didn't you ask Themba to do it for you?"

"You're right, maNtuli, I could have asked him but I saw him early this morning riding a horse and he said he was going to Tayside."

"Forgive me, maShezi, I'd forgotten about that. He did indeed go to Tayside early this morning."

"Do you mean that he's back?" asked maShezi.

"Yes, he's long back."

"That was quick," said maShezi, surprised. "Let's go inside the house, it's too hot outside, especially for me after my trip to the shop."

"I feel for you, since you're a woman who never says it's enough until the plate is spotlessly clean."

"There you go again, maNtuli. You just don't know how cruel the scorching sun was to me today. Where's your man?" said maShezi with a laugh.

"What man?" asked maNtuli.

"I'm talking about the long-toothed debonair guest you're hosting."

"Please, maShezi, give me a break about that strange man. The very reason I'm here is to cool my head off a bit."

"Well, I realise that you seem quite unhappy. What's the matter now? Has he been insulting you again?"

"You know, maShezi, my head is spinning as we speak."

"You are obviously in trouble with this man, MaNtuli. He'd better go now. You've been upset since he arrived on Saturday. When exactly is he going back?"

"Only on Friday, unfortunately."

"*Hhawu*! Only on Friday! What will he be doing till then?"

"Tomorrow he will be attending an *imbizo* called by the chief but he says the *imbizo* has disrupted all his plans and that he would rather leave on Friday as a result."

"That's a great pity and I really feel your pain. Friday isn't like tomorrow. But what has made you so upset so suddenly?"

"If you sit down I'll give you the whole story before the sun sets."

"Let me quickly warm up some water so that we can have tea while we're talking. I also want to know how this man helps people, it's the rumour all over Nyanyadu. There's hardly anything else people are talking about except his amazing work and the huge amounts of money he gets for selling cattle."

"That's exactly what's making my head spin, maShezi."

"I can't wait to hear more! Let me just make the tea quickly and then I can enjoy all the juicy news you've brought, maNtuli."

After maShezi had pumped the paraffin stove and boiled the water, she prepared the tea and then sat down with her friend to enjoy the drink and hear about Ndebenkulu first-hand. MaNtuli gave a long report of the previous morning's meeting.

"Don't tell me! What a pity Mpisekhaya's father is out, or he might be asking this man to help him as well. In any case, these cattle bring us so much trouble and so often we have to quarrel with our neighbours. As we speak, we still have to answer in the matter of the Ndawonde case where yet again our cattle were the intruders."

"What compensation are they asking for?" asked maNtuli.

"They're demanding six pounds. I simply haven't a clue where we'll get that kind of money. Even when I tried to plead with him it was like hitting a stone. That man is stubborn and would not hear of any kind of leniency like we're asking for."

"Do you really think he is being unreasonable?"

"Well, maNtuli, not when one looks at the extent of the damage to his mealie fields. Someone else might have charged us even more. That's why I'm convinced we had better get rid of our cattle very soon."

Then maNtuli raised the matter of the newspaper that Themba had bought in Tayside and brought to the room where she, Mkhwanazi and Ndebenkulu were having a meeting. "When I got out of the room, I was so confused I didn't think my head would ever stop spinning. The very reason I'm here is to try ending the dizziness. I feel as if my brain has come to a complete standstill and I'm going mad."

"Now I get the full picture, maNtuli. This is really difficult. The man could be genuine and because of the newspaper report you could miss a golden opportunity. On the other hand he could well be the crook the newspaper is talking about and the very fact that you got it on time could be a message from your ancestors who want to save you from getting yourselves into a bottomless pit of pain and regret."

"And my biggest trouble, maShezi, is knowing which path is the right one."

"I agree with you, maNtuli. This is too difficult."

"How would you have handled it, maShezi? Be honest with me."

"Let me tell the truth, like someone on his death bed. I don't have a solution either. It's easy to speculate if one isn't directly affected, but it's a completely different matter when one is the bug stuck in the dung. Think aloud. Even if you decide to give him some cows, I suggest you only give one or two, so that if he's a crook you don't lose much."

"Yours is the best advice I've had in a long time, maShezi. I'd better share it with my husband although I believe he thinks this man is everything he has been asking for, and wants to give him no less than ten cows. But I have to try to advise him in any case, and take it from there. Only time will tell."

Suddenly, relief was written all over maNtuli's face. MaShezi had provided the kind of herb she desperately needed to assuage the pain in her throbbing head. She was still not sure the man was not an ancestral envoy, sent to improve their lot in life. But then again, the same ancestors could be waking them up through their children. Indeed, maShezi's plan was the best one to minimise the loss, just in case Ndebenkulu was a criminal.

"You know, maShezi, your advice has brought me untold relief. I'd better go now, and talk to Themba's father before it's too late."

"*Hhawu*! Already on your way out! I didn't mean to chase you away."

"Shezi, you know quite well I'm not being chased, but let me leave at once."

"What about another cup of tea," asked maShezi, trying to keep her friend a bit longer.

"Thanks a lot, Shezi. I'm anxious to go now. Please, don't share what we discussed with anyone else. I don't want the two of us to become the laughing stock of Nyanyadu."

• •

"*Baba*, I truly believe that even if you give him some cattle, just give him two, but not more."

"MaNtuli, I asked you to sit down so that we could finish the discussion and you decided to go out and leave it unfinished. Now, when it suits you, you're bringing up something we could have discussed at the meeting." Mkhwanazi was unrepentant about a decision he had already made.

"In all fairness, *baba*, you know quite well the reason I left."

"Not at all. I don't know it, because I told you to sit down and you defied me."

"What, then, was your conclusion, *baba?*"

"I will ship ten cattle at first," responded Mkhwanazi firmly.

"*Hhawu*! Ten cows! What if he vanishes with your cattle?"

"That's exactly the attitude you and Themba have which irritates me. You're just prejudiced against someone without any good reasons. Why? What has Ndebenkulu done to you? Do you know something terrible that he's done that perhaps I'm the only fool unaware of?"

"We don't know anything terrible he's done, *baba*, but the truth is that we don't know him. I really think you are getting carried away. Ten cattle! Not even five!"

"MaNtuli, your talk surprises me since not so long ago you said I had to do with my livestock as I pleased. Why do you burden me now with the embarrassing task of trying to get out of agreements I've already committed myself to? I know exactly what I'm doing and you'd better leave me alone."

The dark cloud that had engulfed maNtuli when she went out to visit maShezi returned in full force. This time its intensity was like a storm that gathers with deafening sound and frightening speed.

"Well, *baba*, what more can one say to you? Only time will tell." MaNtuli went into her bedroom to lie down.

•••••••••••••••••••••••••••••

At the crack of dawn on Wednesday every man in Nyanyadu woke up with one purpose for the day – to attend the *imbizo* called by the chief at the royal residence. Even those who had missed the Monday meeting were relieved and grateful to the chief for this opportunity to get what they wanted, to get rich and, as they said in those days, to be rich enough to afford a potato that cost no less than two pounds. To be rich enough to afford the niceties of the good life such as spirits and cigarettes, chicken and rice and Coca-Cola! The chief's actions were cause for celebration and applause.

There was so much interest that by the time the meeting was scheduled to start, throngs of men were already milling around in an open area outside the royal residence where the chief would sit on a raised platform and address his subjects. On this day nobody was worried about losing a day's ploughing. Mkhwanazi arrived accompanied by Ndebenkulu, who walked self-importantly as if oblivious to the people who had gathered for the big *imbizo*. Mpungose was also in the crowd but had deliberately sat at the back, so that he would not be noticed. The chief called for someone to bring a chair for Ndebenkulu, since, as someone from the city, he was not used to sitting on the grass.

When everyone was seated the chief arose. "People of my father, I greet you all!"

"*Bayete!*" responded the crowd in unison.

"I greet you all on such a beautiful day." The chief paused, as if to ensure that everyone was paying attention. Then he said: "Some of you might think I'm saying the day is beautiful because the weather is sunny and the skies are gently blue. That's not at all what I'm talking about – the day is beautiful because we have a very important guest in our midst."

"*Ndabezitha*! Chieftain!" responded some in the crowd.

The men were relieved to realise that the chief was not angry at not having been informed of the meeting on Monday. The chief was speaking with a great degree of gentleness and warmth, and there was not even a hint of anger in his voice.

"I must be honest with you all, beautiful people of my tribe. I have no idea how big this man is, but we will find out very soon because Mkhwanazi is here." As he said this, the chief pointed at Mkhwanazi who was seated in the front row. "He is the one who knows this man better than all of us... Who did you say he was again, Mkhwanazi?"

"He is Ndebenkulu, *Ndabezitha*," said Mkhwanazi.

"*Ehhe*! Ndebenkulu."

This was undoubtedly amusing to some men, who were seen laughing surreptitiously and hanging their heads on their knees.

"I too, people of my father, almost missed this wonderful opportunity to meet with Ndebenkulu, since he almost left without the two of us having met. Mkhwanazi kept this man solely for the benefit of his own household and didn't want him to be seen by others. I never realised before that Mkhwanazi is such a jealous man." The chief laughed and was joined by the crowds when they realised that he was joking. "I do hear, nevertheless, that some of you have met this man and were exposed to some of his bright ideas. However, I must tell you that the meeting you had on Monday was not a legitimate meeting of the tribe. That was merely a discussion between Mr Ndebenkulu and the relatives of Mkhwanazi. The only meeting for the tribe is this one."

"*Ndabezitha*!" responded the crowd, in full agreement.

162

"Now is the opportunity for all you people of my father to listen attentively to the words of wisdom that this respectable man is going to share with us. I must also tell you that Mr Ndebenkulu was supposed to leave today and go back to his family. He is here at my request because I wanted him to address you properly at a tribal *imbizo*. I will now hand over to Mkhwanazi to introduce our guest," and the chief took a seat.

At this stage, some shifted a bit to ensure that they were comfortably seated. Mkhwanazi rose at once, faced the chief and bowed as a mark of respect. He looked at the men and fastened his coat properly, looking down as if he was still planning his speech.

"*Ndabezitha* and your dear subjects! Greetings to my honourable chief and his subjects. I am also grateful to my honourable chief for forgiving me after my childish act that adds up to insulting the institution he represents and him in person. My honourable chief knows that I have already apologised for calling a meeting without him, and I do so again in the presence of all the men of the tribe. I hope the chief will not forsake us because of our mistakes. I hope that the chief will continue to lead us as his children."

Mkhwanazi paused, unbuttoned his coat and then fastened it again.

"Let me move on and pay attention to the essence of this gathering. In our midst today is a guest." Ndebenkulu was sitting quietly but with a great deal of self-importance. One leg was crossed over the other and he kept brushing his moustache. His long tooth rested firmly on his lip.

"Although some of you have seen him, I had the good fortune that he came to my house. I have had long conversations with him and discussed the many options available. He has impressed me tremendously as someone who is selflessly dedicated to uplifting his people and is not even concerned about the cost to his own pocket of his benevolence. Such men are rare indeed, and it has been a pleasure to meet Mr Ndebenkulu. Meeting him has been a great lesson for me, and

I hope it will be to all the men gathered here today. Some of you might think that I know him very well but I'm just like the rest of you. I also met him for the first time – but now it may look as if we have known each other for years. I only learned about him through a letter he wrote me, that I received last Wednesday. I've no idea why he chose to be hosted by me, when there are so many men who are better off than me, here at Nyanyadu. *Ndabezitha*, it would also help if Mr Ndebenkulu could explain how he got my name and address."

Mkhwanazi paused again and took out a handkerchief to wipe his face before continuing.

"The chief asked me to explain to the men just how big this man is. *Ndabezitha*, please pardon me, I don't have much information to share in this regard either. I can only say that this man is a rich man, owns properties and is an important man. I also believe that he is learned, knows the law very well, although I don't know how far he went with his education. Anyway, dear men of the tribe, you are not here to listen to Mkhwanazi dilly-dallying. You have come here to hear what our guest has to say. With your permission, *Ndabezitha*, I will now take a seat and let Mr Ndebenkulu speak."

Mkhwanazi sat down and Ndebenkulu took the floor.

"*Ndabezitha* and all men gathered here today, let me state at the outset that I am an urban man. I was born in the city and grew up in the city. I'm not used to *imbizos* like this one. Indeed, I'm not used to them. Please bear with me in case I do or say things that would not be acceptable when addressing a chief, or if I don't appear to be polite in my speech. Please bear with me. I apologise in advance. I beg you not to interpret my behaviour as a discourteous act, dear people. Kindly understand that it would be a result of my ignorance."

Ndebenkulu stopped talking, collected himself and focussed his energies on the task at hand. That his words were a real sweetener was written all over the smiling faces of most men. They were moved by his gesture of politeness and humility. This was a far cry from the impression he had created earlier, sitting at the front and looking too haughty to win the hearts and minds of this humble peasant community. They had expected that when Ndebenkulu opened his mouth he would speak in English.

"Even the very fact that I entered this community through Mr Mkhwanazi is proof of my ignorance. Now I realise that I should have communicated directly with you, *Ndabezitha*, and take full responsibility for having put Mr Mkhwanazi in an embarrassing situation. Indeed, I was at fault and I apologise to the honourable chief, as I intended no insult to you, *Ndabezitha*. I therefore thank the chief for his mercy towards me and for even creating this opportunity to speak to the men in his honourable presence. Although it's true that I should have left today and that my staying longer is a huge inconvenience, all that doesn't matter now. What does matter is that there is a chance for me to do something for the people of Nyanyadu. That I will do, and will do even if I put some of my urgent work aside."

Ndebenkulu told the gathering that he was a well-travelled and well-known person. He told them about his reputation among important white people, who addressed him as Esquire. He also told them about white people who own abattoirs, and that he sold cattle at a good price. He explained how he could be of help to men who wanted to secure bank loans by using their land to obtain a mortgage. He stressed that he was not at all poor and that he did not gain even a penny for his role as an intermediary between needy people and the influential white people he knew. His payment was the satisfaction and the joy that came from seeing people getting help and improving their lives, he said. Had he been selfish, Ndebenkulu continued, he would have stayed at home and not bothered about poor people. He was doing what he was doing mainly because God had not made him a mean person who would turn a blind eye to the gruelling poverty and pain of less fortunate people. He found it hurtful to see his people suffering and being exploited. He had decided to sacrifice his warm and comfortable home because his people meant so much to him. He told them that he hoped his wife would not divorce him because he was hardly ever at home with her and his children. The men laughed in amusement and Ndebenkulu joined them. He was a charming public speaker.

Ndebenkulu then read the letter from Ndiletha Hlongwane, after which he said: "Before I continue, dear people of Nyanyadu, may I first touch on a painful matter? We city people know that there are many crooks out there. Often, when someone is grieving, others go all over pretending to be collecting money for the bereaved when they are actually doing this for their own benefit. Too often, they're not even related to the mourning person but are on a mischievous mission. This behaviour, unfortunately, affects the few of us who are genuinely trying to help, as we are mistaken for these criminals, and one can't blame them for thinking that since there are many shameless people who rob their own people – and even widows – without blinking an eye. I have learnt, though, that people like me, who want to help others, must be strong. One must stay focussed until one earns the trust of the people when they finally realise that you are not a crook and that you mean well."

Ndebenkulu sat down, crossed one leg over the other and stroked his moustache. For a while there was silence, until the chief stood up and invited the men to ask questions or make comments. Shandu was the first to take the floor. "Mr Ndebenkulu, you have given me peace of mind. Indeed, your last words have put me at ease. I regularly receive the Zulu newspaper and when I received it yesterday it disturbed me. With your permission, *Ndabezitha*, may I please read the newspaper aloud?"

"You are most welcome, Shandu. Go ahead and read for everyone to hear," said the chief.

"*Ndabezitha!*"

Shandu read aloud from the newspaper, the same lines that Themba and Thoko had also read at the Mkhwanazi household.

"That is why, Mr Ndebenkulu, I am comfortable with you,

because of your last words. After reading the newspaper I definitely also doubted that you were an honourable man," said Shandu as he emphasised his words with gestures. "I must say openly that I came here with a great deal of concern but I told myself that at least your tongue will reveal a lot about the kind of person you are. Now that I'm here I have no regrets since you've put me at ease, child of Ndebenkulu. When we had a meeting at the school, you said something so profound that your words continue to echo in my ears. The men who were at the meeting might recall those words, and I had hoped that you would repeat those words today. You said, 'For some people, when luck knocks on their doors they don't open until it moves on, leaving them behind'. Your words are hard to forget – they continue to haunt me. I have chosen my way and will surely not be among those for whom luck knocks and only to find the doors shut. It's clear to me that luck is knocking at the door of the Shandu household. I have chosen to open my door. The very kind gesture of the chief to give us another opportunity to listen to the words of this wise man is a blessing from the ancestors, who would like the people of Nyanyadu to turn over a new leaf and realise their dreams. If you're going tomorrow, Mr Ndebenkulu, be assured that you will take along ten bulls – once I have decided on something nobody can stop me. My mind is made up."

Commotion punctuated Shandu's remarks as most of the men suddenly felt under pressure to be decisive as well. They felt they would look stupid to keep on questioning something that seemed so simple and straightforward to understand. This vote of confidence in Ndebenkulu gave Mkhwanazi much joy – at least he was not alone in seeing Ndebenkulu as a saviour – and this turn of events made him understand that women could be a curse in a man's life and could persuade a man to make hasty decisions like themselves.

Even the chief was confused now, and looked for Mpungose but in vain. He also felt let down because while he had expected to meet a young man who looked the part of a crook,

Ndebenkulu was, instead, a debonair and respectable man. The way he spoke also seemed to suggest that this was a man to trust and work with.

"You'd better speak now, men," said the chief anxiously. It was clear that no one wanted to speak, as they simply settled for murmuring among themselves, until Mkhwanazi stood up and said: "I'm also like Shandu, Ndabezitha. If something is clear I don't waste time interrogating shadows. My cattle are going as well."

The men looked at one another, overwhelmed by the gravity of the moment. Most had left their homes unprepared to let Ndebenkulu take their cattle. They felt that to change their minds on the spot would be to be unduly hasty.

Although they told themselves that the men who were ready to sell their cattle had already done their homework, they were worried that by the time they were eager they might be too late to get good prices. The chief was also uncertain, and on the verge of giving his cattle away as well. He decided against the idea, however, on the basis that it would be premature to do so without consulting Mpungose. He therefore opted to hold on to his cattle.

Shandu stood up again. "It is unfortunate, *Ndabezitha*, that Mr Ndebenkulu did not bring along the cheque he showed us on Monday. This would have helped the men to fully understand the great work done by this kind man without expecting to get even a penny for his sweat. I have been fortunate to handle that cheque with my own hands," said Shandu as he held out his hands to make his point.

"I agree with you fully, Mr Shandu," said Ndebenkulu, getting up. "Indeed, he's telling the truth. I meant to bring it but simply forgot. I realise now that I left it in the coat I was wearing on Monday. In any case, those who were with us on Monday saw it and are credible witnesses today. As Shandu said, he was lucky enough it to even touch it."

"You'd better ask now, men," said the chief. "This is your only chance, as you all know that this gentleman is leaving tomorrow."

"In fact, *Ndabezitha*, he will only go on Friday," said Mkhwanazi.

"Thank you, Mkhwanazi, but nevertheless there will be no other *imbizo* before he goes. Speak now, men."

When it became obvious that no one was going to be asking questions, the chief arose, thanked Ndebenkulu for his dedication to his people, and closed the *imbizo*. Reciprocating, Ndebenkulu thanked the chief sincerely for his warm reception. Then Mkhwanazi and Ndebenkulu bid the chief goodbye, and left.

•••••••••••••••••••••••••••••

"*Hhawu*, Mpungose, you let your target off the trap! What happened?" asked the chief with a laugh.

"*Ndabezitha*, I was confused. I don't know this man, and he's not the one I'm looking for."

"I suspected that something was amiss when you didn't surface."

"I was really confused, *Ndabezitha*."

"Are you satisfied that this man is genuine? I didn't suspect anything, I must be honest with you," said the chief.

"*Ndabezitha*, crooks are very smart. Nothing in his behaviour looks suspicious. On the other hand, something in me says that something is fishy about him. It's hard to put my finger on it, but still I'm not entirely satisfied. When he speaks he's persuasive, but that's usual with swindlers. I still insist that something is not the way it looks with this Ndebenkulu fellow."

"Could it be so, Mpungose, or is it just that as a private investigator you're suspicious of almost everything?" The chief laughed loudly.

"Not in the slightest, *Ndabezitha*. I still maintain that he's not telling the truth. I also doubt the authenticity of his surname and the fact that he's an important man.

"I hope you're not serious. Do you mean his surname is a fake? Sometimes, you know, you may find a person unlikeable without any good reason. Maybe he just lacks appeal for you."

"*Ndabezitha*, I'm inclined to disagree. There is something much bigger than that about him."

"Well, Mpungose, you failed when I brought your target to your doorstep as you had requested. Worse still, the men insist that they will not let luck pass them by."

"I also noticed that, *Ndabezitha*, and was surprised to find men having so much blind trust in a person that they would give their cattle away without satisfying themselves about the legitimacy of his scheme."

"They did satisfy themselves, Mpungose."

"Let's just hope, *Ndabezitha*, that they won't live to regret their blind faith."

●●●●●●●●●●●●●●●●●●●●●●●●●●●●

Mpungose returned home walking slowly, greatly disappointed. What disturbed him most was that although he was convinced something was amiss about Ndebenkulu, he couldn't put his finger on it. He had been wise, he thought, to leave much later than the others and on his own, as he wanted to be alone, to use the solitude to think deeply about what had just happened at the *imbizo*, and to devise his next plan of action. In no time he arrived home, having barely noticed the long walk, went straight to his bedroom and threw himself down on the bed. He was even more convinced that Ndebenkulu was neither a philanthropist nor a merciful son as he had proclaimed – but when he thought hard about criminals he knew none fitted the profile of the man. He quickly consoled himself, though, by attributing his ignorance of Ndebenkulu and his tricks to the fact that this man was from Pietermaritzburg whereas he worked in Ladysmith, almost a hundred miles away towards the Drakensberg Mountains.

As Mpungose lay resting on the bed, his mother passed by in the yard. Since his door was wide open, she asked why he had not told her he was back.

"I've just arrived, mother, and the scorching sun has exhausted me terribly."

"Excuses again! The sun is always exhausting you, one wonders how on earth you get your job done! Doesn't it get this hot in Ladysmith?"

Mpungose laughed, and asked if his mother was looking for him.

"No, my son, it's just that I'm surprised that you have returned. Where's your father, then?"

"He was with Shandu and Buthelezi after the meeting," responded Mpungose, adding that perhaps he had gone to Shandu's house first.

"Maybe that's what he did. If I had known you were back I would have brought your mail along."

"Oh yes, it's Wednesday, isn't it? said Mpungose.

"Indeed, it's the day we normally receive the mail."

Mpungose volunteered to go and collect the mail himself and asked his mother where it was.

"On top of the table in the sitting room. I'm just collecting some firewood so that I can make the fire."

"*Hhawu*, mama! Why are you making the fire today? Where are the girls?"

"I just sent them to the Msomi household to ask for a pinch of salt. I didn't know ours was finished."

Mpungose got up and went to collect his mail. There was one letter in a large brown envelope with a government stamp. It made his heart beat faster – what could be wrong, barely a few days before his return to work? He opened it hurriedly. It was a particularly short letter.

"When you receive this letter you must return to work at once. It is quite urgent." What could be so urgent that it cut short his leave? He thought how hard it was to work for the government because once an instruction had been issued one had to obey it without any resistance. He opened the rest of his mail, yet his mind remained fixed on the government letter he had just read.

On his way out of the room, he met his mother. She could

tell from the gloom written all over Mpungose's face that something had disturbed him, and asked what it was.

"I'm on my way back, mother."

"What are you telling me now? Where are you going?"

"Back to work, mother."

"Back to work?"

"Unfortunately. This letter was sent to ask me to return to work immediately."

"But you had said you would only go back next week!"

"You're right, but sadly our work is full of emergencies and we have to expect to be instructed to change our plans at short notice."

"Well, there's nothing we can do. It's a pity, because we were looking forward to spending more time with you. We didn't know what today would bring us. We haven't even washed and ironed your clothes. What's to be done now?"

"I'm as surprised as you are, mother. Don't bother about my clothes. I'll sort everything out when I'm back in Ladysmith."

"I don't like the sound of that, my son. Do you mean to leave your own home with dirty clothes? Why don't you leave them behind? We'll find a way of sending them to you in a few days."

"Please, mother, you don't have to worry. I'd be more unsettled, actually, if I go without my clothes."

"I feel miserable about this, my son. I can't even make you mielie bread and spinach to take with you."

"Don't worry about anything, mother. I'd better ask the Msomi boys to bring back the horses. I have to get going soon, so that I can catch the night train."

"Will you catch it at Tayside?"

"There's no other way. I have to take the evening train from Vryheid."

"When will you arrive at Ladysmith?"

"At Glencoe I'll take the train from Johannesburg, but only arrive at Ladysmith when it's already dark."

When Mpungose reported for duty the next morning he was sent straight to the chief criminal investigator, a white man, to whom they all reported.

"Mpungose, we asked you to return urgently because of the pressing matter of this criminal you're hunting up and down. Incidents of crime are increasing. Now there's information strongly suggesting that the man you're searching for is working as part of a syndicate. I have to say that I personally don't believe this theory, but those who do insist the trickster is working with others. There's a widow from Mbulwana who has just opened a case of theft and fraud, saying he took her cattle and promised to sell them but never kept his word. Of course, both the man and the cattle have never been seen since."

Mpungose was alarmed, and the chief inspector noticed.

"Mpungose, what's the matter?"

"What you just said, *Mnumzane*."

"What about what I just said?"

"Tell me, *Mnumzane*, did the widow give you the name of that man?"

"She did indeed. Just a wait a minute, let me page through my file and I'll tell you what it was.... Here it is. E.E. Mlomo. Have you ever heard of someone with that name here at Ladysmith? Have you?"

"Definitely not. That's a strange surname, *Mnumzane*. I've never heard of anyone called Mlomo."

"Well, Mpungose, that's what the widow says, it's a person with that name who took her cattle."

"But why did she give her cattle to a man she didn't know?" asked Mpungose, at the same time angry and sympathetic.

"That should hardly surprise an experienced criminal investigator like you, Mpungose. You know quite well that people are easy to swindle when there's talk of quick wealth. Even those you think are smart fall prey to criminals just because they are hoping to get money in bucket loads."

"There I couldn't agree with you more, *Mnumzane*," said Mpungose, as he recalled the *imbizo* at Nyanyadu the previous day. He remembered that he had held men like Shandu and Mkhwanazi in high esteem until he saw them trusting a strange man to such an extent that they agreed to give him their cattle in the hope of getting rich overnight.

"Maybe, *Mnumzane*, the story I'm about to tell you will interest you." Then Mpungose told his boss everything he knew about Ndebenkulu.

"You say your man calls himself Ndebenkulu?" asked the chief criminal investigator.

"Yebo, *Mnumzane*. That's the name he uses way over there in Nyanyadu."

"Where is Nyanyadu, by the way?"

"After you have passed Dundee, *Mnumzane*."

"I see. And you say this person has cheques for large amounts with him?"

"That's what those who attended his Monday meeting insist, sir. He actually held two meetings. I didn't see a cheque myself, though, as he didn't bring it to yesterday's meeting."

"Don't you see, Mpungose, that Mlomo and Ndebenkulu seem to be one and the same person? Maybe he interchanges names — at one place he's a mouth and somewhere else he calls himself lips. Don't you think, Mpungose, that our man might be the very same Mlomo who conned the widow? Don't you think he deliberately changed his name when he arrived at Nyanyadu?"

"It's very hard to tell, Mnumzane, because Ndebenkulu does seem to be his legitimate name. He even has business cards with his full particulars and contact details. Nevertheless, I must tell you that since I heard about this Ndebenkulu fellow, I've had no peace. Something about him is not as it may seem."

"Do you have that business card with you?"

"Unfortunately, Mnumzane, I heard this from those who say they saw it."

"Where did you leave that man, Mpungose?"

"I left him yesterday at the meeting the chief had called for

174

him to tell the villagers about his grand schemes to make them wealthy. I must say though, Mnumzane, that the chief had called this gathering at my request. I wanted to satisfy myself about the man's credentials."

"And does your chief also suspect something is wrong?"

"No, he doesn't. He also met Ndebenkulu for the first time yesterday, and the man is a very persuasive speaker."

"That's quite common with swindlers, Mpungose."

"Tomorrow he's supposed to take the train and leave Nyanyadu."

"Where is he going?"

"Probably back to Pietermaritzburg, his hometown."

"At what time is he taking the train?"

"Since I think he'll take the cattle with him, he's likely to take the midday train," said Mpungose. "Maybe he'll leave early to first ship the cattle and then take the train."

"If it's tomorrow, Mpungose, that's fine with me. I'm anxious to see him as well, but would prefer to take the widow with me since I don't have a photograph of him."

"It's very easy to describe him – he pushes his lips out to a point, has a moustache that he likes to play with, and a protruding tooth."

"Well, the widow didn't mention the tooth but she did mention the moustache and some unusual features about his mouth. Maybe we should contact her right away."

The chief criminal investigator and Mpungose went out, and rode straight to Mbulwana on a motorcycle with a sidecar for a passenger. The widow was at home and, quickly informed of the urgency of the trip, was just too pleased to oblige. Losing so many cattle had almost sent her crazy. It was unbearably hard that the inheritance her husband had left for her, and for her children's upkeep, had suddenly vanished.

The chief criminal investigator asked the widow to get someone to look after the children. He explained that they would sleep at Dundee and proceed to Tayside early in the morning.

"Even if we leave here in the morning we'll still make it in time. Tayside is not that far, Mnumzane," said Mpungose.

"I think we had better leave tonight, Mpungose, so that I can also get the support of the criminal investigators based at Dundee." They advised the widow to get ready and go to the police charge office in the afternoon, at the time most shops were closing for the day. That evening they would all depart for Dundee.

Towards nightfall, a police vehicle left with two white criminal investigators, with Mpungose and with the widow. It took the Johannesburg road to Dundee, and avoided the road to Zindumeni. When they arrived at Dundee, they took the widow to the nearby township where her relatives agreed to put her up for the night, then went straight to the local police station.

After intensive discussions, everyone agreed that Ndebenkulu would have to be trapped at the Tayside station. Fortunately, since he was taking cattle with him, this was the only exit point from Nyanyadu. In any case, they were convinced the plan would work, as Ndebenkulu had no cause to be suspicious and change his plans. Late at night, they went to bed, having agreed to leave for Tayside soon after breakfast.

● ●

At the crack of dawn on Friday, the cattle belonging to the Shandu and the Mkhwanazi households respectively were roughly awoken by boys on horseback who had been asked to take them to Tayside station. These cattle were taking a final journey so that in return their owners could get rich and live happily ever after. Soon after, the proud men who owned these cattle followed the boys to be sure that their livestock was well taken care of and would not arrive at the abattoir battered and starved.

"Do you appreciate the unbelievable blessings from the ancestors, Mkhwanazi? When we least expected it they showered us with so much good fortune!"

"I'm still battling to come to terms with it all, Shandu. Can you believe that to this day I have no idea who gave Ndebenkulu my name and address?"

"It's a pity that most of the men got cold feet," said Shandu. "I had expected a bigger shipment of cattle than what we have today. I've never seen men who are such cowards!"

"You see, Shandu, most men are cowardly, as you've just put it. They expect others to think for them and even show them the way to riches and success. Many would like to sell their cattle as well, but would rather wait for Mkhwanazi and Shandu to lead them. What they want is to wait on the sidelines and use our experience to test the waters."

"You're right, Mkhwanazi. I'm not prepared to share my experience with cowards. I can forgive a woman when she's a coward, but never a man."

"Shandu, it's almost as if you know that maNtuli didn't want the cattle to go – exactly because of the cowardice you're talking about. She even suggested that I should send two cows at the very most. And what would I be doing if I only sent two cows? Instead of only sending two, I'd rather do nothing at all."

"I had a similar nuisance at home, Mkhwanazi, and my wife even used words I normally hesitate to use! To stop the nonsense I had to remind her of her place in the household, and that when she arrived to become a wife at the Shandu ancestral home, she wasn't herding any cattle. You see, Mkhwanazi, unless you remind a wife about her place in the family she gets out of hand and causes you embarrassment in front of other men. I'm a proud hater of men who let their wives into their pockets and keep on calling them 'mayi diya, mayi diya'. I've no idea why a wife would become mayi diya and end up thinking she's also the man in the house."

"Shandu, that's exactly the reason why I did what I saw as my duty as a man, and ignored whatever maNtuli was telling me, because it's important not to allow a wife to mistake a man's head for a dance floor."

"I think yours will fetch good prices, Mkhwanazi. Mine aren't that fat."

"Actually, I wanted to send even more, but Ndebenkulu advised me otherwise."

"This is a truly amazing man, Mkhwanazi."

"I've never met such a wonderful man before – and wise too," said Mkhwanazi.

"When he gives advice you can tell that he's well-informed, well-travelled and used to doing business with white people. What's especially touching is that he does all this work for free. Such men are rare nowadays."

"Indeed, Mkhwanazi, he's a rare soul and God blessed him with a giving and very loving heart. I think, Mkhwanazi, that if our cattle sell well perhaps we should give him a goat or a sheep as gesture of appreciation."

"You're right, Shandu, we should show that we're grateful."

As they spoke the horses were moving and they were following the boys taking the cattle to the station.

After they had left, a wagon carrying Ndebenkulu also left for Tayside station. MaNtuli stood outside, silent. Thoko stood beside her, also silent. Seeing Ndebenkulu leave her house filled maNtuli with both joy and anxiety. Thoko was very pleased. "*Ewu* mama, at last this man is leaving us," she said.

"Yes, my child, at last he is leaving us with your father's cattle."

MaNtuli's words seemed to come from a mysterious deep place inside her heart. Thoko didn't need to ask whether her mother was in pain, but still she said: "Why do you look so troubled, mother, do you think that...?" She couldn't finish. She realised that although her mother had initially warmed to the idea of selling the cattle, she had subsequently regretted ever endorsing the idea.

"Let's hope your father won't live to regret his decision, my child." For some time, no one uttered a word on the verandah. They watched Ndebenkulu's wagon until it disappeared behind a nearby hillock, and then they went inside the house.

MaNtuli sat inside the kitchen in silence and looked as if she was too tired even to lift her eyebrows. Suddenly she looked like someone who had been ill for a long time. Her handkerchief visited her eyes regularly in an attempt to wipe away her tears. To see ten cattle leave the household under such uncertain circumstances was no small matter, and she was ashamed of herself for having encouraged Mkhwanazi to pursue this plan at the beginning. Maybe, if she had been obstinate throughout, Mkhwanazi might have acted differently. Now she felt like the Zenzile of Zulu folklore, a person no one could pity because she was the architect of her own misfortune.

After a while, she resolved to pull herself together and get on with her daily errands and to take her mind off the subject of cattle – something she knew would be difficult.

Thoko was also up and down in the house, helping her mother to tidy up.

Themba and Ndebenkulu were travelling. Only utter silence filled the meadows, hillocks and valleys. Themba was so angry that his father's cattle were being stolen in broad daylight that he felt like beating the trickster into cow dung. If he had been given a choice he would not have bothered to take him to the station, and would have made him walk all the way – but then, he had to obey his father. He just couldn't forgive this man who, he believed, was a thief bent on stealing his family's cattle.

Then he also recalled that when Ndebenkulu had come to Dundee with him the day before, he had asked him, Themba, to wait outside while, alone, he obtained the permits to ship the cattle. Themba did not know exactly what the man had told the animal inspector and whom he had registered as the owners of the cattle. All these thoughts made him wild with rage.

Ndebenkulu could tell, from Themba's body language, that he was truly unwelcome in his company, but he told himself that, as Mr C.C. Ndebenkulu Esquire, to worry about boys would be beneath him. As they came to the Kheswa household, Diliza came out.

"Here's this boy again," said Ndebenkulu, irritated.

"That's good, because it means you'll travel together," said Themba rudely.

"Why do I have to travel with this boy? Where is this wagon really going?"

"Where is it going? Don't you know where you're going?" Themba was deliberately provoking Ndebenkulu, who immediately saw what he was doing, and who swore that he would not let a boy's disrespect silence him.

"I'm asking again. Who is being transported on this wagon?"

Themba looked at Ndebenkulu as if at cow dung. Instead of responding directly, he said that Diliza was his friend and he was also going to the station.

"Was this wagon sent out for me or for your friend?" Ndebenkulu was furious.

"That's none of your business," said Themba.

"What do you mean it's none of my business? Where is your friend going, to take up a seat on such a small wagon?"

"Just move up and he'll be able to sit without a problem. You must remember that people like us aren't rich and don't have two cars each. We ride on boxes, as you prefer to call wagons. In future you must remember to come in your car, so that no one will trouble you. Just sit properly, Ndebenkulu, and make way for Diliza."

"What makes you so rude, son of Mkhwanazi? Calling me Ndebenkulu instead of Mr Ndebenkulu."

"Just sit properly, Ndebenkulu, we're in a hurry! What kind of language do you understand?" Themba was unstoppable.

"Does your father know you're behaving like this?"

"If you keep on talking you'll miss the train. You must realise that it's the last time I'll take you to Tayside. So please stop your nonsense and make room for Diliza so that we can get on our way before it's too late. After all, this isn't your car – it's the Mkhwanazi cart."

"I'm really unhappy with your behaviour, boy, and I know

your father has nothing to do with it. When we meet him at the station I will have to tell him about this."

"Are you serious about catching the train, Ndebenkulu, or not? Just move up and let Diliza sit, so that we can go. Tayside is very far away! Ride on, brother. Tighten your knees, you. I have no intention of telling you the same thing until sunset. I see you under-estimate my stubborn will, Ndebenkulu. I can dump you right now and go back home."

"I'm used to college boys like you, who think they are everything because of the little education they have picked up. You know what? You don't surprise me. You really don't surprise me."

"So why are you making such a noise, if you're used to the behaviour of college boys? Let's get going, Diliza."

Diliza had been silent, observing the spectacle. He climbed on board at last and they got going on their way to Tayside. He laughed mischievously, looked at Ndebenkulu and said, "What's wrong with you, Ndebe, don't you want to ride with me?"

Ndebenkulu turned, looked at Diliza menacingly, and said, "My name, boy, is Mr Ndebenkulu."

Mockingly, Diliza said: "I'm sorry, sir, but the trouble, sir, is that your surname is so strange. I've never heard it anywhere in the world. What was wrong with your family, to choose Ndebenkulu as a surname?" Diliza ended his gibe with a laugh, the same mocking laugh that had irked Ndebenkulu during the Monday meeting at the school, and which provoked him into anger again. "What ethnic group are the Ndebenkulus?" asked Diliza.

"I've realised that – unlike your fathers – you Nyanyadu boys are rude, really rude... Oh yes, that's for sure."

"Just tell me, Mr Ndebe, what kind of nonsense is your father full of?" Diliza, enjoying himself, punctuated every line of attack with a guffaw.

Ndebenkulu's mouth began to shake uncontrollably, and he battled to speak.

"Do you have any idea why I decided to come to the station?" asked Diliza.

Ndebenkulu didn't answer.

"I'm speaking to you, sir, and you'd better concentrate when I'm speaking! Do you know what brought me to the station?"

"Just leave me alone, silly little boy. Just leave me alone, you bastard! Why should I care about what brought you to the station? You don't damn well feed me!" The boys almost fell off the wagon laughing especially as Ndebenkulu's angry outburst was peppered with a few English swear words.

"You see, my friend, now the Esquire is speaking English, just as if he's enjoying a good cigarette," said Themba.

"You'd better care about the reason that brought me here, Ndebe. I even know that you've called me a good-for-nothing low-life who needs a good hiding," growled Diliza.

"Where did I say that?" asked Ndebenkulu much to Themba's uncontainable pleasure.

"Are you a coward, Mr Ndebenkulu?" asked Themba. "Now that Diliza is present, you're afraid to own up to the words you spoke to my father on Monday."

"Well, if I said it there must have been a good reason for it. Oh yes, there must have been a good reason. It's just that you boys are so disrespectful that I would have to read the entire Oxford English Dictionary to find the most appropriate word to describe your behaviour."

"I'm surprised that you bring books into it," said Themba.

"I'm surprised that you're surprised. Oh yes, I'm surprised. Don't you see that your words and deeds show how impolite you are? Don't you see that? Mkhwanazi sent out his wagon so that I could be taken to the station in comfort, and instead you use the opportunity to pick up every kind of fool you meet along the way. For you it doesn't matter at all that I'm making all these sacrifices to help your own father."

"Ndebenkulu, this must be the last time you talk that kind of nonsense," said Themba. "You must never again tell me that rubbish about wanting to help my father. Go ahead and tell him it's none of my business, but never say it to me. I don't give a damn – even if you're supposed to be an Esquire."

Ndebenkulu was speechless, as if in search of words to throw back at Themba. Nobody needed to tell him that these boys were ready for anything and were provoking him into a fight. He began to think that perhaps they had conspired to beat him to a pulp. Nevertheless, he refused to let country boys silence him.

"You don't even care that we're uncomfortable in the wagon now, and that my expensive clothes are getting creased because of this. Not even…"

"You're becoming such a bore, Ndebenkulu, with this talk of your clothes. Even on Saturday, when I fetched you, you went on and on about your clothes. In any case, they look very ordinary to us."

Ndebenkulu's anger was growing, yet he did not know what to do.

"To return to the reason I came along," said Diliza. "It's because you said I deserve to be beaten up – and you called me a 'thing'. Just tell me, Ndebe, who are you going to ask to beat me up? You certainly don't look capable of doing it yourself."

Ndebenkulu said nothing. Themba laughed. Ndebenkulu concluded that the boys were looking for a reason to beat him up. If he hit one of them, they could both descend on him like dogs and leave him unconscious. He was also worried that the route to the station was deserted and that no one could come to his rescue if they attacked.

"Tell me, boys, where are you going with this kind of talk?"

"We're trying to warn you to watch out for what you say." Diliza stared threateningly at Ndebenkulu. "Do you think I can easily beat you up? Is that what you think, Ndebe? Do you know that I can hit your teeth out of your mouth?" Ndebenkulu quickly touched his long tooth as if afraid it would fall out. The boys had another good laugh.

Ndebenkulu was desperate. It was too hurtful to admit that, although their fathers held him in high esteem, to these boys he was just dirt. "You'll regret your actions boys, indeed you will." And the boys laughed.

"You can laugh as much as you like, but I tell you, you will regret it, boys."

To which Themba responded: "Before you go, Ndebenkulu, let me tell you that I don't trust you, and I think you're a city criminal. Even your surname is a lie and you know it, you dirty man. All your talk of being big and having lots of money is a tale I refuse to believe. You've fooled my father, and even as we speak his and Shandu's cattle are on their way because they believe you're an Esquire."

Ndebenkulu was at a loss for words.

"You see, your fright tells me something. If you're not a thief why do you look so scared?"

"Mkhwanazi boy!" said Ndebenkulu, shaking with anger. "Mkhwanazi boy! Mkhwanazi boy!"

And the boys laughed.

"Mkhwanazi boy, do you realise how you've just insulted me?"

"Where you come from do they call the truth an insult?"

"You're not only insulting me, you're also harming my good name!"

"I don't care about your anger because I know the truth hurts. I'm even tempted to break your neck with my bare hands and at least go to jail for a good reason. You've made a fool out of my father, and I despise you for it."

"Mkhwanazi boy! Mkhwanazi boy! This demands that I teach you a hard lesson, boy, even if your father was so good to me. Oh no – I can't just leave you without teaching you a lesson. I must, so that in future you'll know how to respect others."

"Why not start right now?" said Themba.

"You are a truly uncivilised country boy and can only think of a physical fight. Well, I'm not talking about that."

"What are you talking about, then?" asked Themba mischievously.

"You can laugh as much as you like, but you will soon laugh on the other side of your face because I will sue your father and take his entire livestock."

"What?" asked Themba as he looked Ndebenkulu in the eye. "I'm not surprised you are making the same threat that you made on Saturday. But why do you bring my father into it when the two of us are not yet done? What kind of man are you?"

"I don't care a bit about your talk, boy. What matters is that you will soon be sorry when I take your father's bit of live-stock. I'm warning you, boy, you'll regret it when I sue your father."

"Is trying to steal other people's livestock what you call charitable work? And just imagine what my father would say if he heard you referring to his livestock as a 'bit' when in his eyes you're an angel sent from heaven!"

"Boy, just stop the cart so that I get off!"

"Get off to where?"

"I said stop the cart so that I can get off! Don't you hear me, boy? Do you think I'll continue to let boys insult me? Mere country boys? Let me get off now!"

"Father said I should take you to the station and I won't stop here because it's not the station." Themba continued with the ride as if Ndebenkulu's request was nothing more than a child's tantrum.

"Don't you hear me boy? I want to get off!" Ndebenkulu grabbed the halter and the lead rope. The horses reared up in fright.

"What's wrong with you, silly man!" said Diliza angrily as he grabbed Ndebenkulu. "Are you mad? Can't you see the horses almost killed us?"

"I wouldn't care if you died. Stop!"

"Themba, just stop and let this lunatic get off."

"Lunatic! You're calling me a lunatic! You boys think you're so smart because you're at college. I'll show you just how stupid you really are. "

"You'd better keep your mouth shut before we show you just how stupid you are. Themba, just let this thing get off."

Themba stopped the wagon and Diliza made way for Ndebenkulu to alight.

"Just make sure you don't kiss the earth again," said Themba. He asked Diliza to give Ndebenkulu his luggage.

"What should we do now, Themba?" asked Diliza.

"We'd better proceed to the station and help father loading the cattle. I also need to tell him about the trouble with this difficult man we had to leave behind."

"It's sad to see your bulls go away, man."

Themba shed a silent tear. After a while he said: "Where is that silly man?"

Diliza looked back and saw Ndebenkulu still standing on the same spot where they had left him, like an abandoned orphan. He was looking at the wagon.

"The Esquire is lost, man. He doesn't know what to do with his heavy luggage and the long walk ahead in such heat. He's to blame and we shouldn't feel sorry for him, he asked to be dropped off."

They went on their way, and soon they saw the cattle also approaching Tayside Station.

• •

At about nine in the morning, the police car left Dundee for Tayside. When it reached Tayside station the driver parked the car at the local shop so that it would not be too conspicuous and could be mistaken for a salesman's car. Mpungose went into the station intending to speak to the people there but was disappointed to realise that he knew no one among those people. He nevertheless engaged them in a conversation, and ended up discussing a certain man who had come to the area to help his people.

In no time, the conversation was interrupted by the blowing up of dusty winds. Mpungose's heart began to beat faster as he suspected that the dust heralded the arrival of cattle. He was right.

The cattle were being led by two boys on horseback, with Mkhwanazi and Shandu following behind. Mpungose looked at this high-quality breed of cattle and battled to come to terms with their imminent departure. It was as if they were his. The shop owners also stood on their verandah and looked at the livestock. Then Mpungose began to doubt that these cattle were really being taken away by a thief – perhaps he and his police colleagues had wasted their valuable time, for surely it was impossible for anyone to have the bravado to steal people's cattle in broad daylight like this. Probably he and his colleagues had to face it – Mlomo and Ndebenkulu were two different individuals.

When the cattle arrived at the station, the boys led them to some grass nearby, away from the road. As Shandu and Mkhwanazi dismounted, Mpungose went to greet them. When he asked them where they were taking the cattle, they calmly responded that as a result of the meeting on the previous day they were taking the livestock to the abattoir with the help of Ndebenkulu. Mpungose asked if they had prepared goods coaches in advance. They told him that all the practical arrangements were the job of Ndebenkulu, who was on his way, with the boys, on a horse-drawn wagon. Mpungose made them aware that unless prior arrangements had been made with the station, it might be impossible to transport all the cattle at once. Shandu and Mkhwanazi simply shrugged it off – Ndebenkulu knew very important white people and would duly ensure that all was in order. As the discussion went on it became clear to Mpungose that, to these two men, the rich man of Pietermaritzburg was both the sunshine and the rainfall.

"We had heard that you were wanted at work urgently. Was it not true?" asked Shandu.

"It was true, Shandu. I really was needed."

"And here?"

"I'm here on work. I'm on my way to Vryheid as we speak."

"How did you arrive?"

"I came by train early in the morning, only to get a telephone message at the shop advising me to wait for a car from Dundee that will take me to Vryheid. That's why I'm restless now, and unfortunately home is too far for me to go and visit my elderly mother."

Mpungose took his leave, saying that he wanted to buy a box of matches in the shop, and once in the shop he reported to his white seniors that Ndebenkulu was on his way. When he told them about the cattle that were now the centre of attraction at the station, they shook their heads in disbelief and amusement. The widow asked why the people who owned the cattle were not warned at once that the person who had made promises of wealth was a thief, and that they would regret their decision, and the detectives tried to make her understand that they were not certain who was taking the cattle away, and could therefore not jump to premature conclusions. First they had to see Ndebenkulu, who might still turn out to be a decent and benevolent fellow rather than the criminal they had in mind. The widow gave in reluctantly and asked no further questions.

The detectives suggested taking the widow over to the station, but the shop owner advised against it. It would be difficult to find a hiding place for the widow in the station, but the shop was perfect because Ndebenkulu wouldn't be looking for anything suspicious there. The detectives took the shop owner's advice, stood around in the shop aimlessly and let Mpungose return to the station for a friendly talk with people there.

At that moment Mkhwanazi's horse-drawn cart appeared — but without Ndebenkulu. Mkhwanazi and Shandu could not believe what they were seeing and grew distinctly nervous. So did Mpungose. Was it possible that Ndebenkulu had eluded them? Why would Mkhwanazi lie and tell him that Ndebenkulu would arrive with his wagon? Although he tried, Mpungose could not hide his nerves from his colleagues. As for Mkhwanazi and Shandu, the absence of Ndebenkulu made them angry, and they quickly flooded the boys with unfriendly questions.

Fortunately, since Mpungose knew these four people, especially the Kheswa boy, he was able to stay very close to the action when the non-appearance of Ndebenkulu was being discussed. The boys explained what had happened, doing their best to implicate Ndebenkulu in wrongdoing and to show themselves in a good light, but their efforts were in vain because the men were too angry for words and, there and then, used all manner of insults against the boys. Mkhwanazi said that he was utterly disappointed that his son was not a real man but a fool of the highest degree imaginable. He tried to hit Themba on the head with a *sjambok*, but Themba shielded himself with his arm, then turned and ran, his father behind. Mkhwanazi was unable to catch his son, and even his effort at throwing a stone at him failed dismally.

Mkhwanazi came back to join Kheswa and the others, frustrated and furious, muttering to himself, uncertain about what to do next. He looked like a man defeated without having waged a fair fight. Themba and Diliza, seeing Mkhwanazi in this state, began to feel very guilty. Despite their misgivings about what Mkhwanazi and Shandu were getting themselves into, they had no right to disrupt their plans so dramatically and humiliatingly. After all, although Ndebenkulu had asked to be left behind, they had to admit that this was because they had been so rude and abusive towards him all the way.

Mkhwanazi said not a word. He simply climbed onto his horse-drawn wagon and rode off in the direction where the boys had dumped Ndebenkulu, furious at Themba for interfering in his affairs because the silly game his son was playing could cost him his luck.

• •

Mpungose pretended to be going back into the shop but in reality he was consulting with the other detectives on how to respond to the situation. They all agreed that since the cattle were at the station it would be wise for them to stay put because Ndebenkulu, if up to his usual tricks, would definitely show up soon to take care of the cattle. In any case, he had intended to come to the station – until the boys had kicked him out, so to speak. Mpungose went back to Diliza and

Themba, to while away the time. Themba was even more angry now, not at his father but at Ndebenkulu, who had caused all this trouble. The boys then shared with Mpungose the whole story of their aborted trip with Ndebenkulu. While they were talking, two wagons emerged from the distance. They could see Mkhwanazi in the first but not who was in the second.

After the boys had dumped Ndebenkulu, he had waited in confusion, looking at Mkhwanazi's wagon until it disappeared behind a hillock. Only after it was completely out of sight did he pick up his luggage and start walking. If you had seen Ndebenkulu at that moment you would have been convinced that, despite his pride and his status in society, he was a man who had really been through hard times in his life before he had struck it rich. The way he carried his luggage and his hat, and sweated profusely, was ample proof. His shoes were dusty in a trice, and he did not even bother wiping them.

Fortunately for him, Buthelezi's wagon came along a few minutes later. Buthelezi was on the way to the station – just to be certain that Mkhwanazi's and Shandu's cattle had really gone. Buthelezi was one of those Nyanyadu men who, despite the great temptation to let their cattle go, were nevertheless fearful about taking the big step. As he travelled along, alone, by horse-drawn wagon, the thought kept on playing itself repeatedly in his mind. Should he send them? Should he not send them? Should he send them? Should he not send them? He was so preoccupied with the matter of the cattle that long before he reached Ndebenkulu he had seen a person with luggage battling against the scorching sun, but he was lost in his thoughts and when he drew close he was so astonished that, for a minute, he was at a loss for words.

"What's the matter, Mr Ndebenkulu?" Buthelezi asked, without exchanging greetings. "Why are you in this state, travelling on foot and carrying your luggage? What's going on, Mr Ndebenkulu?"

After a brief moment of silence, a fuming Ndebenkulu put his luggage down and started to narrate the ugly episode to

Buthelezi. He told him that Mkhwanazi's and Kheswa's sons had not only ill-treated him but also insulted him by calling him a thief. "What! What!" Buthelezi battled to believe what he was being told and, worse, to hear that the culprits were well-brought up, rural Nyanyadu boys. "They did that to you, sir? No, this can't be true!"

"I regret that although Mkhwanazi was very warm to me I am now forced to sue these boys as soon as I arrive in Pietermaritzburg. What a pity there is no police station at Tayside! What a pity!"

"I'm really sorry to hear what you've just told me, Mr Ndebenkulu. Both these boys are trusted around here, especially Mkhwanazi's. Both are well-educated, and grew up in front of our eyes. As they say – you can't really say you know someone well enough."

"That's just the trouble with you rural folk – you keep on telling each other that a complete idiot is educated. A complete idiot! Do you hear me, Mr Buthelezi? For you it's a big deal that someone can write his name. If these boys were as educated as you think, they would have never done such a barbaric thing as they did to me this morning. Never! It's just a pity there's no police station at Tayside. If there was they would be getting a very good idea by tonight of who I really am, and they'd be seriously regretting their impoliteness."

Buthelezi found it hard to believe that Themba could behave so badly. As for Diliza, he felt that perhaps he had been corrupted by city ways, since he now worked in the city. "Fortunately you will meet Mkhwanazi at the station. You'd better get on board and not suffer in this humiliating heat when you're someone who is so used to a comfortable way of life."

Ndebenkulu was grateful, and in no time he was aboard. But then, when he looked at his dusty suit and shoes, he felt his anger rising again.

• •

It was not long before Mkhwanazi appeared from the opposite direction, and in a hurry. When Ndebenkulu saw Mkhwanazi he sulked. As soon as both wagons had drawn level and stopped, Mkhwanazi alighted. "Mr Ndebenkulu, I'm so ashamed, I can't even begin to look you straight in the eye. At times a person thinks he has a child and only realises much later that his wife's pregnancy was nothing but the festering of a sore in her intestines." Ndebenkulu would not utter a word. Instead he stared straight ahead, ignoring Mkhwanazi. After a while, he said: "I regret having come all the way to Nyanyadu in the first place. It was so stupid of me. One's commitment to the development of one's people can cause so much pain and humiliation. What happened to me today has never happened before. I'm still so shocked by it, it's as if I'm having a terrible nightmare. Never in my life have country boys humiliated me like this. The Ndebenkulu elders must be turning in their graves."

"Please, Mr Ndebenkulu, leave it all to me now. I have to deal with that boy when I get home, clearly there are now two Mkhwanazis running that household. If he thinks he's now a man and can set rules, he should get out of my house and go where he can be in charge. I almost killed him at the station just now. Only his speed saved him."

"Boys insulting me and calling me a trickster who wants to swindle people! Me! C.C. Ndebenkulu!"

Mkhwanazi didn't know what to say to this because Themba and Diliza had not told him the whole story.

"They called me a thief, Mkhwanazi. You know, my heart tells me I should not take your cattle any more. It's meaningless to keep on helping you when your very own son is rude and insulting to me. He was rude and insulting when he fetched me from the station, then when he brought the newspaper to you, and now today. At the same time, I'm expected to help the father of a son who thinks I'm nothing but dirt. Mkhwanazi, please take your cattle back. Please do it, Mkhwanazi."

"I have already apologised, sir," said Mkhwanazi.

192

"Apologised? With what have you apologised? With your mouth only? Let me remind you once again, Mkhwanazi, because I see you have forgotten. Dusty as I am with rural dust," said Ndebenkulu, as he briefly examined his shoes, "I am a man of high social standing. Let me remind you that I'm a Very Important Person. Your son and Kheswa's son's actions compel me to sue you and Kheswa and clean up my good name. Indeed, I am compelled. My name and social standing allow me to charge 40 pounds in damages. I could even ask for a hundred pounds if I called on the Supreme Court in Pietermaritzburg to decide the matter — the judges there know me very well. Me, a thief! Something drastic must happen."

"I accept, Mr Ndebenkulu, that the boys have insulted you. Just tell me, how much would satisfy you, as this was caused by children and we weren't responsible for it."

"I'm not a poor person, Mkhwanazi," said Ndebenkulu. "I'm also not trying to make money at your expense. Clearly, this is just a case of boys being rude. Indeed, it's clear to me, Mkhwanazi. It's important to teach them a lesson, so that they will never behave like this again. They must get a lesson, because in future they may do the same to someone who is less kind-hearted and understanding than me. I will therefore be satisfied, Mkhwanazi, if you and Kheswa give me ten cows each as damages. I am just being lenient, Mkhwanazi. Indeed I'm being lenient. If you don't want to give me ten cows I'll go to the police and ask for a hundred pounds."

After this, Ndebenkulu looked even angrier. Mkhwanazi kept quiet, as if he had not heard Ndebenkulu.

"Really, Mkhwanazi," said Buthelezi in a sad voice, "the elders are right when they say that a transgression enters one's house uninvited. Just look at the damage these silly boys have caused you. But then, ten cows is nothing if it can help you douse these fires."

Mkhwanazi was still silent on the side of the road. Ndebenkulu's words were burning him, deep down into his being. It was as if someone had driven a hot metal rod into his heart. Ten cows, just because of Themba! He began to feel as if he was the most cursed person, to have had Ndebenkulu imposing himself on his household. What at first he had considered to be his luck had now become his worst nightmare and misfortune. Ten cows going – for something like this! He began to sweat, and took out his khaki handkerchief to wipe his face.

"We'd better go now if we don't want to miss the train," he said.

"I would like to know, Mkhwanazi, if you will give me the cows I have asked for to clean my name, or not. I would like to know that before I go, so that I know what is the best action to take. I want to teach these boys a lesson."

Although Mkhwanazi accepted that the boys had erred, he was now becoming resentful of Ndebenkulu. Why would this man try to deplete his livestock in one day, for such a childish mistake? He began to see him as a hard and cruel man and regretted having thought, all along, that Ndebenkulu was a benevolent and selfless person. His arrogance also began to irritate Mkhwanazi. Could it be true that his children had seen an unpleasant trait in Ndebenkulu that he had failed to see?

"We'd better go now, Ndebenkulu, and talk at the station. It would be better, as well, for me to discuss this matter with Kheswa first."

"So you want me to wait for your discussions with Kheswa. What is there to discuss? You'd better give me the cows that are already on the way and then later send the ones I have to sell for you. As for Kheswa, I'll simply let the law take its course."

Now Mkhwanazi was growing angry. Maybe Ndebenkulu was lying when he said he was out to help people. The man was cruel. He began to think about what maNtuli would say to him when she heard about this. Without saying anything, Mkhwanazi went to his wagon and called on the horses to get going.

Ndebenkulu followed in Buthelezi's wagon. He still looked

like an important person, and seemed pleased after talking to Mkhwanazi. When he arrived at the station he simply dusted his hat off, and did not bother to offload his luggage, so Buthelezi was compelled to offload it. Ndebenkulu strolled into the station with a great deal of self-importance and looked irritated when he saw Themba and Diliza tittering in the corner.

"I just hope your fathers will do the same when I get closer to them. I'm warning you in person, me, C.C. Ndebenkulu. If you think I'm a laughing matter, boys, you are definitely making a terrible mistake." He was pacing up and down as he spoke.

Unknown to him, the widow had recognised him immediately. The investigators asked her again if she was sure that this was the man who had disappeared with her cows and she answered that she was. "Without a doubt, he is the thief that stole my children's cows. I don't know when he got that long tooth, but he is the one." She was champing at the bit, anxious to get close to the man and do whatever came instinctively.

The investigators told her to calm down. They would take her to the station and see how Ndebenkulu would respond on seeing her. After all, she was from faraway Mbulwana. His reaction would alert them to arrest him.

Mpungose was instructed to move closer to Ndebenkulu for fear that if indeed this was Mlomo he would run away as soon as he saw the widow. So Mpungose proceeded to the station and the white police investigators followed with the widow. As the Ladysmith police team and the widow approached from behind him, Ndebenkulu was busy throwing threats at Themba and Diliza. When they were close, emotions overwhelmed the widow. "What am I seeing, Lord of Heaven and Earth! Here's this Mlomo thief that stole my children's cows!" Her wail was loud and haunting.

Ndebenkulu heard it, saw her, and started to run as if for dear life. To see the Esquire of Pietermaritzburg in flight was unbelievable, and for a moment people just looked on, stunned into silence. The 10-pound hat fell off on to the grass nearby. Could you blame him for not bothering to pick up a mere hat when the going was this tough? As he ran, his coat looked as if someone had pumped it up with air. He jumped the nearby fence and ran in the direction of Nyanyadu. Not using the road, he ran instead into the thick grass, and picked up speed alarmingly quickly for an Esquire. The police and the boys ran after him, as the car was useless in the circumstances.

At this stage the widow began to wail even more loudly, and was heard cursing the police for not running fast enough to catch the thief. She suggested that they grab horses to chase the thief of her children's cattle. Diliza and Themba took the widow's cue, dashed back to the station, and each mounted a horse and returned to the chase. When Ndebenkulu saw the horses coming at top speed, he realised his chances of escape were over. He tried to hide. He tried throwing stones at them.

The boys pounced violently on Ndebenkulu. Diliza wasted no time in depositing a mean fist on him, and the long tooth flew into the air. Themba joined in, and the two boys punched him as if feasting on him.

By the time the police investigators ran up he was bleeding. They greeted him with some good smacks as well, as if to show Themba and Diliza that they could not outdo the police in their job. Ndebenkulu was arrested at once. When Mpungose expressed surprise that Ndebenkulu no longer had a long tooth, Diliza proudly claimed responsibility for its demise. They then took him back to the station, everyone talking about him all the way.

Themba and Diliza were delighted to have finally had an opportunity to beat up Ndebenkulu – or whoever he was. Their only regret was that the white police investigators had come to his rescue rather too quickly.

"What have I been telling my father, who was too stubborn to listen to me?" said Themba to Diliza rhetorically. "At the station he almost killed me, in full view of so many people, and because of a thief. I can't wait to see what he'll say now about his most trusted Esquire."

Meanwhile, Mkhwanazi and Shandu, who had remained at the station, were shocked to the bone to find out that a man they had trusted wholeheartedly really was a crook. Mkhwanazi was thinking about what he had almost done to his son because of this con artist. The thought that if he had caught his son he might have killed him made him shiver in the middle of a pretty hot day.

For Shandu, anger was the main emotion, and he wanted to skin the man alive. He took up his sjambok and went off in the direction of the people who had gone to chase Ndebenkulu. Before he could go far, he saw them returning with the man, now a sorry sight. As he came close, Shandu, quietly fuming with rage, and when nobody expected it, struck viciously at Ndebenkulu with the sjambok. By the time the criminal investigators stopped him, he had already hit him a good few times.

"Why don't you let me sort out this devil, good people?" said Shandu, still hungry to vent his anger.

"Do you realise that what you are doing amounts to a serious offence and that I can arrest you right away?" The white criminal investigator was angry at Shandu.

"Honourable sir, you might as well arrest me," said Shandu defiantly. "This is not a human being but a real devil. The white man's law is just a nuisance, for protecting criminals. Had I had my way, I would landed a knobkerrie on his head. He's here to make fools of us!"

"Even if he's a devil, as you say, you have no right to do what you have just done once he's in the hands of the police."

"Sir, this devil was here to steal our livestock. The cattle at this station are here because of him and his silly English. I wish I could hit him again and teach him a hard lesson."

"There's no law like that, Shandu," said Mpungose calmly. "You're not allowed to attack a criminal once we have him in custody."

"Would you say that if you knew everything this man did?"

asked Shandu. "Just think about him stopping us from doing our work on Monday to gather at the school while knowing that he was making fools of us in broad daylight. Just look at the chief even calling an *imbizo* hoping that this man could help us. On that day we wasted our time instead of working, all because of this devil. Today we even brought our cows to the station because of this devil."

Mpungose responded by telling Shandu to respect the law no matter the circumstances.

"Where is this devil's long tooth?" asked Shandu. Everyone burst out laughing.

"Maybe he left it in the bush. If not, he swallowed it," said Mpungose.

"Obviously it wasn't a real tooth," said Shandu. "This is a real crook, he even crooks us with a false tooth. I wish I could teach you a lesson. I swear to God, the white man's law is terrible."

On the other hand, when Shandu had left to help in the chase, Mkhwanazi had just sat down and begun to sweat profusely. He battled to accept that all his hopes, hard work and sacrifice had been misplaced, and engineered by a hardened criminal. That they were at the station to give their cattle to a thief was just too sad a reality to fathom.

• •

By this time, the station was full of onlookers. It was a real spectacle at the usually quiet Tayside station. Mpungose was asked to seize Ndebenkulu's luggage for further inspection at the police station. Although Ndebenkulu had been silent all this time, when he was near the shop he laughed aloud and said: "You fools! You're lucky to have survived my game!"

"Shut up!" said one criminal investigator as he slapped him.

"You men must prepare to be called as witnesses," Mpungose told Shandu and Mkhwanazi. The criminal investigators, followed by the widow, then proceeded with Ndebenkulu to their car.

"Today I grew up," said Mkhwanazi, as he saw the police car leave for Ladysmith with Ndebenkulu. He walked slowly to his wagon.

"We'd better go now, Mkhwanazi. Boys, take the cattle back home." Shandu's voice revealed a great sense of defeat and betrayal.

Mkhwanazi neither moved nor spoke. Themba was deeply hurt to see his father in this state.

"We must go, Mkhwanazi, staying here won't help us," said Shandu.

After a long silence, Mkhwanazi spoke like someone who had just emerged from a coma. "Let's go home, boys."

I wonder what maNtuli will say when they get home!

Glossary

baba – father, used as a general term of respect for older males

Bayede! – literally 'hail', used in greeting a member of royalty, as in 'Hail Caesar!'

donga – deep ditches caused by soil erosion

halibhoma – sisal

Hhawu/Awu – Goodness gracious

Hheyi bo – come on

imbizo – community gathering

iNkosi – literally 'queen', used as a term of respect in addressing a woman

mayi diya – 'my dear'; a play on the Zulu pronunciation of the English words

mielie – maize plant

mielie pap – stiff porridge made from maize flour

mnumzane – Sir/mister

ndabezitha – chieftain

sanibona – Greetings

sjambok – short, stiff whip, often made of leather

tsotsi – crook/gangster

yehheni – outburst of astonishment, as in 'Really!'